GRIM TIDE

Sever Squad
Book 5

A.R. KNIGHT

ONE

Water World

THE GREAT BLUE snakes writhed through the ship's cockpit, Gillane Four's mammoth water production a marvel from orbit. Aurora, sucking her morning coffee through a steel straw, watched the corporate-morphed world go about its business. A far better sight than deep space's dark nothing, which had been the starry show for weeks as the *Prisa* sped up to and beyond light to make the journey.

As Sever's commander, captain . . . Aurora gave the quietest laugh, not even drawing a look from Eponi. What did rank matter? Sever wasn't in the DefenseCorp hierarchy anymore. Everyone in the squad had a skillset: Aurora coupled hard discipline with strategic thinking, Eponi flew anything she could get her hands on, Gregor swung a big hammer, Sai blew things up, and Rovo handled the talking.

That grin died a quick death as Rovo came to mind. The former rookie had been taken by two traitors, DefenseCorp agents intent on using Rovo's knowledge to improve on new weapons. He'd been stolen off the *Nautilus* by Renard and Vana, used as a hostage to keep Aurora from blowing up the bastards. Now, Sever had tracked the trio and their force all the way to Gillane Four and its watery nest.

"Beautiful," Gregor said, swooping in to the seat behind Aurora's. One of four in the *Prisa*'s cockpit, the rear two meant for appreciating the pilot's abilities. "The blue planets are the best ones."

"This one's not blue by choice," Eponi said. "Used to be all that water sat beneath the ice. I've seen vids of kart races they used to do here. Then Salinity decided different."

Another megacorp, built on the need for most species to suck down water to survive. Aurora didn't know much about Salinity except its H2O logo seemed to be on every liquid dispenser in the galaxy. That, and they believed planets ought to be tuned to their most useful degrees.

Which, fine. Not Aurora's problem if Gillane Four went from a polar planet to one with endless water geysers.

"Where are we landing?" Gregor asked. "Did we find them?"

Them meant Renard and Vana, and with those two, hopefully, Rovo. Gregor had done some meaty work on a couple captured agents before Sever left the *Nautilus* to come here, breaking the two captives with threats not of physical violence, not of mental torture, but with a very Gregor move.

"There is right," Gregor had said to the pair, still in their med bay beds, pushed together in the same room for the meeting. "And there is wrong. Your friend, Zaydi, died for the wrong. Now, you can make it right."

He'd followed up that trite beginning with a recording series. Video captures of Renard and Vana tearing apart squaddies with their new suits. The charred bodies left behind in a *Nautilus* docking bay when the escaping agents blasted out with their stolen transport. The two spies changed their tune as they saw what their side wrought.

Easy enough to pursue a dream when you don't see the cost.

"They're not making it hard for us," Aurora said, answering Gregor's question. "The transport's still in orbit. Hanging at a distance. They've sent shuttles down to the surface, right to the capitol."

"Right where Salinity's headquartered," Eponi added.

Renard and Vana had come to Gillane Four to find a girl named Kaia and the treasure buried in her blood. A young kid with a father specializing in molecular biology. Rovo, before he'd been captured, received a message from Kaia saying she and her father had come to the planet, and Aurora could only think of one reason why a desperate-for-cash scientist would come here.

Salinity jobs had to pay well, and Kashmal might be able to squeeze out a good position there. At least, that's the assumption Aurora would work with until something proved her wrong.

"So we land, go to Salinity, and smash Renard with my hammer?" Gregor asked.

"Almost," Aurora replied. "Sai's going to Salinity with Eponi. You and I are going hunting."

"Ah. Good plan."

Outside, Eponi shunted the *Prisa* into a line of landing ships. Freighters, passenger cruisers, and smaller craft like theirs.

"You think there'll be a trail?" Eponi asked. "Like, Renard will be waiting down there for us with some flags, tell us where to go?"

Gregor didn't answer, and Aurora could tell the man was waiting to see what she'd do. In the past, giving Aurora that kinda sarcasm would be grounds for a strict dressing down. A matter-of-fact reminder about the mission's stakes, to offer something helpful, not a joke.

But the last few months, from Dynas and its swampy hells, to Wexer and the deadly *Nautilus* corridors, had sanded off those edges. The joke didn't annoy Aurora anymore. Didn't do anything except spark a little happiness that Sever *could* still joke after all the garbage they'd gone through.

"They're agents," Aurora said. "Renard will contact the local outpost to get an operation base on the planet. We'll start there, see what we can find."

"And you want Sai and I to wander into Salinity's offices and say what, have you seen this man?"

"You can use your own words, if you like."

Eponi curled up a grin and Aurora matched it, "I'm liking this new you, commander. Giving me some room to fly."

"Just make sure you don't crash."

Leaving the *Prisa* into Gillane Four's bright atmosphere made for a mad biological rush. Aurora, as she did every time she met a new planet, took a deep inhale to get a read on where she'd parked her body. Gillane Four greeted the move with light, dry air meshed with a lemon scent, as if Aurora had wandered into a citrus garden. The atmosphere met the design, as Salinity had put flowing flourishes over its owned world.

The docking bays sat on open ice-blue platforms suspended, as everything was on Gillane Four, above the endless ocean that coated the planet's surface. Spearmint green barriers shone translucent around the platform edges, providing a sign and a slight shocking sensation to anyone thinking about taking the kilometer dive into the churning sea.

Aurora couldn't recall the last time she'd seen clouds

so white and puffy, a circumstance owing to Salinity's precise control of the planet's water cycle. No bad weather here, just optimal conditions for harvesting water.

Deepak had sent along the DefenseCorp dossier on the planet, a deep document describing how Salinity made Gillane Four work. Aurora had devoured it, and suggested the others do the same, with Gregor paying particular attention to Salinity's work capturing and crashing icy asteroids on the planet's far side to keep its giant reservoir topped up.

The work's evidence played over and around Aurora as she left with Gregor, dressed in capable civilian clothes. A loose white jacket helped hide a shoulder holster and the pistol inside, while Aurora had slotted in a knife along her thigh. Hardly the gear needed to break in and rescue a hostage, but if they found Rovo, five new power armor suits sat back on the *Prisa*.

Deepak hadn't fought hard when Aurora made the demand. She'd pointed out the admiral owed Sever for its efforts clearing the agents from the *Nautilus*, and that Deepak had caused the loss of their original suits through the doomed effort on Dynas, coupled with the aggressive tactics on Wexer.

And, though Aurora hadn't told this to anyone else in Sever, she'd promised Deepak the squad would come back after the rescue.

What that meant, well, Aurora would figure that out later. For now, they had weapons, they had targets. Time to go.

The dossier also had the DefenseCorp office location. The official base probably wouldn't be where the agents hung out—the clandestine branch tended to go its own way—but the paper pushers might know where to check.

"So how do we get there?" Gregor asked as they walked from the pad.

A good question. Salinity's liquid focus flowed into everything on the planet, including the blue pads and their central platform, a droplet design funneling the landing crowds to a point. That point appeared to be tied to several giant, clear tubes, all hurtling back towards the stalk-like rise of the city's core.

A flower, with the city at the center and every docking platform a petal.

"Swim?" Aurora said as they joined a motley crowd making their way towards the tubes.

Gillane Four held to its cash-driven ethos, and like everywhere else in the galaxy, merchants made themselves known to new arrivals. That peaceful first breath vanished beneath an advertising onslaught, with shouts from stands offering food and, yes, souvenir water 'straight from the source'. Their targets weren't hooded vagrants like on Wexer, but a functional collection whose obvious income and direction put Aurora on a strange edge.

Maybe she'd spent too long hunting cash in the galaxy's dregs if real civilization made her this uncomfortable.

"I think I need a vacation," Aurora said, both of them now stuck in the line. More species than she'd seen in one spot crowded around her, their languages competing for her non-understanding. "After we get Rovo, maybe."

"Hah. A nice idea," Gregor said. "But too boring for me."

"There's nowhere you'd want to go?"

"To a planet with less peace than this one, perhaps."

Somehow, Aurora figured Gillane Four might not be long for that peace, but before she could talk about it, the last few people ahead broke for a tube and left the Sever pair in front. Two thick poles stood several meters apart, red rings glowing near their tops. Between them, another soft green barrier shone. A pleasant, artificial voice asked that anyone carrying goods announce themselves, and when nobody did, the stalks chimed a trilling affirmation.

Ahead, the three clear tubes ended with their own bays. Capsules, each the *Prisa*'s size, flew into a gentle rest before loading up and shooting out again. One had an orange slice through its silver middle, with blue letters designating it for cargo alone. Directly ahead, an incoming capsule found its rest as the other passenger one jetted away with technology's familiar whooshing whine.

The rings topping the two stalks went blue, and the green barrier shifted, angling the approach for the middle capsule, giving Aurora and Gregor a path.

"I think I prefer Wexer," Aurora said as they went into the capsule, where prim, cushioned seats awaited their entry. "This feels a little too controlled."

"Enjoy it," Gregor said. "I have no doubt chaos will find us before long."

"Or we'll find it."

"Is there a difference?"

"I'd rather be the ones making the chaos, than have someone else do it."

"Ah," Gregor sat next to Aurora, his bulk pushing her up towards the capsule's oval windows. "Let me know, and I will create your chaos."

Aurora laughed, and the capsule shot off. Whatever tech powered the thing, it didn't give Aurora much moving sensation. Like being in a starship when the engines kicked on, riding the tunnel to the city felt like watching a movie. And this movie loved water.

Approaching the city's giant stalk, Aurora saw the various pumps climbing the city's solitary stand, the tubes coming up from the ocean and stretching across it. The vast array no doubt accounted for that pulsing sensation Sever had seen while in orbit, as the glassy tunnels funneled water all over the planet for whatever treatment it needed before getting loaded up and shipped out. Waves snuck in between the tubes, like prisoners reaching through the bars.

"Ready for a rescue?" Aurora said. "Just like Dynas?"

"Nothing will be like Dynas," Gregor replied. "But, I am ready for a rescue. And I am ready for some revenge."

Gregor had detailed Vana's betrayal, a move that hadn't done a whole lot to shake Aurora's opinion of the strange agent. Vana had equipped Aurora well on the *Nautilus*, then proceeded to take Gregor off on a quest to find Renard. The old agent had apparently surprised Vana with some new power armor, lighter versions that were nigh invisible to human eyes. A treasure-tempted turncoat, Vana had flipped Renard's way, donned a suit, and very nearly sent Gregor to the great beyond.

Aurora had taken the news with a shrug and a promise to lay Vana low with a laser next time she saw the woman.

"First, however, I want answers," Gregor continued. "She should have killed me, but she did not. I would know why."

"Because she didn't have the time?" Aurora recalled Vana had gone on a slaughtering spree when some hapless squaddies interrupted her Gregor evisceration. Vana had left Gregor behind, gasping in some damaged power armor, a lucky break that Gregor refused to see that way. "It's hard to think clearly when you're getting attacked."

"She thought clear."

Gregor looked troubled, a frown over that giant face, and dropped into a broody silence that Aurora decided to leave alone.

The capsule approached its destination, and that meant she had to confront the next challenge: getting some DefenseCorp flunkies to rat out their agent friends.

Nothing a little cash or a pistol's pointed end couldn't solve.

TWO

City Walk

CAN'T BELIEVE you took the sword," Eponi said to Sai as they stepped off the capsule into the city.

The crowd gave Sai and Eponi a wide berth, long looks dragging over Sai's katana, sheathed over his shoulder, with a hilt that went out far enough to leer over his back like some animal. Both Sever members had on loose business-wear, clothes that could pass for office-appropriate while maintaining enough flexibility to throw down should the need arise.

And Sai expected the need to arise.

Like Dynas, Sever had come to Gillane Four on a particular mission, for rescue and revenge. Such things tended to end in violence, and after what Renard and Vana had done to Sai on the *Nautilus*, the demolitionist wouldn't mind a crack at the two.

Especially after a few weeks spent healing on the long journey. Salves and exercises had reduced Sai's burns and busted muscles to a ready state, albeit with new scars and off-color patches on the skin beneath his clothes. Everyone serving in DefenseCorp for more than a minute had those, though.

Signs of a life hard lived.

"You know where we're going?" Eponi asked, drawing Sai into the crowded courtyard where the capsule plunked out the planet's new arrivals.

Salinity designed their world like an amusement park. The off-boarding area ran rampant with signs advertising various destinations and services. Want to immigrate to Gillane Four? Head this way. Looking to deliver cargo? Go that way. Planning to tour the watery world? Straight ahead, please.

Bots hovered among the crowd, delivering answers to questions and beckoning people to keep moving: the next capsule and its targets would be arriving soon.

"Uh, no," Sai said. "Haven't been here before."

"Really. Totally seems like your place."

"Why do you say that?"

"Family man. Kids must love all this, right?"

"Crowds? Chaos?" Sai shrugged. "Maybe you're right."

They settled on straight ahead, marching towards a grand sign showcasing the city's formal name, Kaiyo. The five letters had been done up like waves, their tops cresting white while the rest flowed deep blue into a golden frame. Beneath the arch, the broad silver-stone walkway opened into a busy square.

Most modern urban areas relied on aerial taxis, with docking stations posted all over, or underground mass transit, leaving the surface spaces free for walking, shopping, and special needs. Kaiyo played the same game, only instead of the varied kart-and-craft mix flying through the air, those glass tubes and their capsules swirled like veins overhead. Lift-and-stair combos provided access to the stations, and the long lines in sight showed little reluctance to load into the shooters.

The tubes gained their curves going around tall buildings, all designed with a blue or sea green color scheme, and all seemingly without a straight line on the outside. The structures arced above and around them, no doubt trying to convey being lost in a deep ocean. Instead, Sai found it vaguely unsettling, motion sickness making a minor play on his stomach.

"Guess they're committed to theme," Eponi said.

"It's their planet," Sai replied. "Their choice. Let me see what I can find."

After the *Nautilus* misadventure, Sever had loaded themselves up with new wristlets. The small computers served as mobile databases, communication devices, and anything else Sever needed from the digital universe. After losing his on Wexer, Sai had felt a combination of freed and frozen, unable to access knowledge that he'd had ready for his whole life, and, at the same time, untethered from the larger galaxy.

Still, Sai would sacrifice that freedom for a good city map, and Kaiyo's came right up as requested when Sai asked the little computer locked to his left wrist. Turned out Kaiyo's central stalk had levels aplenty beneath the one they stood on, and the wristlet's estimation showed the galaxy's usual income disparity at play: those with money had the top levels and their blue skies. Those without went further and further down towards the churning seas.

"Okay," Sai looked up from his map, straight ahead. "Going to say we should've figured this one out."

"Oh?"

"Salinity's headquarters is right ahead. It's the city's center."

"That is obvious," Eponi said. "Sad."

"Why's that sad?"

"Because I keep hoping these big companies will be more creative than they really are."

"Well, they didn't hire you."

"I know. If only."

Sai chuckled as they set off. He couldn't imagine a spark like Eponi crunching numbers and documents all day, playing diplomat to investors and customers alike. Then again, Sai couldn't picture himself doing that either. After an hour standing in the same place, listening to a briefing, he'd get this niggling itch to do something, to sink his mind into a puzzle—like what chemical compound could best melt a starship hull. Spending days sifting through presentations and preening power plays?

Nope.

Wanting to get a better feel for the world, Sai and Eponi took to walking. They even stopped into a small cafe, one spangled over with sea-creature theming, and ordered up some fresh breakfast and coffee to go with it. After weeks munching on lab-spun protein packs and rehydrated vitamin juices, having something fresh felt, well, life-changing.

Sai bought the round, tapping his wristlet. The cash cost didn't reach high, but the deduction flashed a question to where his next deposit would be coming from. Rescuing Rovo, however important it might be to Sever, didn't come with a reward attached. Deepak had stuffed them full with provisions and gear for helping out with the *Nautilus* but cash hadn't come with it.

They'd made the call in Dynas's orbit to chase money instead of their careers, to ditch DefenseCorp and its damned missions for a more pure sort of profit. Yet, for all that talk, Sai hadn't seen a drop come into his account.

And his family hadn't seen a boost come their way in a long time now.

"You're thinking the same thing I am," Eponi said as they wandered towards the city center, between those flowing buildings and chattering crowds, the ocean planet's crashing waves suffusing the background from far below. "We're gonna be broke if we keep up this way."

"The way I see it," Sai said, "is we get Rovo back, take out Renard, and then ask Deepak for a proper reward. Stopping a DefenseCorp coup ought to be worth something."

"Yeah, a pat on the back and a quick exit," Eponi said. "What's the rationale? We still deserted. They can say our payment is a clear name and a chance to jump back to, I dunno, freaking Wexer to suck dirt for scraps."

"Glad you're so supportive."

"We need one realist on this squad."

Salinity's headquarters spawned from Kaiyo's center like a frozen splash. The building's outer ring rose up and out, culminating in a curving top level with periodic spikes. The center, done up in icy teal, stretched above to a narrowing point ruined at its absolute height by a landing pad. Leading up to the entry sat a glass courtyard, under which ran water in rippling swirls, occasionally sucked up into one of a half-dozen fountains.

Sai would've called it impressive, except not much qualified once you'd seen a nebula from space's dark heart. Nothing neared that interstellar splendor.

"So what's our play here?" Eponi said. "You start chatting up the receptionist while I sneak past and hunt down Kashmal?"

"How about you follow my lead, and we try not to create a scene?"

"The boring way, then."

"Not everything has to end with us getting shot."

"You know it will anyway," Eponi said as they hit the main doors, cascading water curtains that blew aside as the pair approached. "No matter what you and I do, we're gonna get lasers to the face."

"I'm going to ask for Gregor next time."

"Don't hate the messenger, man."

The Salinity lobby broke into outgoing and ingoing halves, marked by glass-coated pathways and water running in the requisite directions. To the left, the stream ran towards Sai and Eponi, beneath a soft scanner-barrier set looking for IDs to open up. On the right, the stream ran inward, past a desk where both bot and human parlayed asks into answers. Beyond them, a second scanner-barrier arch waited.

After all the fuss, the space opened up into an atrium with a centralized waterfall lift. Droplet lights hung every-where, proving Salinity's extreme commitment to theme. The endless liquid had Sai searching out a bathroom, and wishing, just a little, for Wexer's black sand.

Freshened up and ready, Eponi and Sai rejoined at the reception desk, where artificial pleasantries on a human face greeted their approach.

"Hi, yes," Sai started, "we're actually here to meet with someone?"

"The name?" The receptionist, eyes sliding to Sai's katana, already had her fingers at the console, perched on the sea green desk.

The obvious question didn't get asked. Apparently Salinity's customer service training overrode all inquiries about strange blades coming into the office.

"Kashmal," Sai faltered, not sure about the man's last name. "I can't remember anything else. Sorry, long morning."

Technically, the morning had started back in space. Sai had gone from orbit to a planet's surface all before local lunch time. That definitely qualified as long.

The receptionist didn't look all that impressed by Sai's failed memory, but Salinity probably wasn't paying her to interrogate visitors, so she did the typing anyway. Then, flipping the screen, the receptionist invited Sai to pick out which of the employee photos applied to his particular Kashmal.

Three local options, and the top, the newest one, matched what Sai remembered. Black haired, stubble. Looked more put-together than the evacuating refugee appearance Kashmal had sported on the run from Dynas.

"That's the one," Sai said. "We have to chat with him."

"About?" The receptionist asked, her fingers poised above the console's call button.

"Family matters," Sai replied. "He'll understand."

That earned Sai a raised eyebrow. Eponi, for her part, stood a little back, her eyes surfing the room. Standard procedure when one member had an active engagement, the other kept watch for anything weird. She'd give Sai a tap on the shoulder if Eponi spotted something, but so far, Salinity kept things standard.

No Renard, no Vana, no obvious agents.

Maybe Sever had managed to beat them here, or maybe Rovo hadn't given the game away. If that was the case, then Sai owed the rookie some more respect. Being a hostage was never fun—getting injected on Dynas came to mind—and Renard didn't seem like a gentle captor.

"Okay," the receptionist said. "He's coming down. Lucky you came early, he's going off in an hour for a week."

"For what?"

"Salinity on-boarding training. They send you around the planet, see all the processing facilities."

"Sounds fascinating," Sai tried, failed to sound fascinated. "Should we wait here, or on the barrier's other side?"

"You're not getting to the other side with that sword," the receptionist said. "So I'd wait here."

"Fair enough."

Sai stepped back, rejoined Eponi, who pointed out that every Salinity security guard in the lobby, maybe four, had their eyes locked on Sai and his katana. A few had chatted into their wristlets already.

"You're saying I'm popular?" Sai said.

"I'm saying you might get us killed."

"Hi, welcome to Sever Squad."

Eponi rolled her eyes.

Sai, watching the lift, spotted Kashmal first. The lanky scientist, who had a penchant for mid-day drinks and enough genius to get away with it, had a confused look as he came out from beyond the barriers. He had on a Salinity blue lab coat, glasses, and an air that he ought not to be bothered.

An air that vanished as soon as Kashmal saw Sai and Eponi waiting for him. Sai had only once seen a face drop like Kashmal's, and that'd been his own son's when the kid's soccer game had been canceled for weather. A true disaster, that.

"I can't imagine this is anything good," Kashmal said, approaching them with hands in pockets. "I'd hoped I'd never see your miserable bunch again."

"Trust me, the feeling was mutual," Eponi said.

"Not our choice," Sai agreed, "but we're here anyway. People are after Kaia. We're trying to catch them, but we want to make sure your daughter's safe."

Kashmal blinked, tilted his head, "Safe? Last time you intervened, she was nearly taken from me. Now you're here again to, what, take her away?"

"Protect her," Sai said. "Let us know where she is, and we'll set up a perimeter. Keep the ones after her away while Aurora and Gregor deal with them."

Kashmal looked at the floor, the water beneath, for a long second. Looking up, he had a different look, one Sai had seen before: the cornered creature.

"I'm not telling you a damn thing about my daughter," Kashmal said. "I have a job here, Kaia's doing well, and we don't need you messing that up. Leave us alone."

"Not gonna happen," Eponi said. "Not because we want anything to do with you, but because we can't chance the bad guys getting their hands on your girl."

"That, I believe, is not your choice to make." Kashmal backed up a step. "Last chance. Go away and forget you ever found us."

Sai shook his head, "This is for your own—"

"Help!" Kashmal shouted, pulling his hands from his pockets, backing up. "They're trying to threaten me and my family! Security!"

Sai would've called the performance ridiculous, would've called it absurd and pathetic, except Salinity's security seemed to take Kashmal's words for fact. The four guards closed, one jabbering into a wristlet for reinforcements.

"See?" Eponi said, backing up with Sai. "Lasers to the face. Every time."

Sai couldn't argue with that.

Making A Deal

THE SPARKLING WATER buzzed his lips with something beyond the lemon flavor, perhaps the tingle responsible for the water's name: *Jolt*. Not quite as strong as Aurora's coffee on the ship, but for a lunchtime boost, it would do.

Gregor and Aurora held sway over a rounded outdoor table, watching the DefenseCorp offices on the walking avenue's other side. Aurora munched on her sandwich, while Gregor's crumbs blew away in the breeze. Gillane Four had enough birds, likely brought over from other worlds, that'd clean up the scraps. Somewhere nearby, a busker plied his trade, the rough melody bouncing off the buildings in a pleasant echo.

"This is dull," Gregor said. "We have been here an hour."

"Stakeouts are dull. That's the point."

Aurora's plan had changed from a slam-bang demand for Renard's location to a more targeted pursuit. They'd wait for some solo person to exit the office, then jump the poor sap and get the information they needed without risking a problem with bigger numbers.

Thus far, there'd been a few scattered souls heading in and out of the office, but nobody sporting the crimson uniform showing they actually delivered data for Defense-Corp. Aurora and Gregor needed a source, not a random civilian, and—

"There," Aurora said. "That's one."

Sever's captain shoved the remaining sandwich in her mouth as Gregor turned, spotted the newest exodus from the offices. A plum lady with that deep red uniform and harried hair pounded the pavement. Away from the office, and away from the two Sever squad members.

"Let's go." Gregor stood, lurching up with a little too much excitement and catching his chair before it clattered over onto the light-blasted, creamy stones.

The two fell into pursuit. Much more satisfying than sitting and waiting. He missed the heaviness on his back where his hammer used to sit, waiting to be unlimbered for mass destruction. Instead, while Aurora hid a pistol beneath a jacket, Gregor kept his own pocket shooter in an ankle holster, hidden by flaring, billowy pants. Not exactly fashionable, but Gregor met every raised eyebrow with a steady stare, and soon enough any would-be critics blinked away.

You didn't need to use muscle to take advantage of having it.

The target ambled on towards a crowded intersection, a circular square dominated by yet another water-related statue calling attention to Salinity's founder, her family, or some other person Gregor had neither the interest or time to know. Thus far, the target had kept herself around too many people to make for an easy snatch-and-grab.

"She's turning," Aurora said. "Be ready."

"Always ready."

"Of course you are."

The captain called it right, though. The woman angled away from the square and towards a quieter path heading towards a residential collection. The stacked condos up here looked too nice for what Gregor remembered of his DefenseCorp salary, but perhaps she held a higher rank than the uniform would suggest, or Salinity paid the DC staff here hefty bribes to keep things quiet.

No world wanted to be known as a festering crime pit, while DefenseCorp had every interest in publicizing its well-done peace-keeping efforts. Balances tended to be struck between controlling interests, with cash going into the DC coffers and statistics dying out. A mutually beneficial relationship, and one Gregor had always taken without much comment: so long as he had the opportunities to crush the criminals, who cared where the cash went?

The thinning crowd around the target forced Gregor and Aurora's hand. Before, they'd been able to maintain some distance and count on the disparate species, outfits, and their combined noise to keep Sever hidden. Now, with a person here and there, the tailing would be obvious if the target ever turned around.

"Go," Aurora said, soft. "Try to pull her to the side."

The solid block style Salinity put into their buildings negated alleyways and offshoots, the typical spots Gregor might use for take-n-threaten work. Instead, he'd have to play things mild. Try not to make a scene.

Letting Aurora fall behind, Gregor lengthened his stride, closing with the target. The woman had her wristlet up now, appearing to swipe away. Good timing. Reading a message, watching a video, both and either would serve to keep her eyes and attention off the hand about to land on her shoulder.

"Come quietly," Gregor said, feeling the target stiffen

as his hand planted. "No one needs to get hurt. I only have a question."

Gregor steered the woman with his planted hand, taking her to the right and under an overhang for a leasing office that looked, thankfully, closed for the lunchtime hour. Deep glass windows showcased stands covered with projected pictures of glitzy property for purchase, and Gregor used the display to put himself and the target facing that glass.

Just looking at dreams they could never afford, that's all.

"What do you want?" The target said, a tremor belying the tenor tone in her voice. Not used to getting made a hostage, then. "I don't have much cash."

"Not cash. Information." Gregor watched the world through their reflections on the glass. Nobody paying attention. Aurora had herself spotted up opposite Gregor, shape visible. With her hand signals, she'd give Gregor a heads-up if something went sour. "The agents. Where are they?"

Again, the target twitched, the jerk carrying up through Gregor's still-planted hand. Surprise?

"What agents?"

"DefenseCorp. Your counterparts. Where are their offices?"

"I don't know? Do they have any here?"

There were lies and there were liars. Anyone could attempt the former, spill out some words and hope they were believed. The latter performed a skill, manipulated reality for their audience. This poor DefenseCorp staffer fell into the former camp, and her voice, her stature, her lack of conviction betrayed her in the same way a pretender betrays themselves the moment they throw their first punch.

Gregor tightened his grip. Dug the fingers in enough to convey the meaning, "You heard me. Answer."

A sharp breath this time. In the reflection, the target's gray eyes slanted away, pulled towards the ground. Another tell, another breakaway moment to come up with an excuse.

"A little girl's life is in danger." Gregor headed off the attempt before it started. "Help us save her, or live with a four year-old's death."

"Tragedy happens every day," the target said, but her voice lost what little gravity it had. Weakness grasping for a hold. "It's not my fault."

"It is. Give us the location, and we will save her."

The woman's eyes closed. She'd fought the fight, done the minimum DefenseCorp expected of its personnel. Resist, then relent. DefenseCorp would rather not have its low-level employees murdered. Besides, the giant company could extract any vengeance it pleased on the perpetrators. No need for the woman to sacrifice more than she had.

"Okay," the woman said. "It's not far. I can show you, and then you'll let me go?"

"Yes."

The simple answer spurred a walk. The woman led them back away from the residential district, through the intersection, and towards another commercial sector. Aurora stayed well back as Gregor walked alongside the target, keeping herself apart.

The target pointed Gregor towards a glossy-looking store billing itself as an outlet for used gadgets, gear, and whatever else the proprietors happened to find on outer space salvage missions. A cover that might actually serve as a solid side business for DefenseCorp, as they had to get plenty of junk from bashing up pirates and rogue ships polluting the stars.

"In there," the target said. "Ask for the owner. That'll tell them what you're really there for."

This time, no twitch. No tremor. A truth-teller's level voice.

"Thank you," Gregor said.

He didn't need to add anything else.

The big man left the woman standing in the street, heading straight for the salvage shop. The woman wouldn't get far. Aurora would keep tabs on her and, if Gregor's request for this owner came back blank, the Sever captain would reconvene the hostage situation.

Inside the salvage shop, Gregor took a second to find his bearings. Glass lockboxes littered every surface, scanners tuned to open up if a staffer's wristlet approached. In the meantime, the highlighted goods sparkled at their various possibilities. Some boxes held weapons, others spacecraft parts, while still more held what signs claimed to be unique relics from worlds far across the galaxy. Crystals, metals, glowing shards stuffed with energy, these all shared space with random trinkets too, from children's toys to an adult shirt woven entirely from green sand beads.

Two employees coupled with a checkout bot to man the store. One looked to be fiddling with a newly arrived junk dump, picking through it behind the store's wraparound glass counter and putting things in one pile or another depending on, Gregor assumed, their presumed value. The bot hung near the entrance, waiting for someone to place an object on its purchase pad. Its happy monotone welcomed Gregor to the store, while the big man also noticed a nerve-nuking stun shooter the bot pointed right at the door.

Theft prevention taken to serious lengths.

"Help you?" the second employee said, coming around in a peach t-shirt and soft white pleated pants and a look that went from bored to curious as he took in Gregor's sheer size.

"I'd like to speak to the owner," Gregor said.

"Uh, the owner?"

"You heard me."

The employee swung his face to his partner, still picking from the pile. No rescue there. Gulping, the man went back to Gregor and offered up an ill smile.

"Okay, just give me a sec, all right?"

"Fine."

Peaches-and-cream turned tail and ducked back through an employee's only door, leaving Gregor to wander the aisles for a long few minutes. He kept one eye on Parts-picker, who seemed to give not one single care about the large man roving his store. Gregor's other eye found a neat long-handled steel staff, heavy duty walking support or, in a pinch, capable of holding a door shut against vacuum leaks.

Gregor found the price, winced at the mark-up Salinity's planet-wide cost of living threw onto the item's worth. Still . . .

"Hey," Gregor said towards Parts-picker. "I'd like to buy this."

Parts-picker followed Gregor's nod towards the staff.

"Sure thing," the man said. "Be right there."

Gregor turned back to the staff, trying to figure out how best he'd wield it to deliver a good smacking or three. The seconds swam by, until things shifted into the uncomfortable, and Gregor turned back towards the parts pile. Instead of the idle picker, Gregor saw both staffers standing behind the counter, pistols raised and dead set.

"Time to talk, dude," said Parts-picker. "You're not one of ours. What're you after?"

Steady hands, no nerves in those words. These two had

to be agents, or close to it. Gregor couldn't count on a sudden move to throw off their aim.

"Renard," Gregor said. "He's here. I have business with him."

"Thanks," said Parts-picker. "That's what we needed to know."

Their fingers went to the triggers, and the storefront's window shattered.

Gregor took the distraction and moved, using the chaos to get behind the high-stacked lockboxes. Lasers flashed as the agents fixed their broken nerves and shot at him, at Aurora. The trash bin Aurora had used to smash the glass rolled along the floor, coming to rest near Gregor's feet. The Sever captain, meanwhile, returned potshot fire at the two agents.

Shouts, screams came from the broader street as the fight went public. Security would be coming quick. No time for games.

Gregor reached forward, picked up a lockbox holding some special wristlet model, turned and whipped the container back towards the agents. Aurora's lasers had them ducking and weaving, but a chunky box took more effort to dodge. Gregor's toss clipped Parts-picker in the shoulder, bounced him into his own crap pile.

Aurora sprayed covering fire in the ping-ping-ping pistol rhythm while Gregor spun the opposite way, taking three long steps through the store, ending with a crashing charge into the counter. Glass shards bit into Gregor's thick sweater, a few marking scratches, but the big man's momentum carried him through to the other side.

Peaches-n-cream swiveled, bringing his pistol level with Gregor, and took an Aurora shot to the skull for his troubles. The man dropped, and Gregor used the space to tackle the just-rising Parts-picker to the ground. Wrestling away the pistol, Gregor turned the hot barrel on its owner, delivering a whisper with the warning.

"Give it up, or die like your friend," Gregor said.

"Giving it up, giving it up," Parts-picker said. "Don't shoot me, man."

Gregor had another hostage, but going by the sirens outside, he didn't have much time either. Aurora crunched her way into the store, hair frizzed out by the firefight's rolling demands. That white jacket had some new stains, and a single burning black hole that, thankfully, didn't have a match on the captain's body.

The bot issued a hearty welcome her way. Ever on the ball, that one.

Pulling Parts-picker to his feet, Gregor surveyed the ruined shop, the blast marks scouring the walls, the glass-coated floor. A small fire burned where a stray bolt struck something with power.

Now it felt like a Sever mission.

FOUR

Business

How DO you win a fight against an overwhelming force?

Prove that the overwhelming force is a bunch of trumped up bargain-rate bums, that's how.

"I've got the prize, you get the punches," Eponi said, lunging towards Kashmal. She could've pulled out her pistol, started spraying laser, but so far the energy weapons had stayed put. Moving this fight into the lethal category seemed like a bad idea when Sever sat on the number's wrong side.

"Lucky me," Sai replied, stepping into a low-slung slug at the fastest guard to arrive.

Like Eponi, he kept his katana in its sheath. Playing nice today.

Kashmal kept backing up as Sai's swing connected with the guard's gut, dropping the man with a singular *oof.* The scientist and crappy father couldn't manage a backtrack faster than Eponi could pound it ahead, and she grabbed his lab coat's collar before two seconds had passed.

Perfect timing to whip Kashmal into a squishy guard

lumbering her way. The scientist made his biggest break-through yet as Kashmal stumbled into the advancing Lunk, piling them both to the ground.

"Behind!" Sai called, and Eponi whirled from admiring her handiwork, going right into a kick without seeing who came at her back.

With the lovely sound of cracking carrots, Eponi's kick struck an outstretched hand, prompting a howl from the guard, who cradled her smashed knuckles and stepped back. Eponi did the same, buying some distance while closing again with Kashmal as the scientist climbed back to his feet.

"You're coming with us," Eponi said, again snaking Kashmal's arm and holding it fast. "This is your damn daughter we're talking about."

"Talking?" Kashmal asked. "You call this talking?"

"We didn't call the guards!"

Eponi felt hands on her shoulders, felt the heavy grasp as Lunk ripped her away from Kashmal and threw her to the ground. Training kicked in as Eponi hit the smooth floor, rolling along with the stream beneath the glass and popping right back up.

Lunk had a hand moving towards a stun gun, not something Eponi wanted in the fight.

"Shoot him," Eponi said towards Kashmal, looking over Lunk's shoulder.

The security guard started, glanced towards a confused Kashmal, and Eponi used the misdirection to dash forward into a gut-busting shoulder charge. Lunk took the hit better than he had Kashmal's stumble moments earlier, retaining his footing and keeping his waist holster right where Eponi needed it.

Using her momentum, Eponi kept moving forward, spinning around Lunk's bulk and using her left hand to pull the stun gun out. She raised it, flicking off the safety, and firing in a single motion with her left hand. Lunk folded, collapsing with all the wheezing puffery of a balloon loosing its air.

Grabbing Kashmal, who stared at Lunk's downed self with a stunned, broken expression, Eponi checked in on Sai's morning. The man faced off against a single guard, one who had the meaty gleam on his face that said a hand-to-hand combat dream was being fulfilled. Behind the man, another guard had her stun gun drawn and aimed, waiting, apparently, until her partner finished the game.

"Stay still, or I'll zap you too," Eponi said, setting Kashmal as a body shield, taking aim, and firing.

Her stunning bolt hit the second guard, knocking her senseless as Sai delivered a triple-jab combo to his own opponent. The guard blocked all but one on his forearms, taking the leaked hit to the ribs and shrugging it off. Countering with a heavy haymaker, the guard clipped Sai's shoulder as the Sever man attempted to close. The punch knocked Sai wide, and Eponi's shot went into the opening, ruining the guard's hopes and crashing him to the ground with his friends.

"Would've had him," Sai said as Eponi pulled Kashmal up.

"You were taking too long," Eponi replied. "Be quicker next time."

"You're both awful people, you know that?" Kashmal interjected.

"Can't you stun him?" Sai said as they made their way towards Salinity's exit doors, the others in the lobby having ducked behind their desks or made their way well clear of a fight that didn't involve them.

"You want to carry this guy?"

"I can walk," Kashmal said. "I can walk."

"Then walk faster," Eponi said.

Sai reached the doors first. The things should've swished open as Sai approached, but the glassy barriers stayed closed. Sai pushed, using the age-old way to move things aside, and achieved precisely nothing as Eponi and Kashmal caught up to him.

Because, of course. Sever couldn't manage to beat double their number in brawling combat and get away. That'd be too easy.

"Stay put," Eponi said, then whirled, aiming the stun gun back the way they'd run, towards that lobby and the waterfall lifts behind it.

Salinity could mobilize, Eponi had to give'em that much. Two guards picked the rubber-limbed Lunk off the ground, while the wounded others retreated behind a veritable corporate phalanx, led by a poised woman who's folded arms crossed her Salinity blue-gray uniform and declared no bullshit.

Eponi would've believed that stance too, except the perfect pose matched a perfect face, with hair bearing none of the hallmarks of time spent in the rough. The woman looked like a schoolteacher, or maybe an executive, someone who thought their presence, their orders would be obeyed because society demanded it.

Good luck getting away with that nonsense in a firefight.

"Put that down," the woman said, packing in all the scorn a parent might to a disobedient child.

"I'll cut you a deal," Eponi said. "You want me to put this toy down? I'll do it, but before I do, you're going to open these doors and let us walk out. I toss the stun gun back, and we're all happy."

"This part isn't negotiable," the woman replied. "We're

in a business. You've already stunned two of my people. Put the weapon down and we can talk."

Eponi checked, saw Sai had Kashmal held tight. The Salinity guards hadn't drawn their weapons yet, trusting in their leader to de-escalate the situation. Eponi could get two, maybe three shots off before someone fired back her way, and stunning some guards wouldn't get those doors open. Neither would pulling her pistol and adding murder to her pending record on Gillane Four.

"I trust you," Sai said, pinching off Kashmal when the man tried to speak. "Make your choice."

Go down fighting, or stay up talking? Not much of a choice.

"Well?" the woman asked.

Eponi set the stun gun at her feet, close enough to grab again if things went awry. Stood up and flashed the cocky kart racer's smile, "You wanted to talk, let's talk."

"Can we move aside, and let this lobby get back to its business?" The woman said, gesturing towards Eponi's left, where a small coffee stand purveyed its warm wares to thirsty visitors. Several small tables looked to be the proposed negotiating ground. "Or do you require a show?"

"All we're looking for is results," Eponi said. "You do anything funny, and my boy here'll snap this twig's neck before you can get anywhere. Just warnin' ya."

"Eponi," Sai growled. "Not the time."

"Hey," Eponi held a single finger up Sai's way. "I'm busy negotiating. Keep it quiet."

The woman had the grace to look bemused, a crack in the armor that said she might not be as frigid as Eponi took her for. With the opening round settled, the group made their way to the left, Sai and Kashmal stepping along slow. As soon as Sai cleared the last door, putting solid wall behind him and the hostage instead of an exit, the woman signaled two guards to cover those doors. Once they were in position, with Eponi, Sai, and Kashmal at the coffee stand's cookie-shaped tables, someone in Salinity unlocked the entry, giving way to a steady, confused employee and visitor rush.

"Convenient," Eponi said as she sat across from the woman, Sai and Kashmal behind her. "You open up the doors now?"

"Salinity's a company," the woman said. "They'd prefer cash flow continues. That being said, you're outnumbered and assaulting a scientist employed by the company that, effectively, owns this planet. Not a good position."

"Eh, I've been in worse."

That earned Eponi a raised eyebrow.

"Let's reset, all right?" The woman said. "I'm Raquel, and you are?"

"Eponi. Behind me's Sai. We're the two coolest members of Sever Squad." Eponi leaned back in her chair, tried to see if Sever meant anything to Raquel.

Tried to see if Renard or Vana had already been here.

"Sever squad?" Raquel looked as confused as Eponi hoped. "Is that supposed to mean something?"

"It will now," Eponi replied. "I'll keep it short, Raquel, as you seem like you're a nice person and don't deserve to get caught up in a bloody, destructive mess."

"What's going to be a bloody, destructive mess?"

Back in the DefenseCorp days, they sat down every squad member and had them sign off a thousand little documents before giving you a sign-on bonus. Those pages held that you could lose any and all payments should you blab about your assignments to non-DC personnel, or, really, to anyone outside the immediate squad.

Now, Eponi didn't give a damn what DefenseCorp

wanted. She could blab about it all to anyone she wanted.

"Raquel, let me illustrate to you the level of awfulness this man got himself mixed up with," Eponi said. "Oh, and while I'm talking, maybe one of your flunkies can get us some coffee. Sai, you want anything?"

"Black tea?" Sai said.

"I'd like—" Kashmal started, before Sai tightened an awkward hold on the man's arm.

Raquel tilted her head, then nodded towards the stand. A guard behind her, one that had the distinct look of an assistant hoping for some future promotion, scurried off to fulfill the demands.

"Thanks," Eponi said. "As I was saying, Kashmal here played a game with DefenseCorp a while back. I don't know all the nuts and bolts, but short way of saying, he spliced some DNA, made a fancy virus that turns the person it infects into an invincible, murderous mess. Didn't work all that well, but he stuck his daughter with it and found his miracle match. Then, thanks to Sai and I, and the other Severs, Kashmal ran away with his daughter and the prize in her blood."

Kashmal kept trying to interrupt, squeeze in a word or three, but all that came out were yips and croaks as Sai kept him under lockdown. The flunky arrived with the drinks, and Eponi gave hers a hot sip while Raquel parsed the info-dump Eponi had just delivered.

"And you're here because someone wants this prize?" Raquel said.

"Hey, you catch on quick," Eponi replied. "That's a big ol' bingo. There's some nasty folks that hit your planet recently that'd like a piece of Kaia—that's his daughter, a sweet girl—and we're trying to get her location from Kashmal here so we can play protector. Instead, the guy decides to call all you into this."

"How do I know you're not the ones trying to kidnap Kaia?" Raquel said. "It's hard to take all you've said on faith."

"Kashmal, what do you think, did I get it right?" Eponi tilted in her chair, gave Kashmal a sugary look that said pain would be imminent and infinite if he dared object.

"Roughly." Kashmal's answer came with the sullen grit of a teenager caught doing something stupid.

"See?" Eponi said, turning back Raquel's way. "We're the good guys here."

Raquel tapped a single finger on the table.

"Salinity put me in as its local security chief," Raquel said. "Given we own this planet, that makes me in charge of its well-being, and its safety. You're telling me some force is here to capture a little girl under my watch?"

"That's what we're saying."

"Then," Raquel pushed back from the table, stood. "I think I need to see this girl, and find out if you're telling the truth."

Eponi bounced to her feet, the coffee juicing her energy, "Knew you'd come around."

"You've still assaulted four of my personnel," Raquel said. "After this is over, we'll be discussing how you plan to rectify that."

"Raquel," Eponi said, sticking out a hand for the woman to shake. "You could do lot worse than having Sever Squad in your debt."

Kashmal groaned as Raquel sealed the deal, but when the Salinity security chief asked him to lead the way to Kaia, the scientist didn't fight it. Together, they tromped out under that blue sky.

A negotiated truce, not a single dead innocent, and the objective achieved.

Not too bad for a kart racing reject.

FIVE

The Other Side

MOST HOSTAGES DIDN'T HAVE it this good.

Rovo devoured a delectable lunch—fresh fish, verdant greens and fruit pulled from Gillane Four's own gardens and fisheries—beneath a park's clear sky. The swallows had stopped hurting now as wounds healed, though the dark scar on his chest wouldn't go away without some cosmetic work, a surgery that'd require cash Rovo would only get if he went along with Vana and Renard's plan.

But nobody who cared about appearances would join DefenseCorp, would subject themselves to deadly and dangerous missions.

"I see you hated that," Vana said, coming over and sitting beside Rovo on the long sea-green bench.

"Had to eat it quick, to save anyone else the pain."

Vana gave him that accommodating smile she pulled out seemingly every conversation. The agent dealt with Rovo like a patient parent, dealing encouragement and discipline in equal measure, trying to turn Rovo from a loyal Sever squad fighter into a turncoat.

If only she knew what Rovo actually cared about.

"They've landed," Vana said. "Like you suspected, your squad followed without waiting for Deepak's reinforcements. They're alone, vulnerable."

"Wouldn't go that far," Rovo replied, putting elbows on knees and leaning forward. The sweater, the wooly pants, kept him warm enough on Gillane Four's temperate days, but they felt wrong. Meant for leisure, not combat. "Sever's more than enough for you all by themselves."

"Now you're the one underestimating us," Vana said. "We've been watching them. Aurora and Gregor are hunting for you. They destroyed our main site."

"That salvage shop?"

"Quite demolished."

"Oh no."

Vana laughed, "It's a good start. They're moving quick. The other two have Kashmal now."

"See? And you wanted to go in right away and take Kaia. Now you can toast Sever, get the girl, and solve all your problems in a single shot."

Rovo had been spinning the idea in the weeks leading up to landing on Gillane Four and in the days after, holding Renard and Vana from jumping on their plan with a trap instead. The two wanted Kaia's blood for their suits, but taking the girl and leaving Sever alive would only mean continued pursuit and, worse, a widely broadcast reveal from Sever about what'd happened.

Aurora, back on the *Nautilus*, had tried to get DefenseCorp's military arm to rise up against its clandestine half. Renard and Vana insisted that idea wouldn't fly, but the agents didn't have the same control over public sentiment. Throw the idea that DefenseCorp agents were stealing kids and sucking their DNA into the open, with Kaia's disappearance as the evidence, and those juicy contracts would disappear.

Wipe out Sever, though, and everything else would fall into perfection.

"Renard still thinks we are making a mistake," Vana said. "I'm starting to believe him."

"Doesn't matter. Sever's here now. It's our plan or nothing."

And, when Vana and Renard did something stupid, like engage Sever in open combat, Rovo would relish shooting the agents square in their backs.

The sealed skiff, a curved valley craft with a bubble-glass roof, held five in seats meant to absorb a hard crash into the water. Along the bottom, visible when the landing struts kept the skiff a meter or so off the ground, rubbery slats revealed floaters ready for use. Every craft on Gillane Four had to be ready for an ocean landing.

The skiff kept its secrets otherwise. No brands, no sharp color scheme. Light gray and nothin' else, a blandness Rovo had come to accept with the agents and their devices. Who knew keeping a low profile could be so dull?

Renard and another agent, a shining clean, beige man already had the front seats for themselves. Renard's old eyes tracked Rovo as he approached alongside Vana, his drooping frown digging deep divots into that plastic face.

While Vana sought to turn Rovo into a traitor to his squad, Renard had wanted to wring out the rookie for information and then leave him desiccated and dead some-where. The two had kept up an ugly dance for a while, until Renard realized he could neither defeat Vana with words or physical prowess.

Rovo hadn't spoken to the man in days now.

"Happy to see me?" Rovo said, climbing into the skiff. The craft nestled into a small landing pad behind some Salinity office Renard had co-opted through some connec-tions into a makeshift headquarters. "Been awhile."

"Vana thought it would be good if you came along. I thought it would be good if she shot you, now that your friends are here."

"Not my friends," Rovo said, the lie becoming easier to tell with every repetition. "Former squadmates. You're cutting me in on the cash, I'm yours."

"Apparently."

"Let's go," Vana ended the conversation, the bubble roof closing over the craft as they settled in. "Remember, the goal is to get the girl first. Kill the Sever duo second. This might be our best shot."

Rovo tried to get a better look at the tanned agent, also the skiff's pilot, as the man lifted the ship off the ground. He seemed cool, unfazed by waltzing into battle against hardened DefenseCorp mercenaries, but maybe all agents seemed that way.

Not that it mattered: Rovo had seen 'em die plenty fast on the *Nautilus*.

"The others are ready?" Vana asked Renard as the skiff puttered forth into Gillane Four's mild aerial traffic.

"They're in position," Renard replied. "Rovo, I don't believe you've met Abbad here, but let this serve as both an introduction and a warning. When we arrive, his focus will be on you."

"Oh goody," Rovo said. "Always wanted a fan."

Abbad laughed, and Rovo's eyes went wide. An agent with a sense of humor? What?

"Don't worry, Rovo, I'll be by your side every step of the way," Abbad said, his voice like cheerful honey. "Renard's been telling me you're from the fun side of DefenseCorp. You'll have to tell me about it sometime."

Rovo's mouth dropped. He'd specialized in communications, read any number of letters, met and negotiated plenty between all personalities, but this, this just wasn't on the map. Abbad sounded like he was one hour past orientation, but the man's age and position, here in the skiff with Renard and Vana, said otherwise.

"Uh, sure," Rovo said. "A drink."

"Right on," Abbad replied. "Now sit back and relax. Not a long flight, but gotta grab the moments when you can, am I right?"

Rovo glanced over at Vana, hoping to see some explanation in her expression, but all he found there were rolling eyes paired with a small smile.

With the capsule tubes providing most transit around the planet, actual air jaunts seemed to be reserved for those with money and without time. Even Renard and Vana preferred the capsules to the notoriety delivered by the skiff.

Neither one, though, wanted to head onto public transit loaded with weapons. Rovo glanced at Vana's array, with pistols on either hip and obvious knives up both arms. Spare power packs sat on the woman's belt, too, and her coat bulged with the protective vest snug beneath. Her hair up, Vana flashed with life. The opposite of Renard's grim, decaying facade.

Rovo might've been biased.

The flight didn't last long, with Renard settling the skiff onto a rooftop that, like most on Gillane Four, topped a teardrop shape with a broad flat platform entirely at odds with the building's design. Rovo figured some poor sap's beautiful architecture had been ruined by efficiency's needs: in today's galaxy, you had to have a spot for a craft to land, even if it looked ugly.

Kashmal's apartment sat somewhere beneath Rovo, and in it, presumably, waited Kaia. He hadn't seen the girl in a month, not since she'd vanished in the first few hours on Wexer. The rookie never thought he'd see the little sparkle again, so, despite the circumstances, Rovo couldn't be too upset.

The bubble roof popped open and Abbad bounded out, drawing a gleaming-clean silver pistol in the same motion. The man hit the rooftop in a crouch, sweeping the open space for hostiles that clearly weren't there. Beyond the skiff, the only thing sharing the landing pad was a squat opening for a lift and its requisite stairs.

"All clear," Abbad said, looking back at the skiff with a hard stare, before collapsing the facade into a wide grin. "Ah, I'm just playing with y'all. You can see there's nothin' up here."

Renard climbed out second, Vana third, and Rovo came last, still trying to fit Abbad's puzzle piece into something that made sense.

And failing.

On the landing pad, Vana took the lead, heading for the lift and tapping her wristlet. Buildings like these ought to only allow residents or, say, delivery folks in, but Vana's ID did the trick. With Abbad waiting for Rovo, the foursome piled into the lift and started down.

"We're going to hide out next to their apartment," Abbad said as the lift dropped. "The owner didn't mind, especially after I pointed Princess at him."

"Princess?" Rovo couldn't help but ask.

"His pistol," Renard replied. "Abbad may have a peculiar energy, but he is nonetheless effective. I would not underestimate him."

Underestimate? Rovo hadn't grappled with Abbad being a real person, much less giving the guy some skill rating. Abbad seemed to stand so at odds with everything Renard and Vana, the calm and scheming couple, cared about. The man spent the lift ride leaning on the elevator's side wall, small grin never leaving his lips, and watching the trio like they were all part of some vast inside joke.

Every time Rovo thought he had a hold on the universe, it proved otherwise.

They filed out into a hallway, a corridor speckled with blue and gold carpet, with nautical lamps faux-flickering their way forward. A workday quiet suffused the scene, apartments emptied out as their owners plied their trades. Not a bad time for a fight, or a kidnapping. Behind them, the lift closed fast and shot away, with Renard remarking that its next pick-up would be their prey.

Abbad brought them halfway down the hall, then turned and slapped his wristlet against a marble-white door. A lock clicked, and, with Vana playing rearguard, the quartet hustled inside. Abbad shut them in quiet, and Rovo found himself in a quaint, family-photo dominated spot with three people plotting to kill and steal his friends.

Cool. So cool.

"To run it back," Vana said, whispering. "Renard and I lead the way. We'll handle any resistance. Rovo, you take Kaia when she panics. Abbad, you're covering our backs."

"Got it," Abbad affirmed.

Renard nodded, and all eyes went to Rovo.

"Kaia. Yeah, I know," Rovo said. "You're all thinking I'm not going to play along, but I just want her safe."

True enough, and Rovo didn't have a weapon on him anyway. This wouldn't be as simple as just turning traitor, he'd have to be smart about it. Maybe deliver a smack to Renard's deserving face, then grab Kaia, stuff her back in here, and—

"Here they come," Abbad said, eyes glittering. "Get ready, y'all, cause this is about to get fun."

This guy.

Abbad's warning bore out as Eponi and Sai's voices,

mingling with Kashmal's constant protests, floated through the door. Someone else spoke too, presumed authority meshing with moderating attempts. Good luck with that crew.

Rovo took a deep breath as the apartment next to theirs clicked open, the people starting to funnel inside. Vana gave the slightest nod to Abbad, and the man reached for the door's handle.

Next door, Kaia laughed.

Assault

THE WIND WHIPPED ALONG, slicing through the buildings and into the tree-studded park along Kaiyo's edge. Bordered by those translucent, soft green barriers, the park gave a beautiful look out into Gillane Four's endless ocean. The fluttering birds, targeted flower arrangements, and capsule tubes made strange, compelling scenery.

As did Gregor, holding Parts-picker near the barrier. The man looked positively panicked with every step as Gregor brought him closer to what would be a long fall and a hard splash. Aurora wasn't one for torture—the practice, in her experience, tended to result in wild answers attempting to preserve life and limb—but the view and its surroundings gave the Sever duo a chance to look out for any potential pursuit.

Parts-picker had shown them a back way out from the destroyed salvage store, through an employees-only access tunnel cutting through the larger building's core, where trash and supplies could be run without disrupting the daily commerce. While Kaiyo's police tromped through the blown out front, Aurora and Gregor followed their forced friend out to the streets and, with Gregor's persuasive arguments, to their current park locale.

"Okay, I get it," Parts-picker said, his voice gyrating with the panic due someone who'd survived an unexpected shootout. "Renard didn't come to us, no matter how much you wanna hear something different. The man's in our branch, right, but, like, you've got different groups too, I'm guessing?"

Aurora put a hand on Gregor's arm. Just because Parts-picker talked in fragments, and looked as young as he sounded, wasn't a reason to deliver some heavy-handed discipline.

"You're saying Renard's not your boss," Aurora offered up, enticing Parts-picker to speak more.

"Yeah, definitely not." Parts-picker looked past the two Severs, searching the park for any potential spies. "He's in a development group, dealing with projects I don't know anything about. R&D, you might call it, except it's more secret than that."

"That fits," Gregor said. "We know he's on Gillane Four. How can we find him?"

"Does this guy listen? Why does he keep asking the same thing?" Parts-picker looked to Aurora.

"Answer the question," Aurora replied.

"Fine, dude. Like I said, Renard doesn't dance on our floor. So I don't know where he is, but I guess I know where he might be."

Parts-picker paused again, eyes dancing between Aurora and Gregor as if the two were going to offer up some cash, like in some movie. Neither one moved.

"Guess I'm just supposed to talk for free, then?" Parts-picker doubled-down on his strategy. "No bonus for me stabbing my employer in the back?"

"Think about it this way," Aurora said. "You help us, your employer doesn't go totally evil."

"You think a moral compass is gonna turn me around? Me, a DefenseCorp agent? I'm about as bankrupt as it gets on that front."

"What do you want?"

"Out," Parts-picker said, erupting into a grin, nodding a few times as if that made the request more clear.

Aurora's patience had hit its endpoint. Sai and Eponi had tossed a message not long ago saying they were on their way to get Kaia. Without Renard or Rovo in hand, that move came with risk. Aurora and Gregor simply weren't keeping their end of the deal.

"Nah, man, outta DefenseCorp," Parts-picker answered Gregor's obvious follow-up question. "I saw you light up my buddy—RIP, by the way—in there and got to thinking during our run here, maybe you can do the same to me."

"Kill you?" Aurora said. "You give us Renard's location, I'll do it. Gladly."

"Ouch, lady." Parts-picker put up his hands at the searing glare Aurora gave him. "No, I'm saying you make it look like I'm dead, see. Then, my family gets the benefits cash, and I get free."

"Fraud," Gregor said.

"Against DefenseCorp, though," Aurora mused. "Deal. You give us Renard's location, then we'll go back to our ship. You get on the next transport off-world when we start raising hell."

Parts-picker could work out the next steps for himself. Wait a while off-world, then come back to reap the cash benefits. Whether the plot would really work, Aurora didn't know, didn't care. What mattered was that Parts-picker, assured of his delusion, tapped out the potential location on Aurora's wristlet.

With the target in hand, Gregor and Aurora jaunted back to the *Prisa*, enjoying another lovely capsule ride crammed in with people, this time, heading off-world. On the ship, the two donned their new power armor suits, which they'd had painted to match their old ones. Aurora loaded up with her rifles, while Gregor, reunited with his massive hammer, stomped down the *Prisa*'s ramp looking like a metal demon from some old nightmare.

"Ready to smash some things?" Aurora said, her voice beaming now through the radio ties between the suits.

"Been too long."

Aurora couldn't argue with Gregor there. Those weeks spent flying out here had been long and dull. The *Prisa* didn't have simulators, didn't have much beyond movies and exercise. The muscles itched, the instincts buzzed.

Getting to the spot Parts-picker pointed out without causing a massive commotion required hiring a point-to-point skiff ride. Aurora handled the negotiation, asking for a lift right from the *Prisa*'s docking berth. Most skiffs wouldn't have the space for a couple power armor-clad mercenaries, so Aurora had to get a cargo hauler. Any human problems around ferrying two monstrous weapons resolved themselves when the skiff showed up with a bot driver, waiting until Aurora gave the go-ahead for the skiff to get flying.

The windowless ride gave Aurora and Gregor a chance to chat strategy while feeling out their armor's bits and bolts, a tactical intermission that boiled their assault plan from smash'n'rescue to just rescue, with the smashing bit implied.

"You get Rovo," Gregor concluded. "I get everyone else."

"You okay with that?"

"It is all I ever want."

The two bumped power armor fists as the skiff touched down on the targeted landing pad, opening up to an afternoon sky and little else. From the platform, one of several along the building's smooth blue-green side, each one connected via smoothed-over, painted scaffolding, the two mechanized marauders clanked towards a wide entry.

"Big building for a few agents," Gregor said.

Renard's supposed hideout did seem to be in a large commercial space, lingering near Kaiyo's southern half. The building dwarfed those around it, though the reason Renard had chosen the space became clear three steps along: up above, where Aurora hadn't been able to look due to the cargo skiff's closed transport, sat exposed metal. A skeleton not yet clothed with fabricated skin.

"It's not finished," Aurora replied. "He's taking it because nobody else can."

"Guess we ought to kick him out, then."

The landing pad doors, already up and running to facilitate friendlier cargo deliveries than this one, whooshed aside as Gregor and Aurora approached. No security for the in-progress place, then.

Not that it mattered: if the door had stayed shut, Aurora would've rammed the whole thing apart anyway.

Inside, a clean and clear loading dock gave way to an empty office floor, gapped in the center for a hollow core stretching from roof to base. The building adopted a smoothed over and dull aesthetic. Lines marked future floor arrangements, while Aurora looked straight towards the lift bank. Up and running. Light came in through windows dusted from the construction, their clanking armor disturbing clouds with every step.

"Quiet," Gregor said. "We're not hiding, so where are they?"

"Good question," Aurora replied. "That transport could've held a thousand agents. Who knows how many might be here. Stay ready."

"Always am," Gregor did, though, unlimber the hammer, hefting it with both hands as they started towards the lifts.

"Start at the bottom, work our way up?" Aurora said.

"Lotta floors for that."

"Better idea?"

"Smash our way down?"

Aurora took another step, playing out an efficient way to clear a thirty story building with two people. Maybe Gregor's idea wasn't so bad.

"How about we meet in the middle?" Aurora said.

"Done."

Aurora broke into a jog, the power armor playing with her desires and upping its kinetic assistance to shift into motion. Every step pounded along the heavy floor with a rattling shake, finishing off any life left in their stealth hopes. The lift wasn't made with power armor in mind, but with a duck and a dent to the doors, Aurora fit inside. She tapped, with just enough force to keep from cracking the screen, a descent to the first floor.

The lift obliged, shuttling Aurora down past floor after floor of empty spaces. At least, until the last few. Belongings whirred by as the lift descended, makeshift beds and foodstuffs. Tables put up, and a few pop-up walls to create private spaces. Parts-picker hadn't been totally wrong, then. Someone lived here.

But where were they?

The lift doors popped into a bland lobby, walls left in dull primer white, waiting for a fresh coat of personality.

The front doors, spanning a dozen entries, had paper plastered over them, hiding any potential peeks from the outside. The light coming in now rained from above in patches, creating golden shafts and making dots on the floor at Aurora's feet.

The quiet died a sudden death. Gregor's hammer slammed somewhere far above, a quaking blow followed by the scattered collapse as the man dropped through his newfound hole. The power armor landed with an anvil's grace, sounding a sequel boom. Aurora would've felt sorry for the damage, except Renard's aims would bring about so much more if left unchecked.

The cost, she supposed, of doing business.

The hammer blow flipped a switch. Aurora, standing just outside one of those golden shafts, witnessed a surge not unlike a disturbed insect nest. Agents in all clothing varieties swung around walls, burst from closed off sections, and took up posts on floors above, using the open core to try and find firing angles.

"And here I was, thinking you'd all run away," Aurora said, her visor splashing red all around as the power armor found threats everywhere. "Glad I wasn't disappointed."

Ordinarily, being this outnumbered would send Aurora scrambling for an escape. Power armor could take hits, but would melt under heavy, sustained fire. Unfortunately for the agents, they'd found a covert home on a populated, controlled planet. Difficult to get in rifles, cannons, and the heavy gear needed to take on power armor.

The agents had pistols aplenty. Some even looked confident, waiting to see if Aurora would surrender.

That confidence? Badly misplaced.

Aurora punched up the kinetic boosters in her power armor and flew forward, bursting up a huge dust cloud as she sprinted meters in a second. Crossing the middle gap,

Aurora caught one flash, two as the quickest triggers tried to respond. They missed.

The poor agent opposite Aurora didn't. His pistol shot crashed right into Aurora's chest, dissipated through the energy-sapping suit architecture with only the slightest tingle coming to Aurora's nerves. The agent's suit didn't do the same to her shoulder charge, but the far, outer wall stopped the agent when he slammed into it, the floor at his feet providing a suitable resting place for the crunched man.

Standing still in a fight like this meant dying, so Aurora shifted her momentum to the right, charging through some thin dividing walls that split like paper. Agents on the other side, plotting lean-around shots towards where Aurora had been, found their target breaking through behind their backs. Hefting her rifle, Aurora roasted the one to her left, then swung the rifle, one-handed, to her right, squeezing the trigger as she went.

Like a treasure map, the blast mark string led right to the next agent's steaming body.

Calls for position, for help, for anything, rang out around the building. The sounds of a collapsing strategy. Gregor's hammer hit again, collapsing another floor. Aurora's visor picked up new threats, coming in from all sides. Renard had to be in here somewhere.

She'd find him, no matter how many agents Aurora had to go through.

SEVEN

Apartment Rumble

Sᴀɪ ʟᴇᴛ Kashmal lead the way into his own apartment. The move prompted a delighted squeal from Kaia as the door slid open, the four year-old jumping up from a couch and heading Kashmal's way. The father, showing more humanity than Sai had ever seen from him, scooped up his daughter and smothered her in kisses.

The fact that Kashmal kept one knowing eye looking back towards Sai, Eponi, and Raquel only undercut the loving display a little.

"Glad to see she's not in a closet this time," Eponi said as the trio filed into the spare space after Kashmal.

The scientist had said he'd only been on Gillane Four a few weeks, and the apartment showed. Precisely zero art hung on light blue walls. The living room sported a couch, a fixed screen, and a balcony with no furniture. The kitchen, visible right from the door, had the clean look of a space never used.

Kaia, though, seemed happy. She gave Sai and Eponi a second squeal when Kaia recognized them, Kashmal putting her down so she could do a run-and-hug around their legs. Neither Sever squad member had the protective connection Rovo sported with the kiddo, but spend a few weeks bumming around a small space ship and you were bound to find some affection for each other.

"You keep your daughter home alone at this age?" Raquel said, breaking the mood. "Really?"

"I haven't had time to look for daycare," Kashmal countered, backing into his apartment like a cornered rat. "I've been busy."

"Salinity offers—"

Raquel didn't finish her sentence, breaking as the door slammed open behind them. Sai whirled, katana rubbing its sheath on the apartment walls, to see two people he didn't know and two he did forcing themselves in behind the Salinity officer.

The mood, the situation changed so fast that Sai felt a kind of whiplash. Sudden reversals were a Sever fact of life, but the apartment, Kaia, and the orderly walk over had put a safe glaze on everything. Sai's combat nerves had dialed down since the Salinity lobby fight, and he struggled to put them back in the apartment's confines.

Especially when Rovo, third in with an unknown behind him, looked so calm.

Seeing Rovo at all swirled the moment even more. The rookie had been a hostage for weeks now, and with Aurora and Gregor off on the rescue mission, catching Rovo here made no sense. Why would Renard and his agents bring Rovo along on an abduction? It's not like they needed his help to catch a four year-old.

"To the back!" The woman leading the party, an older face that had longtime authority's etched lines, ordered to Kashmal, Raquel, and the Sever duo. "We're not here for you, but we'll shoot if you resist."

The woman's face tickled recognition, and her voice

confirmed it. She'd given Sai a drive back on the *Nautilus*, one holding information on a separate command chain behind DefenseCorp's official version. She'd been on that drive, same with Renard.

But why would Vana help her enemies? Sai would've asked the question if the drawn weapons hadn't demanded closer attention.

Kashmal scooped up Kaia from the floor and complied. Sai pulled Raquel behind him, saw Eponi step back a pace or two as well. That move wasn't quite the retreat it appeared to be: Eponi knew to clear enough room for Sai to draw his katana, and the pilot had moved her hand towards her pistol. No matter the odds, there wouldn't be a surrender here. Not with Kaia at stake.

Not with Rovo standing behind Renard, un-cuffed and ready.

"Name's Sai," He said, reaching a hand up towards his katana hilt. "Mind introducing yourself to my friends here, and then we can get to the fun part?"

Vana gave him a look, one Sai couldn't quite read. Seemed equal parts respect, pity, and annoyance.

"Vana," the woman said, gesturing with her pistol towards Sai's sword. "Keep your hand away from that, please. We're here for Kaia, and nothing else. I promise, should we take the girl, she will not be harmed."

"No," Kashmal said quick. "You can't have her."

"Dude, keep your mouth shut," Eponi said to him, not taking her look from the intruders. "The grown-ups are talking."

Raquel, for her part, dropped back next to Kashmal. Sai couldn't turn to see anything else, but the scientist kept quiet, which was a blessing.

"You're pinned," Vana said. "Trapped. Anything other than what we ask ends in a poor death for all of you. The girl ought to have her father back. Don't make us take that from her."

Sai flicked his look towards Rovo, "Rookie, what's your take on this? I know Renard's an ass, but what do you think? Should we kill him first, or her?"

The man behind Rovo laughed, a hooting thing way at odds with the situation. The noise drew Sai's attention to the pistol the man had, a big toy modified and shimmering with green and gold parts. Anything that extreme meant the goon was either a fool to be ignored, or more dangerous than any of the others.

"I think you should do what she's asking," Rovo said, keeping his hands at his sides, his fingers moving.

Sever's hand signs gave the squad an edge in almost every mission, a secret language Aurora had cobbled together and taught with uncompromising zeal to any new recruit. Rovo, like Eponi, Gregor, and Sai before him, had spent his first days on *Nautilus* getting wrung out in one simulated mission after another, with every hour in between spent learning those hand signs.

The rookie didn't have'em perfected yet, but the meaning came clear enough: Rovo would make a move. Sai and Eponi ought to follow. Keep the girl away.

"Kashmal," Sai said. "If Kaia's going somewhere, why don't you go help her pack a bag?" Vana's eyes narrowed, and Renard started a protest. Sai cut'em off, "No offense, but none of you look like you have kids. I do, and if you try to take this girl without her favorites, you're going to have a miserable time. This apartment's got one exit, the one behind you. Nobody's leaving unless you let them."

Vana kept up the showy grimace, but nodded, "Fine, make it fast."

Kashmal, Raquel, and Kaia hustled away, heading towards the bedrooms and leaving Eponi and Sai with a couch-clad living room. More importantly, the civilians weren't in the firing line anymore.

Which mean it was time to trash Kashmal's apartment.

Rovo broke first, delivering an elbow back towards the laughing man behind him. The dude took the blow in stride, and the way the man's smile only grew made Sai's eye twitch for a microsecond. Rovo, though, followed up the elbow strike with a turning, pulling throw that sent the laughing man forward, barreling into a whirling Renard.

A flash fired as Eponi drew and shot her pistol, moving with the motion to get behind the couch and into some cover. The laser hit true, smoking into Vana's chest, revealing—of course—a protective vest. The agents hadn't banked on their diplomacy, then.

Vana, though, flinched enough at the hit, her own reaction thrown off, that Sai had time to draw the katana. With the smooth weight in his palms, Sever's sole swordsman set his angle and went to work.

Three targets, all trapped together, presented a compelling choice: who to slice and dice with the first go?

Renard, obviously. The older agent had to be the commander here, and Sai couldn't count on infinite swings. Best remove the danger to Kaia and cause confusion among the other two.

Sai went for an overhead swing, swift and ready to detach Renard's annoying head from his annoying body. The blade went in, and the damn laughing man blocked it. That green-gold pistol swung up and caught Sai's stroke as the man, rolling with Rovo's throw, pushed Renard into the rookie.

Sword met gun in a sparking clash. Sai's katana should've sheared the pistol in half, but the man apparently played with better quality than DefenseCorp standard.

The man pushed up on the block, pushing Sai's katana into a ceiling-scarring gouge.

"Abbad," the man said, getting close enough that Sai felt spit from the speech. "Pleasure to meet you!"

"Pleasure's all mine," Sai said, kicking Abbad's ankle.

Abbad danced back from the kick, letting Sai's katana free, but leveling the pistol at the swordsman's face. A sure-fire kill. At least, until Eponi shot him.

The pilot proved her worth a second time in the fight, delivering a solid hit to Abbad's shoulder as Eponi used the couch to absorb Vana's counterfire. Abbad twitched away, his right arm with its pistol hanging. Sai flipped his grip, sliced the katana horizontal, planning on sticking Vana's side.

Vana must've sensed something, because she dove forward as Sai swung, cutting off her fusillade towards Eponi and giving a clear path for Sai's katana to cut a chunk from the apartment wall. A good dodge, a tricky one.

Sai tried to calibrate the battlefield. Vana now moved behind and to his left, while Abbad struggled back towards the apartment door. Renard and Rovo tussled, the old agent apparently able to hold his own when things turned close.

"Take Vana!" Sai shouted, breaking towards Abbad and the rumble at the apartment's door.

If Abbad showed any fear at being charged in close quarters by a katana-wielding soldier, the man didn't show it. Instead, Abbad's left hand snagged his pistol from his defunct right, whipped it up to ankle height, and blasted. The forest-green bolt flashed and Sai felt his left leg burn, then go numb. What had been a charge turned into a fall.

Sai hit the tile floor, swinging the katana wide to keep from stabbing himself. He saw Renard go by, followed by

Rovo. The two exchanged punches, with Renard getting the worse end of a deal that eventually tilted towards raw strength. Abbad followed, stepping on Sai's katana blade to lock it to the floor, aiming that pistol towards Rovo's back.

Shoot a man's ankle, and he couldn't walk. Didn't mean he couldn't fight.

Dropping the katana hilt, Sai reached out and yanked Abbad's leg, pulling the man to the ground. Abbad landed butt-first on the flat katana, and the man laughed again. Just cackled with what seemed like pure joy as that green-gold pistol made its barrel-first aim at Sai's skull.

"Just a brilliant move, man," Abbad said. "Gotta respect that."

"Right," Sai replied, rolling over his own sword.

Another flash, and Sai smelled his burning hair, but the move broke Abbad's aim enough that the shot whisked over Sai's head. Glass shattered off to the right, towards the balcony. Kaia's crying broke through too, along with feet hitting the floor hard.

Vana cursed, loud. Eponi called for them to run.

Abbad pushed Sai away, kicked the swordsman in the side to buy another few centimeters. Sai tried to get to one knee, get his ankle-holstered pistol out. Felt a hard, hot barrel at his skull.

Then felt it disappear as Renard crashed into Abbad, throwing them both in a bundle towards the door. Sai whipped a glance back, saw Rovo start to come his way. Behind the rookie, Raquel looked to be following Kashmal out a broken balcony window and over the edge.

Were they just falling to their deaths to keep Renard from getting Kaia? And where was Eponi?

Vana rose up behind Rovo, looking frustrated and bleeding from a nice cut along her face.

"Behind you!" Sai shouted, finally getting his pistol free.

Rovo wheeled to the side and Sai snapped the shot, struck Vana for what looked like the third time in that protective vest. Those things couldn't take hits forever, and Vana's stumble showed she felt the heat that time.

"C'mon!" Eponi's voice carried through the balcony window. "We have to leave!"

The objective. Kaia. Getting the girl away from these bastards mattered more than anything else.

"Rovo, run!" Sai said. "That's an order!"

Who knew whether the words would have any meaning to the rookie, but Sever taught its squad members to read the situation. Rovo would know he had no chance to get Sai, would know the only option—

The rookie ran, sprinted across the living room, through the open balcony window and over the edge. Nobody even bothered to shoot at him. Sai, still holding his pistol on one knee, aimed back towards the door.

Abbad's kick struck again, numbing Sai's right hand and knocking his pistol loose.

"A good fight, my friend," Abbad said. "But I think this one is over now."

"And not a total loss," Renard added, approaching. The man's tired, bruised, and angry look told Sai all he needed to know. "Time to take our prize and go."

One hostage for another.

EIGHT

Down and Up And Down

THE HAMMER WHISTLED as Gregor swung it again and again, mashing walls, floors, and agents. Gregor descended by disaster, setting back the building's construction by months through sheer devastation. A cleaner offensive might've worked if Sever had hit the tower in full force, but with only two, Gregor relied on chaos to give him cover.

Dust clouds whipped up by the hammer strikes masked Gregor's next swing and threw laser fire off by the micrometers needed to keep his power armor cool. Bashing through floors to the next one kept Gregor's movements unpredictable, keeping ambushes and any snipers from drawing a defined bead. And the occasional leap, using his power armor's boosters, straight up through the floor above knocked whole squads on their heels.

Gregor couldn't be sure when the agents decided fleeing rather than fighting made the better play, but the incoming fire dwindled when Gregor smacked a hapless agent into the tower's central shaft. As if the falling scream signaled a preplanned maneuver, the agents popping around corners dashed off. Glass shattering sounds rang throughout as escapists made their getaways by any means necessary, leaving Gregor breathing hard over that shaft, looking through dust-clouded daylight down at his partner.

Aurora, below, kept up the shooting. Her rifle hummed with pinpoint blasts after the running agents. An admirable dedication to their destruction. Gregor's visor showed his immediate area had no threats, and the man confirmed it with a sweeping look 'round. Yes, the crumbling walls, sparking exposed wires, and a few burst pipes spewing water made for a busy scene, but no real danger remained.

Neither trusted the lifts after the rumble in the tower, so Gregor made his way down to the first floor through a too-tight stairwell along the building's side. Jumping from one landing to the next, and leaving cracks in the tile as he went, Gregor made good time, entering the lobby to find Aurora, rifle holstered, standing still.

"Do they have the girl?" Gregor said.

A pose like Aurora's tended to mean the power armor pilot had her attention swung to the digital world, playing with the power armor's wristlet connection to send and see messages.

"They do, but there's a problem," Aurora replied, voice saying she was reading still as she replied. "Eponi's dashing off the messages quick. They're dealing with more agents. And Sai's been taken."

"Taken? Like Rovo?"

"An accidental swap," Aurora replied. "Rovo's with them now. Along with Kashmal and Kaia. Someone named Raquel, too?"

Gregor shrugged, the suit whirring as its metal shoulders complied. He didn't know any Raquels, in this system or any other.

"What do we do?" Gregor said. "Someone will tell Renard what happened here."

"If they find somewhere else to hide, we're back to square one." Aurora's frustration bled through. "We should have confirmed Renard was here before we attacked."

"Hard to know."

"We moved too fast," Aurora said. "Now we have to change the game."

"How?"

"Eponi and the others are making for the *Prisa*. We can fly Kaia into orbit, make sure she's safe while we go looking for Sai," Aurora said. "We know Renard wants the girl, so that's what we use."

A child as bait didn't strike Gregor as the best plan, but he didn't have a better one. Gillane Four had too many possible spots for Renard to hide, and the man would probably send everything he had after the girl.

It's what Gregor would do. Bury the enemy in your numbers until you had what you wanted.

"Back up, then?" Gregor said.

"Back up."

Running through the streets in the power armor, particularly with Gregor's giant hammer, continued to seem a bad idea. Together, the duo pounded back up the far too many stairs to the lowest landing pad. Aurora once again drummed up a call for a cargo carrier, and the two clomped out towards the silver pad in the shimmering golden afternoon to wait for their ride.

"That was fun," Gregor offered, looking out past Kaiyo's edge towards the ocean horizon.

"It was a slaughter," Aurora replied. "They weren't equipped for us."

"Good thing."

"Means Renard's not as far with his whole revolution as I thought he'd be," Aurora said. "The man has to know most DefenseCorp squads will have power armor access.

Those agents didn't have EMP spikes, didn't know our blind spots. Tarla's crew did a better job on Wexer."

"Confidence can create weakness."

A pithy statement, but in Gregor's experience, the ones most likely to fall hard were the ones too wrapped up in their own presumed success. From corrupt officers believing nobody would dare dig through their records to DefenseCorp targets too vain to think their worlds couldn't be wiped away, Gregor's life had been littered with idiots unwilling to see failure and, thus, doomed to it.

Outside, Salinity security began arriving. Fast response bikes, made to swerve a meter above street level, carted armed duos to the building's blown out entrance. Someone, apparently, had seen or heard the battle inside and made a call. From this high up, Gregor found watching the police force amusing, dots scurrying this way and that, trying to set up a perimeter.

"The cargo skiff's been called off," Aurora said, starting the line with a curse. "Apparently Salinity's cut airspace over the building."

"A new plan, then."

"I don't want to drag Salinity security all the way back to the *Prisa* with us," Aurora said. "If that's what you're thinking."

"No," Gregor replied. "Only that we need to get to a different building. One they aren't watching."

From the landing pad, with Kaiyo spread out around them, several options curled close enough on floors down below. A kinetic-boosted jump could carry the power armor from one structure to the next. A bold play, and one that would need some help.

Large, armored suits flying through the air tended to attract attention.

Heading back inside, the two heard the barked calls

from Salinity forces working their way up the tower. Gregor figured they had to drop five levels to get to a range where they could make the jump. The stairs worked well enough for that, though from the first banging leap, the Salinity forces called out alarms.

"We weren't going to stay hidden anyway," Aurora said as they picked up the pace, now kicking off the landings as soon as they touched down. "Keep moving, ignore them."

That would get harder when they started shooting, but Gregor kept his mouth shut, his concentration on the jumps. Escape aside, this still felt more fun than anything he'd done since fighting those invisible suits on the *Nautilus*.

They broke through onto the target level, one Gregor had already laid low in the earlier fight. Aurora whistled as they clomped to the windowed side, looking across a sizeable gap, with a several story drop, to the next building.

"You did work up here," Aurora said.

"I had fun."

Now came the hard part. Both Severs looked over the gap. The Salinity forces were getting close, and with the noise they'd made, any outside eyes would be looking up. They needed a distraction.

Gregor popped a fracture grenade from the slot on his power armor. While he preferred getting up close with his hammer to tossing bombs, Sai had long ago made the things a standard-issue item for Sever.

"You first," Gregor said. "After I throw."

Aurora nodded, went to the floor-to-ceiling window, and grappled the frame. Pulling at the dark lines between the glass, the captain broke the pane from its slot. The window fell back onto Aurora, shattering as it struck her helmet and littering the floor with shards. Nothing, though, fell outside. No clues pouring onto the street.

Gregor threw the grenade, spicing the throw with

kinetic energy. His hammer-cleared efforts paid off again, giving him a through-line across the shaft to the building's far side. A crackling burst came one breath later, wrecking windows and the spaces immediately above and below, damage hopefully far away from the climbing Salinity forces.

Sever's captain didn't wait for Gregor's go ahead, but jumped as the rippling explosion grew. Aurora flew out the window, curling up, but otherwise keeping her feet down, where those kinetic boosters would do their work and absorb the fall's energy. Gregor started that way next, when a second explosion tore through the building, followed by more pops, bangs, and booms. Like he'd suddenly found himself in a fireworks show.

The power armor adjusted to the shaking, the boots leveling Gregor out as he took one step after another towards the window. Not that he needed many, but, as his visor began blaring, the floor around him was crumbling. That didn't make sense: Gregor's grenade wasn't that powerful.

To Gregor's left, an exposed pipe shivered, with nuts and bolts popping off like tiny bullets. The pipe expanded, then blew out, green and orange fire racing into the office. The answer washed over Gregor with the flames: the fighting earlier must've broken utility lines, pushed explosive gasses into the open. He'd thrown a big match into a building chopped to kindling.

Time to go.

Taking one long step, planting his right foot at the window's edge, Gregor punched the power armor's kinetic boosters and flew into space, smoke and flames bursting out behind him. For a fleeting moment, Gregor's stomach shot up as he plummeted in Gillane Four's beautiful sky. For a fleeting moment, Gregor lived that delirious dream of free-form flight that no human was meant to have.

He struck the target and stuck his landing, smashing through solar panels and shredding the black silicon with Gregor's thick armor. Aurora caught him with a steadying hand, keeping Gregor upright. Her visor, though, looked back where they came. Gregor followed the look, saw several levels engulfed in flames. The building shook, but Gregor didn't think it'd fall. Didn't think there'd be thousands of casualties.

He hoped.

"We have to move," Aurora said. "Skiffs will be coming to put that fire out, and we can't have them see us."

The captain had it right, as always.

The two dashed along the rooftop, doing what they could to avoid trampling more panels. This building, shorter and not quite finishing its teardrop goals, ended on its far side with another sloping glass descent. No landing pad, no easy way down.

And no other building in leaping range.

"No skiffs going to pick us up here," Aurora said, looking towards the ground below. "We might have to ditch the armor."

Make a plain-clothes walk back to the *Prisa*, come back later and pick up the power armor? If it still remained?

"They will notice the broken panels," Gregor replied. "We can't abandon our armor here."

"Then what? You want to jump a dozen stories to the ground, get a whole force after us?"

"No, we use that," Gregor said, pointing to the building to their right. It rose above their rooftop, and did have landing pads, including one a little below their level. "We catch our ride there."

"You're crazy."

"I will not deny that."

Aurora called up the list, connected with another AI-piloted cargo skiff. This one, though, she specified to be open sided. Open topped. A flat, aerial barge meant for oversized goods. The call went through and the two waited, crouching beneath the solar panels as a small Salinity army descended upon the burning building.

"This didn't play out as I thought," Aurora said while they waited.

"Things rarely do."

"Are you insulting me, or talking generally?"

"The latter," Gregor said. "Though this is why I do not make predictions."

"Hard to avoid if you're the captain."

"This is why I am not the captain."

Aurora laughed, fell silent. Gregor checked his kinetic charge, found that the far fall to the rooftop had built back up everything he'd burned in the jump. Ready to go for another leap, this one with a smaller target.

"It's here," Aurora said. "Or, rather, there."

"Then we go."

"Lead on, big man. This is your idea."

Gregor didn't argue. He stood, clearing the panels and putting his power armor in full view of anyone paying attention. Which, considering the disaster unfolding a block away, he figured nobody was.

Three steps later, Gregor punched his boosters, launched into the air, and flew towards a hapless cargo skiff.

NINE

Tactical Retreat

THE POOR COUCH didn't deserve it. Eponi ducked behind the stiff blue furniture when Renard and Rovo's quartet made it clear they hadn't come by looking for a spare cup of sugar. Their leader, a woman Eponi hadn't met but, based on Aurora's descriptions, seemed like the Defense-Corp agent Vana, picked out the pilot as a target and the two dropped into a flashy dual around a living room meant for chill hangs and not much else.

Sai and his katana kept the apartment's exit bottle-necked, and with Rovo showing he hadn't gone all evil, Eponi's first look suggested the fight should be an easy win. No way Renard could keep up with the rookie, and if Sai could take out the laughing maniac towards the back, then they could flank Vana.

Easy.

Until the damn shots started coming from behind. Eponi swiveled to dodge a Vana bolt, etching another black mark into the apartment's walls, and caught another flash burn over her moving shoulder. The couch smoldered as its cushion took the hit, and a rapid glance towards the balcony window at Eponi's back showcased a molten hole. Snipers from across the way.

The look back cost Eponi awareness: Vana pressed the advantage, running along the couch to tackle Eponi, shoving the pilot into the apartment's wall. Eponi bounced off, leaving a chunk falling to the floor in her wake, the bruising ache, and only that, in her shoulder a comforting sign that the hit hadn't broken anything. Spinning to face Vana, Eponi swung her pistol like a backhanded slap, swatting Vana's killshot away before the agent could pull the trigger.

The hit bought a spare second, the two facing each other. Experienced agent, experienced kart racer. One a deadly master of stealth and various means of murder, the other a cocky ball of spice willing to push the limits.

"You're not going to win," Vana said. "Surrender, and I guarantee you'll live."

"Sorry, I have trust issues," Eponi replied, snapping up her foot in a kick towards Vana's stomach.

The agent saw the move coming, batted away the blow with her pistol hand. Eponi tried to use the break to bring her own pistol to bear in an off-balance counter. She pulled the trigger as Vana rushed forward, Eponi's shot flying high and melting through one of Kashmal's kitchen cabinets. Vana hit Eponi square, the latter dropping her pistol in a frantic grab to keep Vana's gun from getting a nasty angle into Eponi's side.

Renard hit the floor hard to their left, barstools clattering, the old agent cursing as Rovo followed up. Eponi marshaled the distraction to spin-and-trip Vana, pulling them both into the living room proper, right in view of those damned windows.

Vana, back on the carpet, should've been in trouble. Should've been telling Eponi to lay off as the pilot pulled back a fist. Instead, the agent pushed back with more strength than Eponi expected, rolling Eponi to the right and off her. Eponi's own back hit the carpet—firm, low quality cream threads, matching Kashmal's crappy sense of style—and she expected Vana to follow, until another laser shot blasted through the window, right over Vana's chest.

Right where Eponi had been.

"Thanks for the save," Eponi said, pushing back to her feet.

"You're not welcome," Vana replied, matching Eponi's move and coming right at the pilot, pushing her back against the windowed balcony door.

The sniper had a clear shot, and Vana had Eponi's arms pinned, her back flat against the glass. Eponi caught the other fighters to her right, with Sai on the ground and the laughing man with him. Rovo threw Renard back towards the apartment door, but the rookie wouldn't be moving fast enough to get to her.

Raquel, however, did.

The Salinity security chief hit Vana from behind, a shoulder charge that pressed Eponi into the blast-weakened door and shattered it. Eponi fell back onto the balcony, the glass getting caught in her clothes. Vana, though, took the worse of it: her taller head caught a dangling shard, cutting a long gash. Raquel stumbled back from the push, drawing a pistol, looking outside, and firing a shot over Eponi's head.

Apparently everyone had their own threats to deal with.

Eponi sent a knee into Vana's gut and the agent grunted, delivered a sock of her own to Eponi's face, then rolled off back inside the apartment. Towards the pistols. Eponi expected the sniper to hit her any moment, but

Raquel continued to fire, each burnt orange bolt blitzing overhead towards the far away shooter.

At that distance, Eponi doubted the bolts could do serious damage, but she wasn't about to tell the Salinity agent to stop firing. Instead, she pulled herself up and saw a way out. Retreating wasn't a tactic that came easy to Sever, but with Raquel's re-appearance reminding Eponi of the objective, getting Kaia away came first.

Gillane Four's droplet architecture did a lot for theme, did little for function. The apartment buildings, like most others on the planet, went from narrow at the top to wide at the bottom, a design that fattened the sides out as things went lower. Kashmal's apartment wasn't exactly a penthouse, and beneath the balcony, the building spread out, creating a curving, somewhat steep slide to the apartment —and its own balcony—below.

Eponi snapped her eyes up, following another shot from Raquel, and traced the line to a building across the way. The sniper had opened an office window, one now littered with smoking holes from Raquel's fire. Whether Raquel had fried the shooter or suppressed him, bolts weren't coming back their way now.

"Run!" Eponi shouted, "Kashmal, get Kaia out of here!"

At his name, the girl's father proved he was capable of decisive action, turning the corner with Kaia in his arms and joining Eponi and Raquel, covering back inside now, on the balcony. Vana, who had to have the pistols, stayed in and didn't try firing a shot once Kaia entered the frame. Instead, the agent tried again to get the group to surrender.

Not happening.

"Run where?" Kashmal said, ignoring Vana's orders.

"Over the edge," Eponi replied. "Like a slide. She'll love it."

Kashmal looked at Eponi like she was crazy, until Raquel repeated the idea, "Do it, Kashmal. Aim for the next balcony down."

"You're both insane," Kashmal said, not moving.

Eponi would've cursed the man out, would've declared him a moron costing his daughter her life, when the sniper returned. The shot struck out, lanced right into Kashmal's shoulder. The hit made him shout, made him collapse to the balcony's edge, with Kaia screaming right along with him. Raquel whipped around, sending pistol fire back. Rovo, showing that at least someone from Sever could win today, came barreling onto the balcony with them.

"Take Kaia and drop," Eponi said, already moving to help the girl's father.

Rovo, like a good rookie, didn't question the order. He kept moving, went around Raquel and lifted Kaia from her father's weakening arms. With one arm holding Kaia, Rovo vaulted the balcony's edge and dropped. Kashmal shouted after them, a combination panic and pain, and a noise that Eponi cut off when she squeezed the man, starting to lift them both over the balcony's railing.

"She'll be fine," Eponi snapped. "Focus, please."

Kashmal offered up groan in reply, but he found the strength to lift his legs. As they went over together, Eponi stole a look towards the wrecked apartment. Raquel flipped over the railing next to them, leaving Sai the last of the bunch inside. Eponi couldn't see him. Instead, Eponi caught Vana's grim stare as she pulled around the balcony, her quarry fleeing without a chance for a shot.

Any worries about Sai had to wait a minute, because Eponi hit the building's glass side and slid. Kashmal's bulk pulled him away from her as they skated the few meters from one balcony to the next, landing in a heap on a patio set already ruined by Rovo. The rookie and Kaia were moving on as Eponi landed, hopping the railing and continuing the slide.

"This is the worst day," Kashmal muttered as Eponi helped him up and over the edge.

"You're alive. It could be worse," Raquel said, pistol up and keeping cover.

"Not sure about that," Kashmal replied, then Eponi shoved him along and watched him drop.

"You know what you're doing with that thing," Eponi said to Raquel. "Thanks for the help."

"Technically, Kashmal's a Salinity employee." Rachel's eyes squinted back towards the balcony they'd just jumped from, and she squeezed off a shot. Vana's head disappeared back behind cover. "It's my job to make sure he's all right."

Eponi wanted to ask whether making sure an employee survived really included countering assaults by Defense-Corp agents, but debating job minutiae wasn't the priority. Eponi jumped the rail, slid on the glass again—an amazing feeling, like an action hero—and landed on the next balcony. Another drop would bring them to ground level, and would mean a four meter fall to hard stone. Rovo pieced together the poor outcome there and greeted Eponi from within the last balcony's apartment.

The rookie, still with Kaia in one arm, and bearing scratches on an elbow, had smashed the glass doors. The apartment didn't like the move, its own security alarms beeping in an awful soundtrack to the moment. At least someone had stocked the place with flowers, which smelled a lot nicer than the burning fabric up in Kashmal's joint.

Kaia's father finally recognized the right thing to do

and lurched on, passing Rovo and heading towards the new apartment's exit.

"Figured I shouldn't take that last plunge without power armor," Rovo said. "You okay?"

"You kidding? That was sweet," Eponi replied. "I'm good, though I'm thinking Sai might be in trouble."

Rovo grimaced, glancing up at the apartment's ceiling as if it'd form a magical window straight to Sai's location. Raquel plopped down next to Eponi and ushered the pilot inside.

"We have to keep moving," Raquel said as they followed Kashmal to the apartment door. "I don't know how many people they have coming after us."

"Plenty, would be my guess," Eponi said. "Tell me you have some sneaky ways to get around this city."

"Sneaky?" Raquel said as they entered the apartment hallway and turned towards the stairs.

Kashmal looked a little rough, though when didn't he? Otherwise, Eponi figured the group had made it away without too much trouble. As they walked, Rovo insisted Vana and Renard wouldn't kill Sai, not if they didn't have to.

"They're big fans of the whole hostage thing," Rovo said. "They'll see Sai as someone to use."

"He won't tell'em anything." Eponi found the stairs, saw they'd lead to the building's lobby, a place with people and plenty of spots for a shooter to set up. "Raquel, we need a different way out of here."

"The service entrance, maybe," Raquel said. "But I don't have access to it."

"Why not?"

"Because I don't work here?"

Eponi eyed her, "Doesn't Salinity, like, own this planet?"

Kashmal coughed, and red stuff splattered on the soft blue carpet. That hit to the man's shoulder must've been worse than Eponi thought. Rovo had Kaia turned away so the girl didn't see, but Kashmal needed better medical care than an apartment hallway could provide.

"We own the land, not all the structures on them," Raquel said. "We do have an office near here. One that might help him." Raquel waved her pistol, frowning. "But I'm not bringing a firefight to one of our buildings."

Eponi nodded, considered Rovo holding Kaia, and came down with a plan. A stupid one, but a plan none-theless.

"You won't have to," Eponi said, hating what she was about to say before she said it. "I'll draw them off, then you head the other way."

"Eponi," Rovo said. "Why would they follow you when they're after Kaia?"

"You just said. They want hostages. I might not get'em all, but it should buy you some time."

"But—"

"Rookie, stay in your lane," Eponi said. "Raquel, sorry to leave you with these two, but you know how it goes."

"I don't, actually," Raquel replied.

"Then, surprise?" Eponi said. "Give me twenty. When you hear the bang, make your break."

The pilot went down the stairs with a steadied rush, tapping each step and moving on to the next, eyes surfing the lobby crowd. A few gawkers, talking about the laser fire from outside, meshed with a cleaning bot and a bug-eyed security guard yelling madly into his wristlet. Nobody cared about the woman coming through the lobby, even though a closer look would've revealed the stuck glass shards, tears in her clothes, and enough cocky poise to suggest she didn't belong anywhere near these apartments.

Eponi searched for and found, within a second, her option. Kaiyo's streets didn't have vehicles—skiffs stayed to the air, the actual walkways were for people alone—but there were bots aplenty. The machinations performed the city's grunt work, trundling along without any notice of the shootout above. One, apparently cleaning the creamy cobblestones making up this section of Kaiyo, gave Eponi the opening she needed.

Any snipers watching from above held their fire. Maybe they hadn't thought to look down yet. They would eventually, though. Eponi had to force the issue. Had to get them focused her way.

Eponi went up to the bot, a green-black cylinder thing with a broad base covered in brushes that whirred away on the cobblestones. Eponi took a deep breath and pushed the machine over. The thing had weight, but Eponi had leverage and enough strength training to get the job done.

The cleaning bot hit the stones with a metallic bang, a sound that did what sounds had done since humans had first erected giant buildings in glass-and-steel corridors: echoed. Joining the clank's aftermath, the bot added its own alarm, one meant to bring forth security to catch the meddler that'd just declared robo war on the cobblestone cleaner. That noise, too, bounced off the glass buildings.

Heads already drawn to the firefight's earlier sounds poked over balconies, stuck their eyes to windows to see whether the day would bring even more chaos to Gillane Four's stuffy, peaceful existence. Eponi figured a little action could do the planet good, get some heart beats going, and she had to fight off a threatening smile when she saw those stares on her.

Like being famous all over again.

Then she ran, hoping death would follow her.

TEN

The Long Way Home

EPONI'S PROPOSED bang didn't really qualify—the sound filtered through the building's lobby as a weak clank—but the quartet used the opening they had. With Rovo holding Kaia and Raquel helping Kashmal along in the lead, they dodged the lobby and continued along the hallway to the building's far side. The last stair there led to a designated emergency exit, warnings of triggered alarms based on the doorway.

"It's for the best, really," Rovo said when Raquel hesitated. "There's a shootout happening upstairs, Eponi's probably getting lit up in the street. The more confusion, the better."

"People could get hurt," Raquel said while Kashmal, providing no useful input whatsoever, continued to groan about the shot to his shoulder. "My job is to keep the people of this planet safe."

"Long term, you're doing that by keeping us alive," Rovo suggested. Raquel's doubting look killed that argument, so Rovo changed tactics. "How about this, then? We don't open this door, we're stuck going back to that lobby, where we'll be caught, Kaia's going to be in trouble, and you're probably going to die anyway."

That, at least, proved more persuasive. Raquel, grimacing all the while, shoved the heavy door open. They spilled into a side street, the cream cobblestones providing a few meters between hulking droplet-shaped towers. Whereas main avenues littered their sides with shops and cafes, the telltale waste bins here showcased a space not meant to be seen, heard, or explored.

"Eww," Kaia said, pinching her nose in a sensible response to the moldering scent wafting through the air.

"Not my best shortcut," Rovo agreed.

Behind them, the building's alarm broke out in a squawking cadence, an obnoxious sound Rovo felt only too glad to leave behind. The small street, not crowded, became less so as people noticed Kashmal's bleeding wound and decided now was not the time to play hero, doctor, or even curious stranger. Rovo caught the ducking away, the hiding.

"What's with this place?" He asked Raquel as they went, hugging the far building as much as possible. "Nobody wants to help?"

"It's not their job," Raquel replied. "You know as well as I do that if someone's hurt like Kashmal, there's cash involved. Nobody gets shot like this because of an accident."

And nobody wants to get entangled in trouble that's not their own. Rovo shrugged off the bitter taste that left in his mouth. The galaxy had so much cynicism in it, so many morals resting on the money to be made. Sever Squad had helped Kaia off Dynas, had helped the Talpa without a payday's promise, but, if Rovo was being honest with himself, he'd championed both those things.

A naive rookie? Perhaps, but Rovo wasn't willing to sell out his soul for cash alone.

Not yet.

"The office is up here," Raquel said as they passed a block without obvious pursuit. "We'll be able to get a Salinity skiff there."

"To go where?"

"Someplace that smells a little better," Raquel replied. "That's not so easy for your enemies to find."

"Then what?"

"Is that all you do?" Raquel said, throwing a look Rovo's way as they cleared the small street, broke into a square dominated by a triple fountain and angled across it towards a first-floor window set blazing Salinity's droplet logo in blue neon. "Ask questions?"

"At the moment? Yeah."

Despite the answer, Kaia kept Rovo from asking anything more. The little girl, still buzzing from the apartment, apparently sensed the immediate danger had passed and used the opening to barrage Rovo with exclamations and questions of her own. Most important, to Kaia, was how Rovo had wound up in her apartment in the first place.

There were a thousand explanations Rovo could've spun together to answer that question, but lying to a child, especially one listed as the top target for a large, deadly group, seemed wrong. So Rovo unspooled the tale as they crossed the square, as Raquel brought them through a lightly crowded office and sat them in an empty conference room while she went off to find some transport.

Rovo concluded the adventure as a kind bot brought in water for the group, along with light bandages for Kashmal. Letting Kaia fiddle with her own hydration, Rovo went to work on her father.

"Thank you," Kashmal said as Rovo finished applying the burn salves and bandages. The shot looked rough, the skin around the impact blackened with heat, but compared to the lung blast Rovo had taken back on the *Nautilus*, Kashmal shouldn't have too much trouble. "I know I gave you a lot of grief back then, but—"

"Don't worry about it," Rovo cut Kashmal off, not wanting to hear the man make some apology. Nothing Kashmal would say could make up for locking Kaia in a tiny room for years, and Rovo didn't have the energy to care. "Keep pressure on the wound. This isn't exactly top level medical treatment."

Kashmal took the hint, kept a hand there. The man then called to his daughter, who bounced over to show off the Salinity-branded cup she'd been using to sip water. Balancing the girl on his lap, Kashmal broke into a soft song, one that Kaia joined in with after a verse. The moment went from cute to awkward in a hurry, with Rovo feeling like an eavesdropper on a family he was very much not a part of.

The bathroom proved a worthy escape, and Rovo spent time at the sink, drawing the occasional look from the Salinity office crowd moving in and out around him. Washing Kashmal's blood out of his hands, picking glass from his hair, and soaping up the skin burns from sliding down the glass building, Rovo turned himself from disaster movie extra to a real human being, albeit one in desperate need of new clothes.

"Look at them," Raquel said when Rovo found her outside the conference room, watching Kashmal and Kaia play—the former stiff but smiling, the latter using the conference table and chairs as an obstacle course to be conquered. "It's almost like they weren't attacked an hour ago."

Rovo tried to gauge the tone on the words. Was Raquel saying they weren't taking things seriously, or admiring their ability to ignore reality in favor of having a little bit of fun?

"I'm not an expert," Rovo tried the center line, "but I don't think a kid like Kaia's going to take to panicking very well."

"Not an expert?" Raquel glanced Rovo's way. "You certainly picked her up quick. Held her close during the escape."

"She's a four year-old girl. What else was I supposed to do?"

"Don't need to get defensive," Raquel switched on a deflecting smile. "I'm saying you did well, is all."

"Thanks?"

Raquel nodded, turned away from the window and nodded towards the office's break room, "I know it's late, but given what we've just seen, would you like some coffee?"

Rovo figured he and sleep would have a dim relationship until Vana, Renard, and their agents were sorted out, so he accepted Raquel's offer. Walking into the squat, corporate space bedazzled with notices for team sports and fridge cleaning schedules, Rovo realized the last time he'd been in a break room like this, he'd been floating over his homeworld, filing forms and watching the hours crawl by.

Taking the offered cup and giving it a good pull, Rovo recalled why he didn't miss the breakrooms all that much: the coffee, despite Salinity's perfect water, tasted thin and dull.

"Not your thing?" Raquel noticed Rovo's lip-sucking frown.

"Normally take it stronger," Rovo said, and when

Raquel turned back to the burbling machine, he put a hand on her arm. "Please, it's fine. Let's go back."

Raquel eyed that offending hand, which Rovo removed, and together the two returned to the conference room. Raquel's wristlet had buzzed during the coffee run, letting her know their designated skiff had shown up, so the quartet bustled to the office's lift, rode it up to a level marked for pick-ups, and hopped into the Salinity-branded, pleasantly-bubbled craft.

Kaia made a ride that would've been boring into a smile-fest, pointing out every little tower the skiff flew by as its bot pilot took them to their destination. As to where that was, Raquel wouldn't say. Didn't want to chance anyone listening in.

"You think it's possible?" Kashmal said.

"You were on Dynas, had Helix watching your every move," Rovo replied. "You know it's possible."

"Ah, true."

Below them, Kaiyo's city-scape gave way to deep ocean as the skiff launched towards Raquel's target. The blue sky overhead, with its puffy clouds, dimmed as afternoon tilted towards twilight, Gillane Four's white star dipping towards the horizon behind them. Without the buildings holding her attention, Kaia's eyes grew heavy and she snuggled up to her father, who joined her in a nap once Raquel confirmed the flight would take a while.

The coffee and niggling concern about Eponi and Sai kept Rovo awake, and he figured he might go nuts if he had to sit in silence, so he turned to Raquel, who watched the skiff's progress on its center console, and went with the only question he could find: "So how does someone get to be Salinity's chief security officer?"

"Long hours and longer weeks," Raquel replied. "Might be hard to believe, but most of my days don't involve cross-city shootouts. Instead, there's forms to fill out. Visitors and employees to background check."

"And you didn't find anything with this guy?" Rovo nodded to the back.

"Kashmal has great qualifications," Raquel said. "I remember because we don't get many ex-DefenseCorp researchers. We called his main reference, a woman, I think, who said Kashmal saved their whole project. Hard to say no to that."

"Saved it by sacrificing his daughter."

Raquel's eyes flashed, "That didn't come up in the interview."

"So surprised."

"You're throwing a lot of heat around for someone who walked in with the people trying to hurt that kid."

"Didn't have much choice," Rovo replied. "They were going to go in anyway. At least this way I helped. A little."

As he spoke, Rovo found himself a lost in the moment. It'd been so damned long since he had a conversation with someone not trying to use him, kill him, or work with him to use or kill somebody else. His instinct pushed him to find an angle with Raquel, tilt her towards some objective, but what would that even be?

She was taking them someplace safe, and once they landed, Rovo would try and find the *Prisa*, get in touch with Aurora and Gregor. Put together a plan. Sever would continue the fight.

But right now?

"So are you DefenseCorp people actually from anywhere, or do you come out, fully formed with a rifle in your hands, from some vat?" Raquel asked.

"Definitely the vat." Rovo laughed, soft so he didn't wake Kaia. "DefenseCorp would love that, actually."

"I don't doubt it," Raquel said. "I'm not lying when I

said we don't see much ex-DefenseCorp. That organization, it kills you. Salinity wanted to contract with them when I took over, said it would be cheaper. Know why we didn't?"

"Because you'd be out of a job?"

Raquel rolled her eyes, "No, because if we did that, this planet wouldn't be ours anymore." Seeing Rovo's confusion, Raquel kept on, "Rovo, DefenseCorp keeps saying they're providing neutral protection for the galaxy. What they're doing is trapping everyone under their guns. What happens when there's nobody left willing to stand on their own?"

"So you and a water company are the resistance?"

"Someone has to be."

Rovo, at least, couldn't argue with that.

ELEVEN

Firework Show

THE CARGO SKIFF dropped them at the *Prisa*, under dark purple skies, with a nastier chill coming in off Kaiyo's edge. Aurora hadn't caught any messages over the squad band, nothing from Sai and Eponi about their pursuit of the girl. That quiet festered as the two inspected the bay around their ship, running scans with their power armor visors to make sure agents hadn't planted bombs or other, subtler forms of sabotage.

"All clear," Gregor said, tapping the lock on the *Prisa*'s front strut to lower its boarding ramp. "Nice fighting back there."

"Same," Aurora said. "You want to de-couple, I'll cover out here."

The *Prisa* barely fit a power-armored squad member in its halls anyway, much less two. If they both went inside, and some agent force followed, Aurora and Gregor would be stuck without much room to maneuver.

"Paranoid?" Gregor joked as the ramp hit the bay floor with a light thump.

"With agents? Always."

The *Prisa*'s bay kept the traditional open top around a circular confine meant for light-sized ships like their's. Arcing walls circled the craft, ready to deploy a dome in case of weather, disaster, or to prevent the *Prisa* from leaving after making the wrong enemies. Littered around the circle's outside were the traditional repair bots, fueling mechanisms—for craft that didn't rely solely on solar power—and pay-as-you-go lockers filled with equipment and refreshments. Unlike Wexer, Gillane Four had the money and motivation to treat its visitors nicely.

Unfortunately for Gillane Four, Sever Squad didn't make for civilized guests.

Gregor had just made it up the boarding ramp when Sever's channel crackled and Eponi's voice flared in Aurora's ear, "Hey hey, anybody home? This girl could use some help!"

Aurora snapped her look over to the docking bay door, saw nothing, "Gregor and I are at the *Prisa*. Where are you?"

"Heading your way!" Eponi's hard breathing came through between the words. She must've been sprinting. "Guess what sucks?"

Aurora blinked. She didn't know how to answer that.

"Running through an entire city with people shooting at you!"

"Did you try shooting back?" Gregor said, his voice coming in over the transmission. A clank behind Aurora announced the hammer man hadn't ditched his power armor yet either. "I find that helps."

"You wanna come shoot, I'm not gonna say no," Eponi replied. "I'm about to get on the capsule, and it'd be awesome if I don't catch a laser between the eyes when I get off."

"You wont," Aurora said.

Gregor didn't need the order to get moving. Giving up any pretense of keeping things quiet, the two Sever members ran from the *Prisa*'s bay, hustling in their power armor across the big docking platform towards the capsules to Kaiyo at the far end. Things weren't as busy as earlier in the day, with people settling into evenings on their ships or out in the city, leaving bots and the last cargo haulers to gawk at the heavily armed pair pounding the cobblestones.

Nobody in their right mind would do anything other than watch the dangerous duo.

Nobody except Salinity security and their too-stupid squad.

Aurora couldn't blame the ten guards orienting their way, with at least two calling for them to stop. They earned cash to keep the docking bays safe, to make sure merchants could make their money without getting lit up by lasers. The Salinity force probably spent their days dealing with minor scuffles, with restaurant recommendations, or the occasional haggle over some docking fee.

Though they packed pistols and stun cuffs, the ten converging on Aurora and Gregor didn't have anything the power armor visors even classified as a threat. Instead, with civilians scattering at their approach, Aurora and Gregor posted up at the capsule unloading point and turned to greet those enforcers of the law.

"I suggest you leave," Aurora said to the first patrolman that came up to her. The man had played it smart so far, not drawing his pistol despite Aurora's big rifle. That said he knew any real fight here wouldn't end well. "We'll attempt to minimize damage, but this is DefenseCorp business."

"I don't care whose business it is," the patrolman replied as his fellow officers ringed the capsule platform.

Some, smartly, kept urging onlookers to get farther and farther away. "This is Salinity territory, and Kaiyo's under Salinity regulations, which means you can't have a weapon like that out in the open."

Aurora tried to think of a way to tell the officer he wasn't going to get what he wanted without starting a fight. If Eponi had people trailing her, the last thing Aurora needed was to be bashing around local security while the real enemy took free shots at her squad.

"Heyo," Eponi's voice crackled over the squad band, clearer now as she came closer. "Looks like Renard's goons don't wanna light up random people, but they're getting in the capsule with me. I think a few are on skiffs too. I'm, uh, unarmed."

Of course she was.

"Here's what's going to happen," Aurora said to the patrolman. "There's a capsule coming out this way that has trouble all over it. When it arrives, things are going to get hot here. Your officers and all these people are at risk. Get them back to their bays, tell them to shut the doors. The fight won't last long, I promise."

"It won't," Gregor added, unlimbering the giant hammer from its back holster.

The hammer, perhaps, struck more sense into the Salinity forces than Aurora's words. You just didn't see a weapon like that and assume what was happening fit into the usual narrative. Aurora could see the patrolman trying to find a way out, figure how he could preserve authority without getting himself and his people slaughtered.

"You're outclassed," Aurora said. "Go, take cover and call for back-up. That's the smart play. Keep your people safe."

The patrolman's eyes flicked to his fellows, looking straight back at him. If Aurora had to gauge their attitudes, she'd put the whole group at *likely to break and run,* "I can't just—"

"You can and you will," Aurora cut the patrolman off, didn't let him build any steam. "I've done it. Plenty. Nothing wrong with getting to a better tactical position."

That last found it. Aurora managed to connect with the patrolman on a level he wanted: peers in a conflict above the day-to-day humdrum that'd dominated his career. After this, if Aurora still worked for DefenseCorp, she would've recommended the patrolman sign up. Ditch the dull duties for something more exciting.

But not now. The capsule had left Kaiyo, its approaching lights flanked by several others. Skiffs flying nearby, pacing the car. The patrolman finally followed Aurora's advice, calling for his group to fall back and take the curious crowd with them. Thankfully, there weren't too many gawkers here, and at the prospect of real violence, the bystanders scattered with the officers.

Leaving Gregor and Aurora to watch the approach alone.

"We're ready for you," Aurora sent back to Eponi. "Any idea on numbers?"

"Lots, and they're angry," Eponi replied. "Hope you're ready for some fun today."

"We already had some," Gregor said. "But I am always looking for more."

Gregor's casual lust for violence stated, the Sever duo moved away from the platform's lights and into the relative shadows. Gregor had his hammer ready, while Aurora raised her rifle, put one of the skiffs in her sights.

"You're confident every skiff outside is an enemy?" Aurora asked.

"I've been ducking their fire for an hour now," Eponi said. "Would be awful nice if someone shot back."

Aurora wondered, at that remark, how Salinity's security forces hadn't made any attempts to take out the agents. You'd think they'd want to destroy a hostile force marauding through Kaiyo, but Renard tended to have his slimy fingers in everything. Maybe he'd bought Salinity off, or threatened them with worse.

Regardless, Aurora pulled the trigger. Again and again.

Sapphire bolts lanced from the rifle, adjusted by Aurora to fire hotter. She'd get less shots per power pack, but the lasers stood a better chance at punching through a skiff's hull.

Which these lasers did with aplomb. A hundred meters out—going by the range displayed on Aurora's visor—the skiffs, closing quick with the capsule, slammed right into Aurora's shots. The bolts struck the leading skiff, an oval thing that, though difficult to tell in the dark, looked to have a half-dozen seats inside, and sent it spiraling down and away. Smoke poured from its front as the pilots fought to get control.

Aurora didn't watch the descent, but raised her rifle slightly to get the next one. The skiffs caught onto the attack and danced, swerving out wide as Aurora kept on the bolts. A turret, with its slower adjustments and trickier targeting, would have a hard time hitting the skiffs. Aurora, with her power armor helping twitch her aim, took the left skiff and made it dance between her bolts, each shot giving the skiff less time to dodge as it closed with the capsule. Stitching the fire between two narrowing sides forced the skiff to go up or down.

"Choose," Aurora muttered, playing a shot dead center.

The skiff went up, breaking its line with the capsule and exposing its belly for Aurora to hit. Without the straight-on path, the skiff couldn't dodge side to side so tightly, and Aurora traced the ascent with enough fire to land two solid strikes to the skiff's center. The craft juddered, like a bird trying to adjust its angle mid-flight, then swanned over into a dive right towards the docking platform's center.

"Gregor?" Aurora called.

"On it."

Using his kinetic boosters, Gregor took a running leap into the air, heading right towards the diving skiff. As he flew, Gregor swung his hammer, timing the swing to hit the plummeting skiff. With a screeching, rending bang, the hammer struck, maybe ten meters overhead. The skiff's fracturing hull broke apart at the impact, flaring out and sending pieces scattering to the ground. Its batteries, their careful structure shattered, burst into a crackling, green fire that lit up the space like an acid firework.

The explosion shot Gregor back to the ground, where he bounced off the stones with a heavy grunt. The blast, though, didn't shatter windows. Didn't blow up spare fuel hanging around the bays or ruin merchant stalls closed till the next morning. A mess, yes, but not a disastrous one.

Aurora flipped her attention to the final skiff, easy to do as the thing had lowered its top, freeing the agents inside to loose rifle and—crap—rocket fire of their own. The Sever captain lunged to the left, near a closed welcome center and its covering darkness, as a missile blew up the spot where she'd stood, scattering cobblestones everywhere.

That Renard had cleared artillery for these agents meant the man had changed the stakes. No longer was this a fight for the shadows. Vana and Renard wanted open war, with Gillane Four the battleground.

Aurora didn't like the idea, but if the two wanted a fight, they'd get it.

Ejecting her spent power pack, Aurora kept moving as

the skiff trailed her. Rifle fire dotted her clomping steps, and two bolts caught her, searing her right arm and shoulder. The power armor's defenses kept anything serious at bay, but every hit diminished her deflective capabilities. Eventually, a shot would melt through, torching Aurora's skin and bone.

Aurora feinted left, towards the capsule and its fleeing occupants, then rolled right as another rocket slammed where she would've been. Slipping the new power pack in as she came out of the roll, a move the power armor made profoundly ungraceful, but still effective, Aurora sighted the skiff and lanced out new shots.

Renard had a good pilot for this one, though. The skiff kicked up its engines and blew over Aurora, forcing her to swivel with it, then dive away as her turn revealed the rocketeer inside sighting up another round.

"Any help here?" Eponi called. "I'm a little outnumbered!"

Gregor groaned, still shaking off the skiff explosion, which left Aurora. A hard look left towards the capsule showed Eponi making hands with an agent trio. The pilot darted like a bee, bouncing from one to the next in an effort to keep any from finding a shot with their pistols. The agents were catching on, though, stepping back as they deflected Eponi's dancing blows and buying space. Soon they'd have Eponi stuck in their center, pinned down and ready to roast.

Kicking in the power armor's kinetic boosters, Aurora jumped as the skiff rained down more fire around her. The jump brought her four meters high, carried Aurora to the platform, and gave her rifle time to line up a shot. She pulled the trigger as she landed, torching the closest agent with a blue bolt and sending him smoldering to the ground.

Eponi took advantage, grappling with the agent closest to her and sending him gasping to the turf with a hard elbow to the man's throat. The third, seeing Aurora bearing down, took off towards the shadows.

"Run!" Aurora said to the pilot.

"Happy to!" Eponi replied, breaking towards the *Prisa's* bay.

Laserfire stitched up Aurora's back, blowing something and sending her to a knee as the assist keeping the armor's weight off her muscles died. Not good, but she still had her rifle. Still had a chance. Falling forward, Aurora rolled, bringing the rifle up and giving her a chance to shoot.

But the damn skiff played things smart again. It'd seen her take the hit, seen Aurora fall, and rather than shoot it out, the craft flew over Aurora's head, spinning around to where she couldn't aim. Aurora couldn't even see the skiff anymore, it'd vanished over the top of her visor, which continued to show the angry red of a threat in its direction.

Knowing a rocket blast would be coming, Aurora thought about evacuating, but jumping armor free as a rocket screamed in wouldn't help. She stood a better chance nestled in her armor, waiting out the attack under its protection.

"Get up!" Gregor roared, the man finding his life and pulling his armor, visible at Aurora's bottom edge, to its feet.

Dropping his hammer, Gregor swung his own rifle up and streamed red, lower powered bolts towards the skiff. The fire must've prompted the skiff to abandon its finale on Aurora, as Gregor's red lines followed the skiff to the right. Gregor should've been running along with the craft, should've been jumping to avoid being an easy target.

"Move," Aurora said. "Move, you idiot."

"Can't," Gregor replied. "That boom knocked out my motors."

Aurora didn't want to think of how much effort Gregor must've needed to stand up in that suit. How much effort it would take to get the power armor and all its kilos to take a step without the motors humming along.

Not that it mattered. Gregor stayed stuck, and once the skiff knew it, the rocket came fast.

Who Holds The Power

Being a hostage didn't leave much opportunity for pleasure, but Sai found plenty in watching, listening to Renard's continual curses as the quartet cruised in a skiff. They'd flown from the apartment building and away from Kaiyo, leaving the city behind for the open ocean. Sai, strapped into a back seat next to Abbad, endured endless questions from the chatty maniac, his hands wishing they held his katana. Vana had stuffed the blade in the skiff's undercarriage, a curious turn and one of a thousand questions Sai held.

Abbad's interrogation ranged from the meaningless, like Sai's favorite color and food, to the meaningful, like how he'd acquired the katana and whether Sever had any other swordsmen among its ranks. Sai tried to ditch off answers that'd let him keep listening to Renard, but Abbad kept coming back with earnest follow-ups.

"Man, please," Sai finally said, a headache blooming to match his sore muscles from the fight. "Can you stop for a minute?"

"Can't, buddy," Abbad replied. "The bosses are talking, and that means I can't have you listening. This beater doesn't have a spot I can stash you, so this is the best I can do."

Sai leaned back in his seat, stared at the night outside the window, and suppressed a groan.

"It's fine, Abbad," Vana said, up front flying while Renard did his thing. "There's nothing we're talking about that Sai can't know."

"For real?" Abbad replied.

"For real," Vana said. "If he's smart, Sai will understand where we're coming from, and make the correct choice."

"The other dude definitely didn't."

Rovo? Sai stared out the window, pretended to be disinterested. They'd tried to get the rookie to turn? Maybe that's why Rovo had walked into the apartment without stun cuffs. Why he'd been with Renard and Vana at all.

"Not yet," Vana said. "There's still time for that one. And just because Rovo might not want to play, doesn't mean Sai will choose the same."

"I'm going to choose the same," Sai spoke up. "Sorry."

Abbad laughed. Sai eyed the man. Wished he could edge further away, but the skiff kept its confines small.

"You haven't heard the stakes yet," Vana said. Beside her, Renard lowered his wristlet with a heavy sigh, one Sai had used time and again when his kids drove him to exhaustion. "Renard, you all right?"

"This isn't going as I'd hoped," Renard exhaled. "This was supposed to be a simple mission, Vana. We have the suits. We're almost there. And yet, we can't accomplish this one single thing."

"The road is never straight and easy."

"Stop with your sayings," Renard retorted. "They won't bring any of our people back, nor will they get us

Kaia. Sever's done damage to our home in Kaiyo. Salinity knows about it now, and we cannot go back there. Skiffs have been lost, and we're still pursuing the ones that made it away."

The words brought a smile to Sai's face. A confident surge. Eponi had made it away then, with Kaia and the others. Aurora and Gregor, too, seemed to have found a target to smash. The image of Gregor laying waste with his big hammer only broadened Sai's grin.

These bastards kept thinking Sever would fall apart. Instead, they'd picked a fight with a force too strong to stop.

A click snapped Sai's eyes to his left, where Abbad, now straight-faced and serious, held his pistol up to Sai's temple.

"Want me to blow this one apart right now?" Abbad said. "Guaranteed to make you feel better."

"It would," Renard replied, looking at the back seat. It wasn't like they were flying through heavy traffic in Gillane Four's vast, empty oceans. "But I think this man might be the only card we have left to play."

Nonetheless, Abbad spent the rest of the ride with his pistol up and ready, just in case Renard changed his mind.

The agents brought Sai to a smaller platform, one ringed with flashing yellow lights. Vana, playing mediator for the group, described the spike sticking up from the ocean as a heater. Using solar energy and a deep drill towards Gillane Four's center, the spike threw warmth into the waters, enough to alter the planet's currents and keep the water moving how Salinity wanted it. The intense heat at the spike's bottom also served to melt away trash caught by those same currents.

"Salinity has these spikes all over the planet," Vana said as the skiff's top popped and the passengers began climbing out. "Not the easiest way to bend a world to your will, but it's the one they chose."

"Your endless trivia always impresses," Renard grumbled.

"I read the reports, Renard," Vana replied. "Always have. You should try it."

"The relevant reports matter, Vana. Everything else is just a distraction."

They'd landed in the open air, next to several other skiffs. The landing pad, this time, served as the spike's entire top. Salinity coated the spike's surface in black solar-sucking paint, a color that mingled in the crashing night to make Sai feel a bit like he was stepping into a void. Only the yellow light ring, blinking in an attempt to fight the dark, gave Sai any bearings.

A smaller, steady yellow ring sat in the top's center. A panel, coated in weather-resistant plastics, stood up, beckoning their approach. Abbad assisted Sai, who, without free hands, found getting out of the skiff a difficult proposition. As they went over to the platform, Renard kept his gaze on his wristlet, while Vana inhaled the windy sea air, seeming without concern.

"You're cheery," Sai said to the agent as they walked towards the console, Abbad carrying Sai's katana in one hand, pistol in the other.

Of the three enemies, Vana seemed least likely to burn a hole in Sai's skull, most likely to have some sense. He also couldn't shake the question of why she'd given Sai the drive back on the *Nautilus*. Sever had pored over its contents during the trip to Gillane Four, ending up deciding the charts, the messages, the meanings pointed to a project far larger than just Renard on a quest for glory.

"Perhaps an overestimation," Vana said, turning and

tapping a finger on the salved cut along her forehead. "It's not been a day without pain."

"How many of those do we get?"

Vana chuckled, Abbad laughed. Sai felt the man's pistol dig into his back, prodding him along faster towards the middle.

"Not enough," Vana said, dropping the funny for the real. "Hopefully, should our project do as we hope, there will be more days spent laughing, feeling safe and happy."

"Invisible suits are really gonna do that much?"

Vana went to the console, started tapping away. Abbad directed Sai to stand apart, while Renard, deep in his own wristlet adventure, stood off on his own.

"Alone, no," Vana replied. "With the proper communication, contracts, and enlistment, they will give DefenseCorp an unbeatable edge."

"Just what you want when you're looking for peace: a military organization without a threat."

"Isn't it?" Vana's console beeped and the platform's edge lighting flashed green. A railing rose from the floor to Sai's waist, clicked into place, and the descent began. "Even now, DefenseCorp doesn't face many threats. But who would risk a challenge, who would risk being a simple pirate, when utter destruction waited for you?"

Sai bounced on his feet, kept the blood flowing while he played with Vana's response. Abbad moved the pistol away as Sai shifted, giving the swordsman some room. The katana rested on the maniac's shoulder, blade gleaming.

"My concern is, who decides?" Sai said. "Who gets to say where DefenseCorp points its guns?"

Vana, nodding, came over to Sai. Put a hand on his shoulder, like a mother about to tell her child an important truth.

"You will, if you want it," Vana said.

By virtue of his own doings, Sai had dodged the command structure within DefenseCorp. He'd managed his children through their youth, he'd managed teams in his earlier career running security on his home planet. The last thing Sai needed, and why he'd made the jump to Sever and its high paying, high risk missions, was more responsibility.

Even if it didn't mean teaming up with Renard and Vana to embark on some mad power play across the stars, being the one pulling DefenseCorp's massive trigger sounded like Sai's own personal hell.

"Think you need someone with less morals for that," Sai said.

"That so?" Vana replied. "Would you trust Renard with that power, or the man behind you?"

"Hell no."

"Then perhaps it should be you."

"Or nobody."

Vana shook her head as the platform made it beneath the landing pad's fortified base and into the spike proper, "It will be someone, Sai. Even if it's not DefenseCorp, it will be another. Better to have a hand in the choice than not, right?"

Before Sai could respond, a blue light splashed over the platform as it continued down. Running the spike's length, lined with aqua diodes, were large transparent glass tubes. Like the ones marking transit around Kaiyo. Each one looked filled with rushing water, the liquid almost seeming in stasis as it moved.

"Circulating heat," Vana explained as the platform continued its descent. Sai had yet to see another stopping point. "The water rushes through here, picks up the spike's heat and carries it back into the ocean."

"I don't understand?" Sai said, not really sure why Vana cared so much about Salinity's processes.

"Salinity sets the galactic standard for water generation," Vana replied. "Everyone who wants to compete with them must meet their quality or exceed it. These spikes are expensive, specialized. No planet, hoping to bring their water to a broader market, could match the quality."

Now the idea became clear.

"So you're saying Salinity is the DefenseCorp of clean water?" Sai said, trying to keep from laughing.

"We're not there yet," Vana missed the joke, "but we will be."

Sai had to assume they'd reach the spike's bottom and wherever the housing unit, or wherever Renard and Vana were going, soon. Once they made it down there, Vana would set Sai up in some cell, where he'd sit and wait for hostage negotiations. Maybe Sever would get him out, or maybe Sai would find himself burned out when he refused Vana's weird offer for the last time.

Either way, it all sounded awful.

Abbad didn't have the pistol against Sai's back, thanks to Sai's continual bouncing up on his feet. That breathing room gave Sai a chance, and the man took it.

With the platform going down, Sai threw himself backwards. His left shoulder barreled into Abbad, the maniac man barking out in surprise. Sai felt the man fall away, heard the katana clatter as Abbad hit the platform's edge and fell over the side, blue light washing him the whole way.

Sai ran at Renard, the older officer looking up from his wristlet at Abbad's sound. Seeing Sai's bullrush, Renard reached for his pistol. No way he'd draw it in time.

Except Sai never quite made it to the old man. Vana, stepping in with a low trip, caught Sai's ankles and sent the

Sever swordsman splaying out onto the platform's floor. The stun cuffs flared to life a second later, splitting Sai's nerves apart and sending him into numbing spasms.

At least, though, he'd taken out Abbad.

That thought held for another moment, until the platform settled into its base. The water tubes rose up around them, the gaps filled in with solid steel flooring. Abbad, rubbing his shoulder, stood there shaking his head, having fallen a few meters without much damage to show for it.

"Bad timing," Vana said, looking down at Sai. "But I like the spirit. Now, let's see how much your friends want to pay for your life."

THIRTEEN

Local Interference

WHEN HE HIT the falling skiff with his hammer, Gregor knew the reason Aurora called for him to strike was to save lives. To keep potential destruction to a minimum. Gregor, though, followed orders because he wanted to swat the craft like a ball in some game, wallop it with his kinetic hammer and send the ship beaming into Gillane Four's night sky like a low grade comet.

Instead, smashing the already-burning craft had caused the skiff to disintegrate, letting the hammer plow through into the skiff's battery packs. Hit with force, those packs blew open, sending their energy out like a nova blossom, catching Gregor's power armor with their crackling blast and sending him back to the pad's surface with nothing more than a flickering visor, sparking insides, and a tingling numbness cascading up and down his nerves.

As Aurora and Eponi fought their way around, Gregor strived to get his muscles back under control. He issued one verbal command after another, prompting the power armor to reset itself and its various components, each one bringing an arm, a leg, the visor back into some operational order.

The static on the last, the thing driving Gregor's ability to see anything in the power armor, faded away in time to see another skiff lining up a clear shot. A man in that skiff, holding what looked like a black tube up on his shoulder, centered Gregor in his sights and launched an orange-glowing rocket right at the downed Sever man.

And as much as Gregor had lived through, he figured that was it. Already-damaged power armor wasn't going to take a rocket straight to its core.

Bright flashes came over Gregor's head, skittering green bolts lacing the space between Gregor and the skiff, turning it into a deadly energy sheet. The rocket struck those lights and blew up, a somewhat hollow puff as the missile's concentrated energy didn't find the impact it looked for.

Those green lasers climbed as the skiff realized its predicament, trying to swerve up and away and getting precisely nowhere as the beams found their mark in the skiff's engines. The heat overloaded the skiff's thin protection, sent doom coursing deep inside the ship, and the agents on board jumped over the edges before the thing blew, popping small chutes on their way down.

So the agents had been prepared for disaster. Smart.

But their chutes brought them to the dragon's mouth. Rebooted and revitalized, if not quite back to its perfect form, Gregor's power armor helped the big man spring up to his feet. While debris littered the landing pad around him, Gregor had no trouble picking out his hammer from the wreckage, grabbing it, and turning to catch the first of the quartet as they hit the ground.

Before Gregor could make his fatal strike, bright light shot down from above. Gregor's savior, Eponi in the *Prisa,* killed her laser barrage for less lethal illumination and highlighted the dropping group in her sights. Aurora limped over, rifle at the ready, calling for Gregor and Eponi to let the agents live.

"They won't talk," Eponi's voice came over the band. "Bet you all the cash in your accounts we get nothing from'em."

"We have to try," Aurora said.

The captain didn't hold much to torture tactics, but Gregor wasn't above a little intimidation. Holding the hammer, he stomped over to where the four agents touched down, the group cutting loose their chutes and throwing up their hands. Gregor patted the hammer's shaft against his other palm, a warning and a promise in one.

The agents, in their smooth, deep black and blue suits padded with laser-cushioning vests, spanned an impressive age range. Belts holding pistols and arm-slung rifles complemented their outfits, though none made the stupid play to go for the weapons.

Unfortunate.

"Hold up!" A new voice shouted, one coming from the section's outskirts. Gregor's visor lit up with potential threats from all around. "Fight's over now. You four, in the center, are under arrest for threatening the health and safety of this city and its citizens!"

Salinity's security force and the scurrying patrolman who'd ditched out on Aurora's advice came, nervously and slow, back into the spotlight. They had their pistols raised, the little weapons a pathetic counter to either Sever's power armor or the agent's heavier arms.

"We surrender to you," called one of the agents, reading the situation and making the right call.

The clanks as the agents threw their pistols and rifles to the ground hid Gregor's growl. Their potential hostages were escaping, not by means of athletic or combat prowess, but by, somehow, the local law.

"Want me to scare them off?" Gregor said, using the squad band to keep the message tight between the Sever trio. "I don't care if they put a price on my head."

"But I do," Aurora said as the Salinity group drew closer. "While we're still on this planet, we can't afford to make too many enemies. We might need their help getting to Renard."

"Sever backing down to the local boys?" Eponi's disbelieving laugh came through loud, clear. "Never thought I'd see that, Aurora."

"I don't like it, but it's the only choice," Aurora replied. "We fight for this group here, and even if we get away, you'll have Salinity fighters on your tail in moments. We'd never be able to land. Right now, we're on their good side. Let's keep it that way."

Gregor wondered if they'd still be on Salinity's good side if the knowledge of who torched the big tower back in the city came to light. Not that he'd be the one to tell.

Eponi took the *Prisa* back to its docking bay spot, letting Gregor and Aurora board, shuck off their power armor, and take some much needed showers. They ate dinner in shifts, one person always ready in the cockpit in case Renard's agents attempted an attack on the ship itself. Neither Gregor nor Aurora could fly the *Prisa* away, but either could use the turrets to mow down any invaders.

But no attack came. No threats. Not even a follow-up from Salinity security about why two power-armored people were tramping around Kaiyo's docking platforms.

"And you don't find that suspicious?" Eponi said, camping out in the cockpit after their protein-packed meal.

"I am always suspicious," Gregor replied. "Trust nobody, be ready with the hammer at all times."

"Uh huh."

"Thank you, by the way," Gregor said. "For the rocket."

"Saving your life is like a second hobby for me."

"Is it."

"Well, all of Sever, really." Eponi leaned back in her captain's chair, arms over her head. "You'd all be so screwed if I just left."

"I agree," Gregor said, and meant it.

The tone threw Eponi for a second, and Gregor could figure why. Sever had a camaraderie, sure, but real affection? Honest appreciation beyond acknowledging the skills they all had? Eponi apparently couldn't find a good response, because she defaulted to a smile, then launched into her story leading up to that very same rocket.

Aurora hadn't yet come back from her own refreshing, leaving the pilot and Gregor to pick over the day together. Eponi's story had Gregor almost wishing he'd gone with her instead: sliding down a building's side seemed like all kinds of fun. Although, smashing through floors and walls, setting a tower on fire, that wasn't so bad either.

"Where do you think they went?" Gregor asked. "Rovo and this Raquel?"

Eponi shrugged, sipped on a steaming coffee thermos. Everyone figured they'd be blowing out of the docking bay soon, seeing as it was folly to remain where your enemies could find you. The question hanging over the minutes was: where to go?

Gregor couldn't call himself a detective, but he'd spent enough time around DefenseCorp, around their agents— Lani, on Dynas, no small part—to gather that they'd always have another spot to fall back on, each one more secretive than the next. Also, they'd seen no sign of the big troop transport the agents had taken from the *Nautilus,* suggesting either Renard had a massive, hidden base on Gillane Four, or the transport had dropped an agent contingent and moved on to somewhere else.

The musing died when the *Prisa*'s console rang up with an incoming hail. A targeted one too, not from an open band like Gillane Four's security alerts or docking control. Eponi punched it, grinned as Rovo's face filled the grainy feed.

"Hey look, it's the traitor," Eponi said.

"That's right, just me, the traitor," Rovo replied, then he squinted at the camera. "Gregor, that you? Still alive?"

"Still alive." Gregor moved up, took the copilot seat next to Eponi. "You too, I see. Your wounds were severe."

"Renard and Vana didn't want to let me die, thankfully," Rovo said. "I'm beaming over the coordinates for where we're hiding out. Figure we can meet here, plan our next moves."

"Where is that?" Eponi said, swiping Rovo's face aside to bring up those coordinates. "It's not in the city?"

"Raquel figured it'd be safer outside Kaiyo." Rovo tilted the camera away from his face, showed a tight crew quarters. "It's a Salinity facility with open spots now. These cots feel like home."

Cots: stiff, small, and prone to giving Gregor back pain. The *Prisa* had better beds, put in by the cargo runners that'd had the ship before Gregor's own fast talking and hard punching ways had let him hijack the craft. Nonetheless, putting some distance between where the agents figured Sever was and where they actually were would be a good thing.

Aurora put her approval on the plan, and Eponi swung the *Prisa* into motion, sending the ship back into the night sky. Aurora settled in as co-pilot, and Gregor took the opportunity to head for a turret, squeezing into the gunnery chair and looking out over Kaiyo's bright blue-white city lights.

The techno-majesty of the galaxy's greater cities always awed Gregor, who'd spent his childhood in a frozen rock's dim and dark. So many people clustered down there, whiling away their lives, unaware that above them, around them, forces that could completely ruin their plans fought against each other. Gregor knew he preferred to wield the hammer, to be one of those forces, but somewhere down there, Parts-picker put together his getaway.

The man had chosen to abandon the life Gregor had adopted. A life that would either kill Gregor, or render him, eventually, unable to keep up with it. What would Gregor do then? Sell salvage? Try to train new recruits, barking orders he himself could no longer perform?

The turret's console buzzed. Eponi's voice, coming over the ship's internal band.

"Hey, you're not asleep back there, are you?" Eponi asked.

"Not yet."

"Then do me a favor, kick yourself awake. Looks like we might have company."

"Renard?"

"Suspecting so. I don't think they're done with us yet."

Gregor swiped the console to the near-field scanner, saw the approaching dots. Smaller ships. Maybe more skiffs, or single-man fighters. The kind you could stash on a planet without getting too much attention.

His fingers finding the turret's stick, Gregor settled in. Juiced up the power. Figured that he could, at least, do this long after the rest of his body turned to mush.

Shooting things was, after all, almost as fun as smashing them to bits.

Before the fun could get started, though, Eponi called

back through the ship. The oncoming fighters didn't belong to Renard or DefenseCorp, but Salinity. An escort, taking the *Prisa* outside the city.

Gregor let his hands drop from the turret controls, a little disappointed, a little relieved: Eponi noted the flight would take an hours at atmosphere cruising speed.

Perfect timing for a nap.

Save And Swap

THE MESSAGE CAME in the morning, the hour where dawn's aura first played with the smooth rippled sea around the Salinity facility. Aurora caught it first, her wristlet on the open band while she spent the early morning sitting on a viewing deck, sprayed with tables and chairs for people like her. Eponi found the captain doing her reverie thing, the pilot on an early wander herself.

Eponi had spent the few sleeping hours on the *Prisa*, along with Gregor, though the man snored loud enough to rattle the ship. Ear plugs worked well on that front, but blocking the sound did nothing for her mind. Despite the bravado yesterday, she kept pulling herself back to the apartment, to those seconds where she snapped the shot at Vana, at the manic man in the back.

Could Eponi have taken a different angle? Hit Renard with the bolt instead, bought both Rovo and Sai time to get out?

Leaving the *Prisa* to its noisy sleeper, Eponi wandered out dressed in casual layers—Salinity kept their damn facilities chilled—and tried to step slow enough to keep the automatic lights from turning on. That way, Eponi could use the starlight reflecting from one wall to the next as her guide to the deck.

She'd been taken hostage before. On Dynas, she'd given Sai up, put him in the hands of a ruthless scientist that'd injected the swordsman with a trial virus. One that needed a few more turns in the incubator. Sai had nearly died there, and not in the way most DefenseCorp soldiers want to go out. Nothing flashy about losing your mind and your muscles to a devouring disease.

And now she'd done it again. Left Sai in the hands of people who might do who the hell knew what to him. Who had no reason to keep him alive.

Guilt made for a poor sleep companion.

"Soaking up the stars?" Eponi said as she opened the door and joined Aurora on the deck.

"I'd be grateful if they gave me some answers," Aurora replied, not turning to face Eponi but raising her wrist and its bright screen. "Up until a minute ago, I hadn't heard a thing."

"Tell me it's Sai." Eponi read the gesture well enough: the wristlet's screen had the paused playback frame flashing. "Or is Deepak back to sending you love notes?"

Now Aurora turned around, narrowed eyes measuring the distance to Eponi for a much-deserved gut punch, "He never did—"

"Chill, captain," Eponi said, meeting Aurora at her table and taking the other seat. If Salinity kept its buildings cold, and Gillane Four's relentless breeze nipped at her bones, the chair proved a respite: solar-batteries on the black furniture turned on warmers when Eponi's pressure landed. "It's too early to get worked up."

Aurora measured Eponi with a silent stare that said she'd filed away the crack about Deepak for later. Eponi would've shrugged, by this point everyone had something to get Eponi for. Most of'em weren't serious enough to earn a laser in the back, but Eponi figured she'd cross that line eventually.

And shoot first when it came time to collect.

"Vana sent the message, not Renard," Aurora said, like that was the most important detail.

"So?"

"It muddies things," Aurora said. "I prefer a clear leader. A clear target."

Aurora hadn't hid Sever's ultimate goal. Save Kaia, yes, but the girl would be in danger as long as those agents on Sai's drive survived. Everyone on that org chart had to go. Deepak said he'd put out feelers for every name, try to find their location, but transmitting anything across a galaxy-wide net would take a long time.

Best to start with the targets you knew, and take out the most dangerous ones first.

"We'll get'em both," Eponi said. "They deserve it."

"Agreed." Aurora looked at her wristlet, laid her arm out on the table where Eponi could see it, then tapped for the message to play again.

Vana laid out the terms as simple fact. A place, one of Gillane Four's few landmasses built up by Salinity for the sanity of the planet's populace. Turned out it helped people's minds to get into real nature for a bit, not just a city park.

Sever would report to that landmass later today. They'd bring Kaia and Kashmal. In return for the girl, Vana and Renard would give back Sai. The two groups would depart without a single shot fired, and the galaxy would go on turning.

At least for a little while.

"Sounds like a crap deal," Eponi said when Vana's

weathered voice finished with a plea for Aurora to think it through. "Sai's definitely not worth the little girl."

Eponi had been joking, but Aurora's frown, coupled with a turn back towards the purple sky, put some doubt into the moment. Vana had been straight: if Sever failed to show, Sai would be tossed into the sea with two lasers into the back of his head.

"They won't expect us to play fair," Aurora said. "We've already tried to ambush them, and we've cost them lives and locations. Vana might contain herself, but Renard's going to want payback. His agents want it too."

"Hate to tell you this, Aurora, but they're not the only ones that want a little action."

Aurora gave a short laugh, "Get in line."

The line, turned out, included more than just Aurora. The Sever captain circled up the squad, including Raquel, the Salinity security officer who declared her involvement important because the potential fighting threatened her planet's peace. Eponi couldn't argue too much with that, seeing as yesterday's firefights had torched one building, shot up another, and left one of the main docking pads outside Kaiyo littered with bodies and debris.

Aurora's briefing mingled with call-and-response suggestions from the crowd, ending with an affirmative message to Vana and a plan in place. A plan that put Eponi back in the *Prisa*'s cockpit, with a full load headed off towards the appointed rock.

Kashmal and Kaia took the *Prisa*'s center, the girl's dad coloring the day by telling Kaia they were going on a field trip. At first, Eponi cocked an eye at the explanation, figuring a rock in the middle of an ocean wouldn't be all that special, but then she remembered Kaia's life had been spent, largely, in closets, ships, and apartments. Putting the kiddo out where she could feel a real breeze, see a horizon on all sides, might be magical.

Especially because, if Sever blew this one, Kaia might not last the day.

Everyone pulled on their power armor, Eponi excepted because the *Prisa*, unlike DefenseCorp drop shuttles, hadn't been designed for power armor in the cockpit. Rifles were loaded up, pistols checked. Gregor grabbed his hammer, and Rovo plugged in the strange scythe weapon he'd won back on Wexer.

"Good to have you back, rookie," Eponi said as the *Prisa* soared above the sea, the ship's intercom beaming the message to the squad's band. Nobody else shared the cockpit with her now, and sitting on a straight flight path over an ocean didn't exactly require all her attention. "You miss all this?"

"Better than getting interrogated, for sure."

"What'd they do? Clip off your fingers? Threaten your family?"

Rovo stayed quiet for a minute and Eponi wondered if she'd crossed some line. She'd gone for the exaggerated play, but maybe things were too real. Maybe these nerves shouldn't be calmed.

"They said I should join them, because they were going to make sure DefenseCorp ran the galaxy."

Now it was Eponi's turn to sit for a second. She'd never bought into the power lust that types like Renard held as the ultimate goal. She preferred action, albeit without the lasers and the death, coupled with a healthy cash salary so Eponi wouldn't have to worry about her next meal, or her next ship. If Renard and Vana offered her that for a little girl's life?

Kaia's laugh echoed through the *Prisa*, followed by Gregor's bad singing as the man ran through one of the songs they'd sang while slicing rock on the comet. What had Eponi wincing any other time now turned up her lips, all because the delight of one child.

"You made the right call," Eponi said.

"Definitely the right call," Aurora interrupted. "Vana or Renard would've shot you the moment they had what they needed. People like them don't divide their power willingly."

The captain's words killed the conversation, and Eponi returned to fiddling with the *Prisa*, tinkering its systems to make sure energy found the right places. They were flying into dangerous territory, and given a likely landing, plus people on the ground, Eponi figured juicing the engines wouldn't be the right call. Shields and weapons, that's where the *Prisa* needed to be sending its power.

And, per Raquel's request, Eponi had the ship's outboard cameras ready to roll too. Grabbing proof that Vana and Renard had evil motives could get them kicked off the planet. Eponi didn't give that line too much credit, as the DefenseCorp agents could twist just about any company to their ends, but hey, when this inevitably blew up in Renard's face, Eponi would enjoy watching the failure on replay.

The target, a bulging green-and-brown mass erupting from the ocean like a tooth, faded in on the horizon. Eponi relayed the first calls, getting Gregor and Rovo in position. The rookie had protested this part, wanting to be there when Kaia swapped sides, but Aurora insisted otherwise. Rovo's emotions might blow the whole thing, and they couldn't set Sai up with that kind of risk.

Besides, Vana's message insisted Kaia wouldn't be hurt. Right.

"Cutting speed down, get ready for the drop," Eponi

said, angling the *Prisa* towards the rock in a downward slant.

The landing pads were all in the top center, from which visitors could embark on any number of hiking trails across the kilometers-wide rock. Climbing opportunities dotted the massive cliffs, the rock often covered in thick vines taking advantage of the climate and endless water resources. Thick temperate forest covered the top, massive pines spearing up towards the sky. Birds looped the island, no doubt shipped in by Salinity to provide that bit of real, natural excitement.

White-crested waves lapped the rock's base, their salty spray nearly catching the *Prisa* as Eponi slowed the ship before angling it almost straight up. She'd called for everyone to strap themselves in, but bangs and a few curses suggested not everyone had done it right. Going straight up was a hard move on the body, but critical to keep any prying eyes away.

If there were any: thus far, Eponi hadn't seen a single other ship on the scanners. Either Vana and Renard were already here, or Sever had made better time. Regardless, less than a dozen meters separated the *Prisa* from the cliff-side now, with Eponi shooting up. She began a countdown, at first silent and then aloud.

Zero brought a tap on the console and a hard opening of the *Prisa*'s cargo hatch. Normally, that hatch would've led into a cargo container, meant to be attached to the ship's bottom for long haul trips. Without that, the hatch whistled a free shot into the late morning air. The sudden roar ripped through the *Prisa*, and an alarm beeped its notice that things were, perhaps, not quite right.

"They're gone," Aurora said. "Close it."

Eponi hadn't seen the drop, the power armor boosters kicking Rovo and Gregor from the *Prisa* and onto the island, but Aurora's tone said the plan's first real part had worked. They had two fighters on the island now, armed and ready to play.

Now came the hard part, where Eponi would either save her friend or lose a little kid.

Or both.

FIFTEEN

A Trade

THE ORDER STUNG. Stung even more as Rovo followed Gregor up the rock, both doing what they could to move quietly in their power armor, gear designed for loud assaults on enemy forces and not stealth approaches on an island cliff.

"You won't be yourself," Aurora had said, back on the *Prisa*, after the briefing.

She'd excluded Rovo from the party leaving the ship to greet Vana, to hand over Kaia and get Sai back. At least, the trade made the title line, but Aurora promised to negotiate. The little girl wouldn't be leaving the rock with Renard and Vana if Sever could help it.

The issue, so Aurora felt, was that Rovo might take out his rifle and start blasting before talks could reach a solution. Rovo didn't have a good counter back on the *Prisa*, and he still didn't have one now, as his metal suit brushed aside pine branches and his armored feet squashed ferns.

So far as brooding went, the climb made pleasant enough surroundings. Gillane Four's wind, a more pleasant gusting than Wexer's dust-blown shredders, cut in with a sharp bite on the rocky slope. The breeze did, though, carry fresh pine scent mingling with far up ocean spray, a blessed combination after sterile ship confines and Renard's musty quarters back in Kaiyo. Proper food and a good rest without mortal enemies stalking the hallways did wonders too: Rovo almost felt like a real human.

Almost.

Kaia's looming fate kept any comfort from taking full hold.

"The child won't be hurt," Gregor said, his voice cutting through on the near-field band. "Do not worry."

"How do you know?"

"Because they will be dead before they touch her."

Gregor spoke the words with the same hard finality the big man had used to razz new recruits back on the *Nautilus* before stomping them in training simulations. Gregor didn't leave room for doubt in his threats, and Rovo found himself nodding alongside the hammer-wielder.

"Glad we see things the same way," Rovo said. "They're monsters."

"I once thought we were," Gregor replied, the iron drifting off into a contemplative weight, a musing with meaning. "Sever squad, DefenseCorp champions. Called in to destroy what could not be destroyed, to win when loss was certain. Now, I am seeing it differently."

Rovo waited while they stalked to the left, angling to reach a high point where they could view the full landing pad and plot whether a sniper's post or a close-range ambush would prove deadlier, but Gregor didn't continue.

"What do you mean?" Rovo finally prompted. "Differently?"

"I am a weapon," Gregor said. "Always have been. Started with the rock mine, then to planet patrols, and then to Sever. A weapon to be pointed at the enemy and unleashed."

"Like so many of us."

"Except now I am thinking, perhaps it would be better if *I* chose where to use my skills."

Rovo blinked, "Isn't that what you're doing right now? You're not a DefenseCorp employee anymore, man. You can do what you want."

"Hmm. A good point." Gregor looked back and down at Rovo, the big man's face brightening behind his visor. "I think, what I want, is to destroy this agent and her army."

Rovo waited till Gregor turned back, continued the climb, before rolling his eyes. Quite an epiphany there. At least Gregor's big ideas kept Rovo distracted for a little while, long enough that they reached their target point in time to catch the event's beginning.

The landing zone sat in the island's center, suspended over a pool with thick cables branching out to the surrounding crags. With enough room for twenty skiffs or more, the zone embraced the island's theme, diagraming spaces out in tropical lines. Today, though, Rovo counted not a single civilian ship.

"Raquel did it," Rovo said. As soon as Aurora began the brief, Raquel had started tapping away on her wristlet, claiming she was going to close off the island to visitors for the day. No innocents losing their lives in this trade. "Guess she's more powerful than I thought."

"Companies are easily scared," Gregor replied.

True enough. DefenseCorp's business practices generated enough protest, from victims and collateral damage alike, that Rovo had seen more than one reminder flow through the company's galaxy-wide nets demanding units make every effort to get civilians away.

So long as those efforts wouldn't negatively impact the profits, of course.

Salinity's higher moral bar allowed Eponi to land the *Prisa* on the right side. The ship covered numerous skiff spots. Its ramp was down, and clustered in front stood Aurora, Raquel, Kashmal and Kaia. The little girl had her hand clamped around her father's, though by the waving of her free arm, Kaia didn't know what was about to happen.

Across the way, Rovo frowned towards the opposing group. Unlike the *Prisa*, Renard and Vana showed up in the expected bubble skiffs. Several, all parked with spaces in between. Standard practice to minimize the damage should one take a hit. Vana and Renard had themselves standing free, with Sai and Abbad behind, the manic man holding a pistol near Sai's stun-cuffed self.

Other agents had positions near the skiffs. Weapons weren't drawn yet, but slung rifles made the threat a visible one. Easily double Sever's number.

Rovo kept forgetting Renard had close to a thousand agents on the *Nautilus*, all working to advance the suits and keep tabs on Dynas. That planet had spun off the charts, but square in the *Nautilus*'s assigned sector, an easy place to drop in on while Helix, that dummy company, spun its lab-devised disaster. Now Kaia, the only, wonderful success, was about to be claimed by the worst of the worst.

"Can I shoot them now?" Rovo said.

"You cannot." Gregor's words were truth in more than one way. The big man carried the long-range rifle, thanks to Aurora's order preventing Rovo from getting it. The rookie's role up here was only escort, only protect. "Yet."

Together, Rovo and Gregor laid flat, leveraging some small pines and the big-leaf ferns beneath for cover. Gregor unlimbered the rifle and brought up the scope, settling into the earth. At least up here, things weren't just stone: pine needles provided something of a bed, enough cushion to let Rovo get a good look at the gap between the two groups, where the trade would take place.

Using the power armor's visor, Rovo zoomed in. The focus gave him a clear view as the Sever quartet started walking, with Renard's own foursome moving to meet them. Getting this close with the visor brought a disorienting swirl with every head twitch, a vulnerability if anyone came at the two Severs from behind. Technically, Rovo shouldn't have been doing this at all. Technically, he should've been several meters behind Gregor, watching the forest for any ambush.

Technically, Rovo should've been on the damn landing platform, telling Vana where to stick her deal.

"I'll be fast, because I don't think anyone here cares about the pleasantries," Vana's voice came through Rovo's visor, scratchy and distant. A power suit mic tuned up to the highest sensitivity, broadcasting along the open band. Aurora making a concession for Rovo. "The deal remains the same. The girl for Sai."

Rovo's jaw clenched. He hadn't thought the big moment would arrive quite this fast, but here they were. His right hand traced back to the rifle on his back, ready to swing it forward. Without a scope, he'd be hard pressed to hit accurately from here with the bolt-spraying weapon, but, at the least, he could throw some agents into cover.

"We're altering the deal," Aurora came back. "You don't need the girl. You need her blood." Aurora nodded at Kashmal, who, reaching into a pocket, produced a sealed syringe and vial for just that thing. "We can draw it right here. You get what you want, we get Sai, and Kaia gets to go home with her dad."

The words sounded so small on that landing zone, in

island's center, but Rovo tensed up all the same. Vana, holding up a single finger, turned to talk with Renard.

"You have them centered?" Rovo whispered to Gregor. "This is where it'll all go wrong."

"Patience, rookie," Gregor replied. "They will take the deal."

"How do you know?"

"Because they do not want to die today. They dream of bigger things."

An interesting rationale, and the idea kept Rovo from whipping his rifle around. Instead, the rookie took a long, deep breath as Vana and Renard broke their conference. The lead agent patted her finger with her lips, looked at Aurora in all her power armor, then crouched and smiled towards Kaia.

"Such a tiny one to have all that we want inside her," Vana said. "We can agree to your terms, with one change." Vana rose, gestured at Kaia and her father. "There's no guarantee that the sample we take today will have enough of what we need. We must have access to the girl. Whenever we need more, *if* we need more, she will be available."

"Kashmal can keep you informed of his movements," Aurora said. "Blood draws aren't difficult."

Now Renard shook his head, and Vana ceded the ground to him, "Light years span the distance between this planet and where we'll need the blood. We can't wait that long if this isn't perfect. What happens if the vial is contaminated before we arrive?"

"That's your problem," Aurora countered.

"No, no," Renard replied. "That is being foolish. We want the girl's blood, and we will have it. Until such time as we can reproduce the right infection. Once we have that, the girl will be free. And properly compensated."

"Also," Vana tagged onto the end of Renard's words,

"we will take Kashmal as well. The girl doesn't need to be parted from her father."

Kaia's blood. That was the deal. The girl didn't get to go with Renard, to get slapped into some cage on whatever planet the damn agent was going to take her to. Rovo didn't believe for a second that Kashmal and his daughter would get some plush accommodation. She'd be mined, like any resource, and her father would probably catch a laser to the back by the second night.

"Kashmal?" Aurora said. "This is your decision."

Rovo felt his own blood chill. Sever's squad leader wasn't fighting back? Wasn't declaring the whole charade for what it was? With her power armor and the pistol holstered at her waist, Aurora could have both Renard and Vana gunned down in seconds. The whole thing could be over.

"Sai," Gregor said, apparently sensing Rovo's agitation. Pretty obvious, Rovo noticed, given the pine needles the rookie had been throwing around as he did the lying down equivalent of pacing. "She will not risk Sai."

"She's not even trying," Rovo replied. He reached back, pulled his rifle up. Tried to sight down it. "She's giving her up."

Kashmal's voice came next, nervous, but forcing through some confidence, "How do we know you will keep your word?"

"Trust is all you have," Vana replied. "But we will. We need Kaia alive and well, and the best way to do that is to keep her father happy."

"And," Aurora added, "if you don't, I'll hunt you down myself."

Rovo caught Vana's grin, the woman's slight nod. His captain's threat only made Rovo grip his rifle trigger tighter. Vengeance didn't matter to the one already dead. Killing Vana after the fact wouldn't save Kaia.

"Rookie," Gregor warned as Vana beckoned to Kashmal and Kaia. "Take your fingers off the trigger."

Rovo didn't reply. He just watched as the little girl he'd saved back on Dynas, who'd crawled around on his shoulders during the weeks in space flying towards Wexer, who'd sent those messages beaming across the stars to Rovo almost every day since, just to say good night, went away from safety towards . . .

The rifle pulled away, free from Rovo's grip. Gregor had the weapon, threw it into the woods behind them. Rovo sprang to his feet, looking at the long gun in Gregor's other hand.

"Couldn't trust you with that," Gregor said. "Stand down, Rovo."

"Yeah, see, you said it yourself," Rovo replied. "We're all our own weapons now."

The rookie didn't wait, but sprang on his sentence's end, activating the kinetic boosters and crashing into Gregor, hands going for the rifle.

For the only chance to keep Kaia from those bastards' hands.

SIXTEEN

Laser Burn

AURORA MADE the call the moment she saw Sai. With her visor down, face fresh to the world, she watched as Renard and Vana led Sever's swordsman from the skiff, stun-cuffed and looking like he'd endured a long night. With bags under the eyes and bruises to match, Sai walked with a limp and a listless grin, the look of a man trying to stick it to his captors when he had nothing left to lose. Following him came a strange looking agent, dressed in an immaculate crimson suit—nicer, even than Renard and Vana's outfits, who seemed to be having a great time pushing Sai forward. Sai's katana hung over the man's back, resting in its sheath.

Around Aurora, Raquel formed up with Kashmal and Kaia behind her. The Salinity security chief had a pistol, a laser-sucking vest, and little else to recommend her in a firefight. With Aurora in her power armor and Eponi manning the *Prisa*'s dual turrets, though, Raquel wouldn't have to do much. Not to mention Gregor and Rovo in the trees.

Aurora didn't look to the left, where the duo ought to

be. The forest kept things thick enough, but any halfway decent inspection towards the pines would likely reveal the two, and Aurora didn't need that complication. Instead, she went forward, meeting Renard and Vana halfway.

Keeping the focus on herself.

Vana and Renard appeared to have slept better than Sai. Both had bright eyes throwing hungry looks Kaia's way, though Vana had the grace to cover it up when Aurora approached. Their crimson uniforms showed more of the on-the-run wear and tear Aurora would've expected after yesterday's events, and both agents wore pistols on their belts: Vana two, Renard one.

The negotiations went quick.

Aurora operated on principles. Squad first, mission second, outside casualties somewhere else down the line. Kaia, because Aurora had spent so weeks with the girl en route to Wexer, wasn't exactly a random civilian, but put up against Sai, there wasn't much of an argument. Sever's swordsman offered the squad a chance to continue fighting against the agents, a chance to embrace the short-lived mercenary lifestyle Sever had started on Wexer.

Even if Aurora didn't trust Vana and Renard to treat Kaia, or Kashmal, with anything approaching the sweetness in Vana's promises, getting Sai back took first priority. Hell, once the swordsman had himself a rest, Sever could launch back in pursuit of the girl and her father.

What Aurora didn't want, didn't need, was a firefight. Vana and Renard came in with four skiffs, agents popping from some, with empty seats lingering in others. Thinking back to the *Nautilus* and those near-invisible suits, Aurora couldn't bet that those empty seats actually were, well, empty. Not enough firepower to challenge the *Prisa*, but enough to risk her squad in the field.

Kashmal and Kaia took the trade in stride, the father

wearing a nervous frown, the daughter seeming oblivious to the danger as she walked towards Vana's motherly smile.

Sai started his own walk across the landing pad, acknowledging Aurora's rescue with a half-hearted nod. After two steps, though, the swordsman turned, looked at the agent holding his sword.

"I'll have that back now," Sai said, leaving no room for negotiation.

"Nah, think I like it," the man replied. "Consider it repayment for that nasty trick you pulled yesterday."

Sai froze, and while Aurora could only see the back of Sai's head, she knew what the man was thinking. No way would he be leaving without that sword. Aurora flipped a look at Vana, warning that their boy better return the weapon or everything would go to hell.

"Abbad," Vana said, catching the meaning, "we'll get you one of your own later. Give Sai his blade back, please."

Get you one of your own later? What the hell kind of talk was that?

Abbad put on a pout worthy of a three year-old, then shrugged, reached up and slid the katana from his shoulders. The crisis would've, should've ended there, except a new noise rippled across island's center: a scratching, breaking noise followed by a tremendous splash off to Aurora's left.

Gregor stood at the cliff's edge, the long gun in one hand, looking down at the water. Rovo swam there, the power armor not doing much to keep the rookie afloat. A thousand questions hammered Aurora's mind right that instant, and she tossed them all, because lives were about to be lost.

"Ambush!" Vana shouted, diving into the worst possible reaction. "Take the girl, kill the others!"

Everyone moved after the first word. Aurora ran for Sai, who charged Abbad, stun cuffs still on. Beside Aurora, Raquel broke for Kashmal and Kaia as the first laser shots blitzed the air. If Aurora had been a better diplomat, or been more interested, she might've tried shouting for everyone to calm down. Might've pushed things back from the brink they'd fallen over.

But, really, Renard and Vana didn't deserve the girl.

Aurora kicked in her power armor's boosters, launching forward and hitting Sai from behind. She pushed him to the pavement as shots streaked in at her from those skiffs. The power armor took hits, flaring red on the visor now clamped over her face. Knocking Sai and his unarmored self down, Aurora kept the momentum moving, rolling and coming back up standing, rifle at the ready.

To see Abbad, grinning like he'd just arrived at his own birthday party, holding Sai's katana in a high stance. Aurora leveled the rifle, took aim on the trigger, and, despite the chaos unfolding around her, felt a distinct anticipation at leveling this fool.

Abbad's forward slash came faster than Aurora anticipated. Sai's blade swished through the air and sliced Aurora's rifle barrel clean off, sending the black metal piece spiraling off the pad into the water below. Abbad didn't wait to follow through either, twisting the blade back for a return cross-cut that would've bisected Aurora's power armor if she hadn't hopped back.

"Watch it!" Sai shouted as Aurora's booted feet nearly crushed his hands, the man's voice rising over a suddenly crowded battlefield.

With a few meters between herself and the advancing Abbad, Aurora tried to do the squad leader thing and register the battlefield as a whole. Sai, stun-cuffed and useless, crawled away behind Aurora. To the left, Vana and Renard pulled Kashmal and Kaia towards the nearest skiff. Raquel laid back on the landing pad, smoke rising from her chest where laser fire had burned in.

Gregor had the long gun up, taking shots at the agents from the forest and catching withering fire in return. Rovo was nowhere to be seen. Maybe the rookie was still swimming, maybe he'd drowned.

All in all, not good.

"C'mon," Abbad yelled over the battle, "give me some fun!"

Oh, this guy was going to die.

Keeping her mouth shut, Aurora whipped the ruined rifle at Abbad. The man deflected the weapon with the katana enough to catch the hit on his shoulder instead of his face, but the move took the sword out of the way. Aurora kicked forward, her boots not yet charged enough for much more than a spirited puff, but when you're a rushing metal monster, that's enough.

Abbad tried to get the katana back, but Aurora swatted the sword aside as she barreled through. Her left hand gripped Abbad's all too pressed collar, and threw him to the ground, following the toss with a boot stamp on the katana. Aurora slid her right foot back, tearing the katana from Abbad's grip and sending it skittering across the landing pad while, with her left hand, fresh from giving Abbad a concrete deposit, drew her pistol and leveled it at the man.

Two lasers burned into Aurora as she stood over Abbad, but the pistol fire didn't take too much from her power armor's defenses.

"How's this for fun?" Aurora said, pulling the trigger.

In the split second between Aurora finishing her line, her finger pushing through the slight resistance on the pistol's trigger to send the weapon's superheated gas from its power pack up and through the barrel, the air around Aurora lit on fire.

Like a thousand papers tearing at once, molecules split as Eponi opened up the *Prisa*'s twin turrets and the ship's central gun. Made for space combat, for punching through heavy opposing hulls, the white-blue bolts—tuned to their hottest levels for reasons Aurora couldn't fathom—laced the agent skiffs and the poor souls behind them.

Their cover melted away, blew apart, or simply disintegrated as Eponi laid a steady line, stopping only at the skiff Renard and Vana sprinted to, and only then because they still had Kaia and Kashmal with them.

Aurora's visor went dark to shield her from the laser's searing light, its noise filtering flicked on to keep her ears from ringing as the firing continued. Through that sonic cut, Aurora heard one strange sound, from real close.

Laughter. Wild laughter.

At her feet, Abbad had his mouth open, tears streaming from his eyes, even with a smoking hole in his chest where Aurora's pistol shot, twisted ever so slightly by Eponi's onslaught, hit its mark.

"Eponi!" Gregor's voice, over the squad band. "Stop shooting. You will kill the girl."

"Thought I was doing pretty good avoiding them?" Eponi responded, but she cut the lasers, their silence coming as sudden as their destruction. "They're still standing."

Aurora couldn't argue with that: Eponi had turned Renard and Vana's crew to ash, and blown all but one of their skiffs to shrapnel. The two leaders, though, still had their escape route. Still had Kaia.

"I'm on the girl," Aurora said, bringing the pistol back

in line to finish the job. "Eponi, get out here and help Sai and Raquel. Gregor, find Rovo."

This time, when Aurora pulled the trigger, nothing stopped the shot.

Aurora didn't double-check the results, kicking off towards the skiff. Vana and Renard were nearly there, but Kashmal, the stubborn man, seemed to have realized his best lift didn't lie in going with the agents. He pushed back against Renard, tried to pull Kaia away from Vana.

"Watch out," Gregor said, as Aurora's visor lit up with a bright red to her right.

Crunching over shrapnel, Aurora glanced that way, expecting to see a half-dead agent crawling from a wreck, maybe waving a pistol in her direction. Instead she saw dying fires, smoking bodies, and the slightest glitch in the light, like a small crease running through reality.

The suited agent hit Aurora hard, coming in with a dagger-length knife Aurora couldn't see. The strike bounced off Aurora's thick, armored right arm, sending sparks out and giving Aurora time to square herself up to the suit. Facing it directly, Aurora saw the reflective coating had been marred, with blast streaks patching the suit's sides and chest.

"I don't have time for this," Aurora growled, bringing up her pistol.

The suit went for it, grabbing the weapon and, in the process, showing Aurora right where to punch. She kicked in the power armor's kinetic boost and laid in a strike to the suit's head. The blow crumpled the target, the agent maintaining his tearing grip on the pistol and sending Aurora's weapon flying back with him.

As soon as the suit struck the ground, a bright red flash lit over Aurora's shoulder, sizzling into the suit's chest. Another one followed a half second later.

"Finished," Gregor said.

"Thanks." Aurora's visor showed clear ahead. "The agents?"

"Rovo."

What? Aurora whirled, saw a different scene than she'd left playing out around the skiff. Vana still held Kaia now, with Kashmal stock still nearby with Vana's pistol at his head. Rovo, his suit soaked and dripping, had Renard in a headlock. With the power armor, in a spot like that, he could crush the life out of the man without a second thought.

Aurora burst that way, clomping as fast as her feet would allow.

"You heard me," Rovo was saying as Aurora came closer, "Kaia for Renard. That's the trade."

"Tell me you have a shot," Aurora said, beaming to Gregor. "Vana."

"Working on it," Gregor replied.

"Work faster."

Vana was shaking her head, "Renard knows, just like me. The girl's the treasure. You let me leave, she lives. I guarantee it."

"You don't get Kaia," Rovo said again, as if by demanding it, the rookie would make it so. "You don't get her!"

Kaia, eyes like saucers, turned from Rovo, to her dad, to Vana. She wasn't crying, and Aurora figured it was shock that kept her standing. How could a four year-old make sense of what was happening?

"Think, Rovo," Vana said, low and even. "You let us in that skiff, you get a chance to take her back. You can live with that. You don't want to know what it's like on the other side."

Renard tried to speak up, but Rovo tightened his grip,

the man wheezing out into nothing. Aurora came up beside the rookie, tried to find a weakness in Vana's hold on the kid. Didn't see one. Vana played things smart, she kept Kashmal between herself and Gregor's position, and with Kaia in her arms, any shot would risk hitting the girl.

Like a standoff in some old movie, the two Sever members faced off against Vana and her hostages, the only sound now coming from the crackling skiffs and the wind whistling through the surrounding pines. Smoke clouded the sky overhead, but beyond it, Gillane Four's white star gave the day clarity.

"Rovo," Aurora said. "Let her go. We'll chase and get Kaia back, but not here. Not now."

"That's not an option," Rovo said.

"It's an order," Aurora replied. "Stand down."

"You don't get to give me orders anymore," Rovo said, left hand reaching for the pistol on his waist.

The move proved a line too far for Vana, and she swiveled her pistol from Kashmal to Kaia, stepping up against the skiff's side. Rovo's hand froze, but Kashmal did not. Aurora didn't have children, didn't have anyone in her life that could claim that kind of hold on her, or maybe she would've seen it coming.

Maybe she would've caught the man in time.

Kashmal ran at Vana, and the agent flicked her pistol back and fired. Kashmal dropped, and Vana, twisting Kaia away from the sight, pushed the girl into the skiff. Rovo started forward, but Aurora grabbed his arm, kept the rookie from adding Kaia to the day's casualties.

"She'll kill her," Aurora said into the space. "She'll kill the kid, Rovo. Vana can take the blood from a body if she has to."

The skiff's engines started up, Vana telling Kaia to get herself buckled in, still holding the pistol to the girl's head.

"I can take the shot," Gregor said. "She's clear."

"No," Aurora replied, still holding Rovo, the rookie swearing up a storm. "That skiff's on. It'll crash. We can't risk it."

Vana pulled back, the skiff rose up, turned, and burned away, vanishing into the smoke. A hard clang sounded at Aurora's feet, and she looked, saw Rovo on his knees, hands on the ground. The rookie formed a first, pounded the concrete.

Beyond him, quiet and frail, lay Renard, his neck snapped.

SEVENTEEN

Results and Revenge

Using Sai's katana, Eponi cut away the stun cuffs in the fight's fizzling aftermath. Sai had spent the battle largely on the ground, cheek pressed to the landing pad as laser fire zipped along overhead. When the heat stopped flaring, when the shouts dwindled, Sai dared to look up, to try and stand.

Despite his charge at Abbad—the idea of that man having Sai's family sword blotted out all logic—Sai knew that the best way to survive a fight when you couldn't, well, fight, was to stay down and out. The swordsman wouldn't help anyone by making himself a target, and the agents had left him in the civilian dress from yesterday's venture: no armor, no chance.

Thus, while Eponi torched the air with her fusillade and Vana escaped with Kaia, Sai watched. Though he had no love for Kashmal, Sai's heart lurched when the man took Vana's bolt. He couldn't, wouldn't imagine what it would be like for his own children to watch their father gunned down before their eyes.

No child deserved that, much less Kaia's glittery, happy self.

"You hurt?" Eponi asked, helping Sai get up. The pilot's trademark sarcasm, her laughing tinge, didn't make an appearance this time. "If not, mind taking a walk around, see if there's anyone left we need to worry about?"

"What're you going to do?"

"Get the *Prisa* ready to leave," Eponi said. "Unless you want to stay in this disaster longer?"

Sai definitely did not. Taking his katana back from Eponi, Sai took a new look around, trying to find those telltale signs of life. Aurora had carried Raquel back into the *Prisa* already, and Rovo brought Kashmal quick after. Whether the rookie's haste meant the man still lived, Sai couldn't be sure. He didn't have any device to listen in to the squad band, much less ask any questions.

And, really, Sai could live with the quiet for a minute.

His eyes landed on Abbad next. Aurora's pistol shots had put the final stamp on the man, leaving Abbad frozen in a laughing look. Last night, held up in the Salinity structure, Abbad had pestered Sai relentlessly for stories about Sever. The man had claimed he wanted to be a drop trooper, but had made some missteps along the way, with Renard coming in for an unexpected rescue. Sai wouldn't go so far as to say Abbad had made a good impression, but the man had been a loyal protector.

Not that Abbad's chosen hero fared any better. Nobody had bothered to scoop up Renard's body, and the broken form sat alone. Without the skiff and anything else around it, lacking the burning debris elsewhere on the landing pad, it seemed as though Renard had simply given up and fallen dead. A far more peaceful tale than reality.

Sai found he had no pity for the officer. Renard had ordered Sai, Eponi, and Aurora shoved into vacuum on the *Nautilus*, had tried time and again to get them killed. Fail to finish off Sever for long enough, and it would catch up to you. Even so, Sai didn't find much satisfaction in the man's demise.

Would it have felt like a greater victory with Kaia in their arms?

Probably.

The other burning wrecks and torched agents didn't give Sai any surprises. Eponi and the *Prisa*'s turrets had done a final job against an overmatched enemy. That Vana and Renard had even tried to fight made little sense. They couldn't have won. Even if the agents shot true, even if Abbad had cut Aurora apart with the katana, Eponi would've had an almost invincible vantage to deliver devastation.

"Then why?" Sai said, kneeling to check another non-existent heart rate on a body covered in debris. "What was the point?"

The smoke from the smoldering skiffs, rising into the sky, offered few answers.

RAQUEL LIVED. Kashmal, barely. Vana's quick shot had burned the man's lungs, an injury Rovo commiserated with and that necessitated better medical care than the *Prisa* could offer. Raquel, numbed and juiced by the military-grade concoctions Sever had onboard, made the calls to get medical staff ready at the Salinity facility Sever had used the day before.

"It's not a hospital," Raquel said, sitting in the *Prisa*'s central lounge area. Kashmal had Rovo's room, where the man continued to lie unconscious. "But it's not nothing, either. They'll be able to stabilize him."

Sai, sitting across the space from her, gave the woman a

nod. Rovo hung with them too, while Aurora sat up front with Eponi and Gregor, still cleaning his power armor up on the second level, kept an eye on Kashmal.

"No agents either," Sai said. "A good call."

"You don't know that," Rovo said, head leaning against the wall, glaring at nothing and nobody. "They could be anywhere. Could be anyone. Could even be you."

Rovo looked towards Raquel, who took the accusation better than Sai would have. Rather than turning Rovo's words around on him, or delivering some shouting take-down, Raquel drew in a breath and delivered an empathetic look the rookie's way.

"I'm sorry, Rovo," Raquel said. "We all are. We were all trying to protect Kaia."

"Not Aurora," Rovo replied, turning his heat Sai's way. "She only wanted you. Squad before civilians, isn't that right?"

"It is," Sai said. "Not that it mattered. They were going to take Kaia regardless of what we did."

"Because we brought her right to them!" Rovo pushed to his feet, hot head going full steam now. "We should've left Kaia and Kashmal back at the facility. They didn't belong in a fight like that!"

Sai raised an eyebrow Rovo's way, "If we came without Kaia, they would've attacked. Probably would have executed me."

For once, Rovo's frustration didn't deliver him another path to walk, and the rookie paced. Sai could understand that too: wanting to be angry at something, wanting to have a target, a plan to dish the heat against your enemy.

"It's not over yet," Raquel said, and both Sai and the rookie looked her way. Salinity's security chief had her wristlet up, tapping away. "Vana flew off in a skiff, but that won't get them to space. You said Renard had a special ship, right?"

"I flew in it," Rovo said. "Why?"

"Give me its description," Raquel replied. "I'm sure Renard didn't have it docked under his own name, but if we can find where it's berthed, I can lock it down. Salinity won't let it leave."

"Then we have all the time we need to track Vana." Rovo's fists clenched at the idea. "You can really do that?"

"It's like you think my role is meaningless," Raquel said, her smile now not so sad.

Sai watched the interchange continue, the rookie walking Raquel through Renard's ship and its contours. The idea made sense, though Sai wasn't sure how much he'd bet on Renard docking his prized craft in a standard bay. The dead officer had been high up within DefenseCorp's clandestine hierarchy, no doubt he could find a bay off the common spots.

But when Sai brought that up, once Rovo had finished his ship tour, Raquel batted away the concern.

"Think like this planet is one of your ships," Raquel said. "Yes, there might be places we don't pay close attention to, but nobody gets a ship on or off this planet without us knowing. If DefenseCorp has a private bay, we have eyes on it. I make sure of that."

"And once we find them, it's over," Rovo said. "Next time, Vana doesn't get away."

AFTER A LONG SHOWER and a change of clothes, Sai found Aurora eating a light dinner on the facility's outdoor deck. Altogether more pleasant than the narrow, dark confines of Vana and Renard's chosen shelter, Sai breathed in the salty sea air and took the chair opposite Aurora without asking first.

When Aurora smirked, Sai shrugged. Took a bite of, naturally, some white fish. A sip of non-salt water. Leaned back and enjoyed a long look at the orange and purple sunset show starting on the horizon.

"Rovo's not happy with me," Aurora said after a long minute.

"He's not happy with anyone right now."

"If we were still with DefenseCorp, he'd be fired for what he did with Gregor." Aurora's smirk vanished, her right hand drummed its fingers slow on the table. "Or shot."

"I know," Sai replied. "And I know you want me to push back on it, so you can tell me all the ways he risked the mission, how he screwed up your plan, all so you can get it out of your system."

Aurora laughed, the mood broken, and shook her head, "You know me too well."

"We've been shooting up the stars for a long time, captain."

"Today was a hard one," Aurora said. "I don't like to lose, Sai. And I really don't like to lose to an agent."

Sai shook his head, "We didn't lose. Not a single death on our side, and we took out Renard. By my counting, that's a clear victory."

"If you ignore the principle objective. You've seen those suits, Sai. If Kaia's blood really does have the answer, then you could have invisible agents anywhere without the slightest warning."

"You say that like it's our problem," Sai said.

He expected another laugh, another head shake and an acknowledgement that, no, Sever squad wasn't the galaxy's police. It wasn't their little band's fault if DefenseCorp loosed a bunch of invisible killers on anyone who didn't sign a contract.

But Aurora didn't bite. Instead, she set her look hard to that horizon. Those fingers started drumming again.

"You and I came to Sever for the cash," Aurora said. "We've fought and fought and fought and I always thought that bank balance would prove to be the most important thing." She stopped, glanced at Sai, threw up the slightest grin, "And it still is important, but it might not be the only thing anymore."

"The girl means that much to you?" Sai said, then shook his head. "Sorry, that came out wrong. What I'm wondering is, we've blown up and burned down cities. We've battled parents, and we've shot sons and daughters. I don't want anything bad to happen to Kaia either, Aurora, but right now, we're all here. We're alive, with a fixed ship and a full power armor suite. Who cares if DefenseCorp tears itself apart?"

"If I tell Rovo we're leaving, he won't follow," Aurora said.

Sai felt there was a bigger response to his words than that, so he waited. Ate his now-cold food. Still better than lab-spun protein packs.

"Sai, we left DefenseCorp over Dynas because we wanted to be different. To make our own choices, and not deal with their bullshit. I think we have to make this choice now," Aurora looked his way. "I'm going to need your help. Rovo's too angry to keep himself together. Eponi's too flighty, and Gregor just wants to be told where to punch. If we're going to find Vana and get Kaia back, I need the old Sai standing with me."

"The old Sai?" The swordsman grinned. "What's that mean?"

"When's the last time you built a bomb, my friend?"

Down Deep

THE CONSOLE BLINKED BEFORE HIM, its broad black screen waiting to take Gregor's command. Or, rather, his dictation. Eponi had set up the communications program and left Gregor alone in the *Prisa*'s cockpit, the ship docked safely at the Salinity facility. Kashmal had been flown away in a Salinity medical skiff, while the rest of Sever, Raquel included, finished out a long night on the platform's open deck.

Gregor would join them eventually. Squads had to bond after a day like this one, trash a night or two together to relieve the tension. Gregor would have to talk to Rovo, especially. Explain why he'd thrown the rookie into the water. That he'd done it to save Rovo from a mistake he couldn't climb back from.

That throw, though, had snapped the tight line threading the negotiations. Gregor had witnessed the descent into a shootout through his visor, safe at distance from easy pistol shots. Like viewing a true-to-life movie, and a bad one at that.

Guilt hadn't played a major role in Gregor's life. He

made a point of accepting his choices as he made them. Being in DefenseCorp, or in the mines before, you couldn't dwell on mistakes, on what you might do different. There wasn't time, and, anyway, you couldn't go back. So Gregor refused to revise the hours and play out different scenarios, ones that would've left Kaia in Sever's hands.

Too many maybes there. Too many ifs.

He'd spent the ride from the island to the Salinity facility with one eye on Kashmal, though the man looked so far gone from functional life that to focus on Kashmal was to slide into a sickening frustration. Gregor couldn't hit the man with a hammer to make him healthier, and Gregor didn't have the tools or skills to perform miracle surgery.

He could, though, wait and see if Kashmal needed water. A hand to grip while his life slipped away, if such a thing had to happen.

Gregor waited out the awful display with his weapons. He cleaned and rebuilt the long gun, its barrel scored by the laser fire, but otherwise in good shape. He wiped the power armor, ran the systems checks across its various parts, and nodded as they came back positive. For once, the hammer man hadn't been in the fight's center. For once, Gregor hadn't been a target.

Doing all that killed the time, but did nothing to sate an increasingly urgent nudge. Gregor had been with Defense-Corp for decades, and in that time he'd fallen off talking with his family. Sending messages across the stars always took time, and with his parents hopping from one space rock to the next in their mining work, there wasn't much guarantee any notes would find them anyway. The gradual quieting came back Gregor's way as his family's words came in drips, drabs, and then nothing.

And now, here he sat, trying to think of what to say when he hadn't said anything for so long.

Easier, by far, to swing the hammer.

The console buzzed, its black screen flashing green for an incoming hail. Eponi's identifier scrolled by, and Gregor tapped in.

"Hey, you done writing that love letter yet?" Eponi's voice came through, slurring ever so slightly.

"Love letter?"

"Whatever. Point being, Aurora's declaring a squad meeting, right now. Drinks required. So, you coming?"

Gregor glanced at the dark, empty box on the console's right side.

"Gregor? You there big guy?"

He blinked, focused on Eponi's green, put on a small grin, even though Eponi couldn't see his face, "I will be right there."

"Okay, but hurry, because Sai's already pouring—"

Gregor swiped away the call, stared at the black box for another second, then swiped that away too.

THE SKIFF DIDN'T REPRESENT the optimal way to recover from a hangover, but the drug cocktail making its way through Gregor's body did a nice job nixing the after-effects from a squad briefing gone awry. With Eponi up front at the stick, Gregor and Sai rode with her towards Kaiyo. Eponi seemed to have a limitless pep supply, though Gregor figured her upbeat vibes came more from her choice to abandon the disaster last night at an earlier hour than, well, dawn.

But few things healed rifts better than truth-telling at the hands of a bottle, particularly one shared beneath

Gillane Four's rather astounding night sky, with the roiling waves beneath bouncing light above.

"So you're best friends again?" Eponi asked as she flew.

"Rovo understands," Gregor replied, his voice even lower and wanting water. "And I understand him."

"Sounds boring."

"Eponi," Sai said, "not everyone resolves their differences by slugging it out in the street."

"Like I said, boring."

Gregor leaned back in the seat, shut his eyes. Rovo had been stiff at first, perhaps expecting Gregor to deliver some monologue about duty and handling the mission over one's emotions. Gregor, though, was never one for discipline. Aurora was the squad's leader, all that lay in her domain. Instead, Gregor took the forgiveness route without actually saying a thing about forgiveness.

"I'd have done the same, if I knew the girl better," Gregor told the rookie, and Rovo had taken that and run out the rest of the night on its kindness.

That Gregor would never actually burn a mission for a civilian didn't matter. Sever ended the night whole again.

Eponi banked the skiff, following a light green projection on the skiff's bubble glass telling her where to go. Raquel's sources hadn't taken all that long to find Renard's ship, parked in a little-used bay meant for repairs and salvage. The bay itself sat deep in Kaiyo's structure, and while Eponi had asked about flying right into it, Raquel had suggested a more subtle method.

Apparently Salinity wasn't a fan of big fights breaking out in its cities.

As such, the Sever trio had to go in the long way. Raquel, Rovo and Aurora were staying ready for response with some more Salinity security forces. If Vana and Kaia popped up elsewhere, they'd go in for the rescue. Once again, Rovo had balked at getting left out of the primary force. Once again, Aurora had persuaded the rookie to stand down.

Raquel, though, pushed one other requirement. One that Gregor and Sai had protested, that Eponi had shrugged off. No power armor. Kaiyo itself still buzzed from the earlier fights that'd ruined a landing pad and almost brought down a building, not to mention the torched salvage shop. Now Sever had broken up a vacation spot too. Any more destruction, and Raquel would be compelled to kick the squad off the planet, no matter the reason they'd come.

"She picked the wrong crew for a quiet mission," Sai said as Kaiyo's sparkling city came into view. "Gregor's going to get us on the news before we've even left the skiff with that hammer."

"Or your sword," Gregor countered.

"That's why I'm here," Eponi said. "You two draw all the eyes, then I get the girl out. Easy."

"After we compromise the ship," Sai corrected.

"Yeah, whatever. You do your thing, I do mine."

Gregor couldn't see Sai's face, but he knew the man's eyes rolled all the same.

Eponi docked the skiff in a Salinity loading dock two levels beneath Kaiyo's surface. The space, cluttered with cargo bots and workers handling purified water in tanks and boxes of all sizes, hummed with an industry that had nothing to do with destruction. Sheer work for industry's sake hit a note for Gregor, and he took his time walking from the bay, taking in the effort.

And giving everyone in the bay a chance to take a look at Gregor's hammer.

For all Sai's joking, stealth wasn't the play here. Aurora, Rovo, and Salinity hoped Vana might see the trio making their way towards her ship and act on it. Give herself away. Then they'd swoop in, rescue Kaia, and put a hot laser between Vana's eyes. A good plan, particularly if being a diversion meant Gregor would find plenty of targets.

A sniper's shot just didn't satisfy like a hammer swing.

Sai led, his katana in its sheath on his back. Though he didn't wear power armor, the man, like all three, wore an ankle-length coat, procured from Salinity resources meant to keep workers warm while on the spike across the planet. The garment served to hide everyone's pistols, knives, and, in Sai's case, a few makeshift bombs designed to short out nearby electronics.

Plant the bombs on Vana's ship, and if Sai beamed a message at the right frequency, Vana would find that ship wouldn't make it off the ground. Crucially, the bombs would leave any young kids feeling nothing more than a little buzz in their hair.

But, to get those bombs where they needed to be, the trio had to get to the ship, and maybe even inside it. Nobody figured Vana had left her best escape route unguarded. Some hoped she'd left it reinforced.

Gregor, holding his hammer on his right shoulder, trailed as they left the bay and stalked through a different world. Up top, Kaiyo's clean, metro vibe fulfilled the future prosperity look Gregor expected from wealthy planets. He'd spent his career largely on the opposite—planets with healthy societies tended not to need DefenseCorp's services —so walking Kaiyo's clean streets, seeing bodies zip through the transport tubes and hearing not a single violent shout had been a pleasant break.

Down here? Where the ceilings pressed in, glowing with standard-issue yellow lighting?

Well, Gregor had to nudge his own jaw back into place.

Those boring lights showcased a sprawling level, one

whose walls, bordering stores and houses, held murals embracing every artistic style Gregor could imagine. Live music played, clashing and then harmonizing with each other as musicians, staking out their own corners, led and followed in equal measure. Crowds flowed like rivers, mixing and mashing workers with shoppers and families alike. Every breath brought with it a hearty weight as lunchtime meals cooked to life.

Sai's sword and Gregor's hammer assured the trio space and slight suspicion, but like animals in a nature preserve, these people didn't walk with violence biting at their footsteps. Cash concerns weren't cloaking their every word, digging claws into their eyes.

"Damn," Eponi said. "This might be the happiest place I've ever seen."

"And we are going to ruin it," Gregor said, the fact almost putting a damper on his hammer-swinging desires.

"Maybe not," Sai replied. "The ship is levels away from here. If we're lucky, they'll never know what's happening beneath their feet."

If they're lucky. Gregor didn't have to point out how unlucky civilians tended to be when Sever or DefenseCorp were around.

"So where's the drop?" Eponi asked as they hit the level's center, a circular courtyard mirroring the larger spaces on Kaiyo's surface. No fountains or tall statues here, but benches had been scattered around a small stage in the center perfect for a band. "I'm not seeing a sign for a lift."

Sai, looking at his wristlet, responded, "The lifts open to us are that way. Not far."

The person-size lifts were not, in fact, lifts. Rather than the flat floor that'd take Gregor up or down in a comfortable stand, the lifts Salinity gave to its people were the damn tubes. Individual capsules—big enough for two if the second was a small child—whisking along pressurized paths. The lift station had four tubes on display, one for up and one for down, with two more whose capsules whizzed by holding folks not interested in stopping at this level.

"I'm not getting in there," Gregor said.

"Aww, is Gregor scared?" Eponi taunted as they settled into a short line heading down.

"Not scared, just don't want to." Gregor patted the hammer. "Too big."

That, though, wasn't strictly true. The capsules had enough size for Gregor and his hammer, despite their single-plus-one seating. He just didn't have any desire to get stuffed into an egg and shot around.

"Don't think we have a choice," Sai said, returning to his wristlet for a check. "I guess we could get Raquel to approve us using the freight lifts, but who knows how long that would take."

"C'mon, Gregor. Don't be a baby. Ride the ride with us," Eponi laughed.

There were times when Gregor wished he worked alone.

The capsules operated by pressure plate. The next passenger would walk up to a white-gold painted square, one complemented by a textured pole for those missing sight or needing a second guide. The signal pulled the next capsule going by into the pick-up slot, though most times it seemed a capsule would already be there after dropping off another rider.

Sai, and then Eponi, climbed into their capsules and shot off, aiming three levels down. A seconds-long blitz. Gregor went next, the sea green and silver capsule stopping for him like an egg turned on its side. The big man stepped over the lift, a bright red countdown giving him thirty seconds to complete the loading. As soon as Gregor settled into the hard seat, though, the capsule performed its magic: scanning the man's size, belts adjusted and swept over, locking Gregor into place.

The hammer didn't have a holder, and Gregor didn't think it'd fit in the cargo slot, so he held it in both hands as the capsule's timer hit zero. A protective canopy closed around him and the egg rotated, pointing straight down. A cheery chime sounded and the capsule launched, blitzing into the main pipe and heading down.

Fast.

Too fast.

The levels blurred by, far more than three, well past the one Gregor had selected, as the capsule threw him deep into Kaiyo's depths.

NINETEEN

Dangerous Games

THE KART-RACING RUSH when the capsule shot ahead lasted about as long as it took Eponi to notice the level counter hadn't stopped at the floor she'd chosen. Instead, after several seconds too long, the capsule shunted off to the side, depositing Eponi three floors below the target. The canopy slid aside and a short timer told Eponi to leave now or suffer some undefined consequences.

The pilot stepped onto a deserted platform, onto a level lacking its higher partner's cheer. The orange-yellow lights remained, but instead of a broad layout, the capsule platform narrowed to a secured gate, one shut tight with a glowing red scanner alongside it. To her left, the upward shooting capsules whizzed by, offering an easy-on option.

And yet.

Eponi had picked the right floor, the one Sai confirmed with each of them before getting into the capsules. The swordsman wasn't here, and, as capsules shot by behind her, Gregor clearly hadn't stopped on this floor either. Which meant the capsule had misfired, or someone else had told it where to go.

She wouldn't call herself suspicious, but Eponi knew what they were facing: agents preferred to operate in the shadows, not in front. Splitting Sever apart and taking them out one by one? First page of the agent's playbook, right there.

Sliding her hand to the pistol beneath her jacket, Eponi stepped away from the capsule tubes and towards the windowed booth set near the locked gate. A console's glow clashed its blues with the overhead bar lights behind the glass, and a chair's arch spun in a slow circle.

"Well, if that's not ominous," Eponi muttered, taking her time on the approach.

She wanted to raise her wristlet, send off a question to Sai and Gregor, maybe a warning to Aurora and the others, but Eponi didn't want to die, and taking her eyes, her concentration away from the scene before she'd secured it was a good way to take an express trip to the afterlife.

Coming up to the glass, to the little oval where visitors, obviously, were expected to show identification, cash, or whatever, Eponi looked inside, then immediately back-stepped, drawing her pistol and offering a sweep around the area. Nothing, nobody rose up to greet her.

Inside that booth, Eponi had seen a cold corpse. The guard who'd been manning this station wouldn't be doing his job anymore. Several seared-black holes through the man's Salinity uniform gave the cause of death in final fashion. But why murder a random booth attendant?

That question didn't find an answer in the sudden noise as the locked gate banged open, but it did get shoved to the back of Eponi's mind.

The opening gate revealed several Salinity security officers, these armed with rifles, belted pistols, and the mean looks of people called off an early lunch to deal with a problem they didn't want. Two saw Eponi with her drawn pistol and made the expected calls to drop it, while the third turned towards the booth and cursed in the loud, shocked style of someone who'd never seen a body before.

Eponi lowered the pistol, but didn't drop it. She did raise her left hand though, tried to put on a face that said she wasn't going to shoot anyone.

"Hey there," Eponi said, "I know what this looks like, and I'm going to tell you, this isn't what it looks like."

"It looks like you're still holding onto that pistol," the trio's lead man, who hadn't yet taken a look into the booth, said. Of the three, he seemed the oldest, flocks of grey leading their way around his brown hair and clean-shaven face. "Drop it, or we shoot."

There were scenarios at play here. Eponi could do as the man said, let the three take her to some Salinity processing center where a call to Raquel and video evidence—there had to be some recording in that booth— would clear her. A few hours spent sweating, and Eponi might get away.

A few hours spent off the trail, during which Vana might be able to ditch the planet with Kaia in tow.

"Sorry, buddy," Eponi said, "know that I really don't wanna do this."

The lead man cocked an eyebrow, raised the rifle, but these were Salinity security forces. Like the ones in the lobby above, they hadn't seen real action in too many years. A cushy job on a cushy planet spent guiding tourists and the occasional drunk to where they needed to be.

Eponi broke right, heading for the booth while drawing her pistol and dialing its energy low. The shots would still hurt enough to take the breath away, but shouldn't burn through the skin. Shouldn't torch a lung.

The trio reacted with a mix between bravado and

panic. The leader managed to pull his trigger, sending hot energy scalding into the wall behind Eponi. His buddies tried to get their rifles raised, all the while backing into cover beyond the gate. Two frantic seconds and the confrontation had turned into a standoff, with Eponi lingering behind the booth and the guards on its other side.

"Tell you what," Eponi shouted. "You send one of your guys to look at the video. He'll tell you I had nothing to do with this. My capsule went to the wrong floor. This is a setup."

"If that's the case, the video'll prove it. Why're you pulling a pistol on us?" The leader did, to his credit, sound genuinely confused. No doubt wondering how his ham sandwich had turned into a potential firefight. "This doesn't have to play this way."

"Because I got places to be that aren't here," Eponi replied. "Let me get on a capsule and you'll never see me again, promise."

The leader, apparently, didn't agree, because the next sound Eponi heard came from a rolling gas grenade as it came along the concrete floor towards her. The beautiful thing about grenades, though, was that if you acted fast, you could turn'em back on the ones that threw them in the first place. Eponi scooped the grenade in her left hand and launched it back towards the security trio in one smooth motion, just like DefenseCorp taught her to do.

The gas billowed out, a red gray cloud taking full advantage of the enclosed space. Eponi heard coughs, the leader trying and failing to get out a complete sentence. Time to go. Holding her breath, and thanking Defense-Corp for training its recruits to do it well—water landings were no joke—Eponi sprinted towards the capsule tubes. She stood on the calling platform, whirling around in a crouch, pistol pointed back towards the gate.

She couldn't see the trio, and they couldn't see her, but the grenade didn't have all that much gas. It might clear before an empty capsule came by this lower, less-traveled level. Eponi should shoot, should force them back into cover.

But these weren't the enemy, and Raquel might not be so nice if Eponi started blasting her co-workers.

Eponi really, really hoped there weren't any heroes in that group. Nobody dumb enough to try a charge through to get to her. She watched the gas with tearing, stinging eyes, heard the coughs, and saw not a soul.

A ding sounded behind as a capsule slid into place. Eponi fell back into the opening, spots starting to form in front of her eyes as her oxygen ran out. She had to take a breath now, or risk showing up at the next destination unconscious. She swatted in the proper level, hoping the capsule would get it right this time, and blew out her lungs as the canopy slid shut overhead.

The inhale had her coughing—enough gas had found its way inside to make everything unpleasant—but soon enough the capsule dropped her three levels up, allowing Eponi to make a gasping exit where she needed to be. Shuffling off to the side, eyes a bleary mess, Eponi pulled herself together.

She'd escaped the trap. Vana, or one of her agents, had set Eponi up. All about getting Sever delayed, or killed, without putting her own agents at risk. But, yet again, Eponi had escaped. Because she was amazing, awesome, and brilliant all put together. Eponi found a wall, leaned against it, and coughed and laughed at the same time.

They'd failed again, the losers.

Enough blinking, enough coughing cleaned Eponi out for her to take in where she'd landed. The capsule's red level lights had assured her, even through the gas, that she'd found the right spot. And the big, silver-lit sign confirmed it: Salinity Salvage.

Any thrill of finally getting where her mission demanded she go died as Eponi realized she didn't hear the noises belonging to a salvage yard. Didn't hear the conversation between workers, the humming, slicing, cutting of metals. No bots trundling from one work site to the next. The salvage yard, apart from the steady sounds inherent in any modern facility, sat quiet.

Unlike the lower, locked level, the salvage yard didn't have a booth guarding its entry. Didn't have a locked gate. Instead, the capsule platform opened up into a broad space loosely organized by hanging signs indicating what parts belonged where. Far to the back, near what Eponi supposed would be the level's outer edge, hung a label blazing out a notice for ship repairs.

Eponi would've gone right there if not for the motion she caught. Shifting shadows, playing in the lights. A group, walking through the area. Eponi's wall, a short span meant to cut off the capsule platform from any encroaching debris piles, wouldn't serve as any kind of cover.

The pilot went low, dialed her pistol back up high. A level like this should be covered in people, and that it wasn't meant the agents had either created some excuse to empty things or—Eponi grimaced as she slunk—wiped them out. Which meant anyone left surely deserved whatever shot Eponi decided to give them.

Crouching in the cylindrical shadows of old engines, Eponi sidled down. She pulled out her wristlet and dashed out those messages, one to Sai and Gregor asking where the hell they were, another to Aurora and Raquel, suggesting Salinity ought to send some reinforcements to their salvage yard.

"About done?" said a happy voice, and Eponi glanced up from her wristlet, right into a rifle's business end. The face of the woman holding it stretched into a wide smile, one that seemed way too happy for the circumstances. "I'm so happy I found you! The boss didn't even think you'd make it this far."

Eponi, lowering her wristlet with as little speed as she could muster, tried to equate the smile with the words coming from the person's mouth, "Uh, yeah? Here I am?"

Her right hand still held her pistol, and with the slightest motion, Eponi flicked its barrel up, ripe for a gutshot. Eponi would've had the trigger pulled too, would've, except the agent kicked out fast, hit Eponi's hand and sent the pistol flying.

"So tricky," the agent said, shaking her head. "I like games too, how about we try mine?"

There were times Eponi would brave a hot dive, would try for a gut punch and a roll away, but the agent's fast kick had proved this wasn't some stupid goon. Any sudden moves would likely end with a rifle blast to her face, so Eponi responded in the only way she could:

"Okay, buddy. Let's play?"

TWENTY

Who Pays?

When Raquel asked Rovo, standing in a Salinity conference room on Kaiyo's surface, what'd happened on the island, the rookie didn't quite know how to answer. The first and best explanation was that he'd fallen into emotions and instinct. The struggle with Gregor had ended fast, with Rovo able to neither overpower or out-skill the older, stronger fighter. So Gregor had thrown Rovo into the lake below, telling the rookie to get his head on straight.

"From there, I just tried to get Kaia," Rovo said, looking out tall windows into the endless ocean. "Our power armor has emergency grapples to use, so I threw it towards the landing pad and pulled myself into the fight." Rovo flinched, glanced her way. "I'm sorry, I didn't even see that you were down."

Raquel nodded, matched Rovo's outside stare, "It was stupid to go out there without more protection. It'd been so long since we'd had anything approaching a real fight here that I just . . . assumed the talks would happen without a pulled trigger."

"Never seems to go that way with us."

"Apparently." Raquel frowned. "You haven't said anything about the other one. Renard?"

There wasn't much to say. Rovo had grabbed the officer because he didn't want to risk Kaia by heading for her. He'd thought a trade, a flip of Renard for the child would be an easier trick to pull off. When that'd gone the wrong way, when Vana shot Kashmal and ran with the girl regardless, there hadn't been much reason beyond a flashing, burning red. The power armor had done its work and delivered a verdict.

"I didn't mean to kill him," Rovo said, "but he deserved it all the same. He wasn't a good man."

Raquel didn't give a hint as to how she took that reasoning. Instead, she sucked in a breath that barely seemed to touch her lips, "In the several days since your squad has been here, almost thirty people on my planet have died. All affiliated with DefenseCorp. Our own media networks are covering this as some sort of corporate fight, keeping Salinity clear for now, but there's a panic growing in my streets, Rovo. Nobody wants to go outside if there's a chance they'll get caught in a crossfire."

"This won't last much longer," Rovo replied. "Either Vana will get off-world with Kaia, in which case we'll chase after her. Or we'll get them first, and then we'll leave."

"So who do I hold responsible?" Raquel asked. "When this is all done, how can I face my bosses and the people that live here and say all that damage, all that destruction, was just an unfortunate mistake?"

Rovo didn't have an answer for that one. Sever, and most of DefenseCorp, didn't handle the clean-up from their missions. Most contracts he'd seen explicitly excluded that part: any damage, any public relations work, that fell on whomever hired the company to come in. Except, now, Sever had kinda gone their own way.

"You can blame DefenseCorp for everything. Maybe try billing them for the damages," Rovo said. "They have the cash."

Raquel laughed, a dire one, "You think they'll pay? Make a statement taking the blame?"

"If we win, they might. If we don't," Rovo shook his head, "it won't matter anyway."

Behind them, the conference room hummed. Aurora played orchestrator, talking with Salinity security about where Vana might be, arranging for her and Kaia's photos to be splashed all over Kaiyo and Gillane Four's other cities—Eponi had been smart enough to record the whole exchange on the landing pad with the *Prisa*'s cameras. Raquel, at first, tried to hang with Aurora, but she'd floated Rovo's way when it became clear the Sever captain's experience trumped official rank in this scenario.

"You think it's that serious?" Raquel said. "I know I'm newer to all this than you are, and not as familiar with DefenseCorp, but you're making it sound like the whole galaxy might pay."

"It'll have to," Rovo replied. "That's Vana's goal. Make DefenseCorp an invincible machine, populated with suited soldiers nobody can see, that can go anywhere. Right now, you want DefenseCorp protection, you choose to pay for it. If Vana gets her way, you won't have that choice."

"But she would need trillions of soldiers to cover the galaxy. Trillions of these suits," Raquel shook her head. "Not possible. Not possible anytime soon."

"My father always told me that a stable life was the one worth seeking," Rovo nodded out there, to the horizon, as if this existence waited just beyond their sight. "The one that had the best chance of letting you get to the end in good shape. Once DefenseCorp proves it's unstoppable, how many people are going to decide it's the best way to that life?"

This time, Raquel didn't have a comeback. Rovo could guess why. Salinity had to operate on a similar ideal: a beautiful series of planets—Gillane Four was only one of twenty Salinity had turned into aqua operations, steady cash into your account, and a ride along with a corporation that had been there long before and would be around long after your life.

DefenseCorp could say the same, but its ranks flushed with turbulence. Power armor went its way towards preserving lives, but battles still took their tolls. Garrison duty, on the other hand, was about as cushy a gig as someone could want. Planetary management, orbital taxation, all those jobs offered time to sip your morning coffee and ponder what movie to watch that night.

And for those that wanted the thrill, well, Vana's suits would offer ample opportunity to lay waste to any hesitant planet. Any executive that didn't want to sign a contract. Any pirate adamant about their independence.

"Right now," Rovo continued, "DefenseCorp has a reputation to keep itself in check. It can't wander into unwanted territory without making enemies. That'll end when nobody will dare fight back."

"So instead we fight back now."

"Try, anyway."

The calls came in at the same time. One, from Salinity security protecting power supplies on Kaiyo's lower level, reported an attack by a solo agent. A woman, who they thought had murdered a booth guard before fleeing in a capsule to another spot. And the second, Vana.

Raquel took the first, ordered her forces to sweep the lower Kaiyo levels, excepting the salvage and repair bay. That one, still the target for the Sever mission, had to stay free of interference. And Raquel didn't want her troops turning into casualties when Gregor started swinging his hammer.

Vana, though, asked for Aurora and Rovo, so the two went to a private office, flipped up the feed on a wall-mounted console, and took in their adversary's tired-looking face.

"Where's Kaia?" Rovo opened the conversation, seeing only Vana's head in front of a gray-metal background that could've been anywhere. "If you've—"

"Relax, Rovo," Vana said, though no smile, no parental touches came in this time. "The girl is fine. We've done our draws, and the tubes have left the planet already."

"So you have what you need," Aurora said. "You can let her go."

"I'd rather be cautious," Vana replied. "A few more days, a few more draws, and we'll have enough to make leaving the girl behind a possibility. Give us that and I promise Kaia will not be hurt." Vana frowned, tilted her head and went on before either Sever could find a response. "Her father? Did he survive?"

"Why do you care?" Rovo asked.

"Because I'm not Renard, and I'm not a monster," Vana replied. "I didn't want to shoot him, but I had to keep Kaia. Unlike your pilot, who murdered my agents, or you, Aurora, killing them as they cause nobody any trouble, I prefer fewer bodies left behind."

Rovo started to stand, simply because getting on his own feet would make the sudden anger feel better. Sitting felt too passive, and he wanted to reach through that screen and throttle the agent. Aurora, though, grabbed his arm below the camera and kept the rookie in his seat.

"You called the ambush," Aurora said, icy and even in a way Rovo couldn't figure.

He'd been a diplomat of sorts, but always impersonal, always drafting messages between two sides Rovo didn't give a damn about. Aurora could turn off the emotion like a switch, even at the most personal.

A skill to learn.

"Your words prompted the fire," Aurora continued. "We hadn't pulled a weapon, hadn't sent a laser. The bodies on that landing pad are your fault, and yours alone."

"I suppose a soldier like you has to find some way of massaging your conscience," Vana said, not bothering to engage. "My offer remains, Aurora. Three days, and you can have the girl."

Aurora had her head shaking along with Rovo's, this time, "Three days will cost you a lot more agents, Vana. Bring her back now, and save your people, as you say you want to do."

"They know what they are fighting for, and the cost it may exact," Vana said. "I'm sorry we couldn't find an agreement. I really wanted to return the girl to her father, but if you insist, we'll continue this little game."

Vana cut the message then and there, leaving Rovo and Aurora staring at a blank screen. Sever's captain, though, had a half-smile gracing her face, the kind that had Rovo shudder. Aurora, the predator, had found a way to catch her prey.

Once Aurora made the call, the decision rippled through the ranks with a rapidity that stunned Rovo. Despite not hearing from the Sever trio sent to sabotage Vana's ship, Aurora put the strike plan into smooth motion. Vana had let slip she'd sent blood draws into orbit and beyond, but the skiff the agent had flown hadn't made any recorded docks at Kaiyo. The agent had to be on another platform, which meant there would be runs going to and from, carrying supplies and ferrying back the blood.

Salinity, as tight a corporation as existed, knew their regular skiff routes. They found several unplanned, extra flights cutting through their airspace, all with the proper codes, and all going to one spike in particular. A few hours travel outside Kaiyo, well within range for the island conflict, and Sai had mentioned they'd stayed on one of the isolated platforms during his hostage overnight.

"The other three Severs will keep Vana from any last-ditch escapes," Aurora said, briefing Rovo, Raquel, and a security squad that'd been readied up since the operation began. "Rovo and I will lead the assault. You will come in behind, secure the area and prevent any flight with the girl."

"The spikes only have one lift," Raquel said when Aurora turned it over to Salinity's leader. "We hold that and the landing platform at the top, and it's a bottle that can't be opened. Let's keep it tight, simple, efficient. We do this right, we make our planet safe again."

Rovo sat next to the woman on the skiff, blitzing out over the water. Five others trailed, stocked with armed and dangerous security forces, though most hadn't seen action in years. Farther up, Salinity had some of its meager air force providing fighter support in case Vana managed to make a run to orbit.

A tight operation. A perfect plan.

"Ready to get Kaia back?" Raquel asked, once again vested up, and looking small next to Rovo in his shining power armor.

"More than that," Rovo said. "We're not letting Vana get away. Not this time."

TWENTY-ONE

Into The Spike

AURORA SPENT the flight over scanning Kaiyo's news, running up-to-the-second headlines through her visor, coupled with checks on Sever's band. Gregor, Sai, and Eponi had gone dark several hours ago, and given their mission, that didn't bode well. Aurora couldn't imagine Vana, even if she'd grouped all the agents together, being able to take out all three Severs without a single distress call . . . and yet.

Raquel and Rovo flew behind in another skiff. The Salinity security director said she'd pushed out an alert to her entire force on Kaiyo, asking them to keep an eye out for Sever. There'd been some strange contacts already, and when Aurora had pressed Raquel to get more details—the body in the booth and the associated gas grenade encounter bothered Aurora most—the woman only shook her head and promised Aurora would know more than Raquel.

All that to say, Aurora had her nerves humming, had her eyes narrowed, and she wanted to do something besides sit and wait for news. An assault on an outer ocean spike seemed like it'd do her a world of good.

The skiffs didn't try to hide their approach. Broad daylight under another Gillane Four featureless sky haloed the assault, with Aurora's ride in the lead. The spike, their target and where Vana ought to be hiding, stuck out from the ocean like a silver peg in rippling blue paper. Its top, a broad, flat platform with those laser barriers ringing the edges already had a skiff on it.

"Fly over the skiff," Aurora said to the pilot. "And open the roof."

"Open the roof?" The pilot looked up at the bubble top over the skiff. Salinity's droplet branding graced the otherwise spotless glass. "When we haven't landed?"

"Do it," Aurora replied, again drawing on the tone that brooked no disobedience. Authority didn't have to be given. "Maintain control of the skiff when I jump and circle back around to drop the others."

She saw the pilot mouthing a question to herself, but Aurora didn't care. So long as her orders were followed, it didn't matter what the pilot thought.

The roof, pulling in the howling wind with it, opened. Aurora felt nothing, safe in the skiff, but the pilot's hair and the shorter locks of the two Salinity soldiers packed in behind, swirled. Aurora's armor treated the new variable the way it had treated everything so far: not a threat to its optimized systems, ready and repaired after the hits taken around the Kaiyo docking bays.

The spike's landing pad flew below, and Aurora kicked in the suit's kinetic boosters as she jumped. The boosters gave Aurora a few extra meters in a snap, enough to clear her ride and send Aurora plummeting right at the docked craft. As she fell, Aurora drew her rifle, aimed down, and fired two bolts before she struck.

The lasers hit the skiff's roof, burned two holes and weakened its cohesion. When Aurora's full, plummeting weight landed, the glass had no chance. It shattered as Aurora crashed through, the seats beneath faring little better. The power armor's heavy boots went clean through the skiff's floor, breaking pipes and causing the battery to spark into flame.

Aurora didn't wait to burn up, but, lifting legs boosted by the power armor's fall-recharged kinetic supply, she climbed out and onto the pad proper. Salinity's force landed to meet her.

"Decided to make an entrance?" Rovo quipped as the damaged skiff popped and cracked behind Aurora.

"Decided not to chance an escape," Aurora replied. "Now they can't run."

While Salinity's forces disembarked Aurora and Rovo went to the lift leading into the spike. The sole console sticking up from the thing demanded credentials, which Raquel provided. The woman hesitated before sending the platform down, looking Aurora's way.

"If we all bunch up on the platform, we'll be vulnerable," Raquel said. "But . . . "

"We'll be fine alone," Aurora said. "Send us. When it returns, come back with your forces."

"You don't know how many she has down there," Raquel protested, but Aurora knew a real argument when she saw one, and Raquel wasn't fighting here.

The Salinity forces around them were armed, yes, but they were green. They couldn't go up against trained DefenseCorp agents, not without losing five to one or worse. Aurora didn't want to have to watch their backs along with her own.

"We'll be fine," Aurora said. "Send us."

"She'd the deadliest person I know," Rovo added.

"Except Gregor with a hammer. Maybe. Trust her, Raquel."

The endorsement seemed to do it. Raquel punched in the command and stepped off the platform as it counted down to its descent. Aurora directed Rovo to stand opposite her, both apart from the platform's center. Better to place themselves away from the easiest spot to shoot, better to get an edge to look over and around.

"She trusts you," Aurora said to Rovo over Sever's close-range band. "That's good."

"We both want to see Kaia safe," the rookie replied. "Turns out, it's easy to bond over rescuing a kid."

"Keep that bond strong," Aurora replied. "It'll help us later."

The lift cranked down, dropping below the pad. Immediately beneath the surface, Salinity's commitment to functionality became clear: decor, beyond a big white-painted label giving the spike a number, was absent. Ghostly blue light flooded up from below, wrapping around the platform and coming from water-pulsing tubes.

"Help us later?" Rovo said. "What, are you already thinking about future contracts? I don't think Salinity's going to want us on the planet after all the destruction we've caused."

"We'll see," Aurora replied.

She'd worked with DefenseCorp long enough to know that some of their best repeat clients suffered all kinds of disaster at DefenseCorp's hands. What mattered was, at the end, through all the fire and the explosions and the smoke and death, the job finished the way it needed to.

This one would be no different.

"When this falls apart," Aurora said, scanning the walls, the blue light for any hidden surprises, "I need you to listen to me. Do what I tell you."

"Thought this wasn't about orders anymore?"

"That changed when you screwed up on the island," Aurora said. So far, no agents hanging from the walls. No bombs blinking away, mines set up to blow Sever to bits. "I'm risking my life, Raquel and her forces are risking theirs. You will be professional, and you will be competent, or you will be out."

Rovo didn't reply right away. A good sign. Aurora hadn't wanted to lay down the level like this in front of the squad, but she'd come to the decision as the hours had passed from the island disaster. Rovo's desperate performance had put the squad at risk, and his rash snapping of Renard's neck had killed a great chance to get information. Aurora could handle loose cannons.

She wouldn't babysit a child.

"Wait," Rovo said, matching the word with a clomping turn. Aurora would've asked what the rookie was talking about, except his tone said he'd gone past his disciplining into something more dangerous. "You see that?"

Aurora matched his look, though they stood on opposite sides of the descending lift. The blue tubes now rose alongside the platform, putting the two Sever members between their twin aqua tunnels. Rovo looked at the one nearest him, at a spot two meters and counting over his head.

The tube, there, seemed to flicker. Black shadows flitting through what should've been perfect water.

"Move!" Aurora shouted, snapping her rifle up but holding her fire. She couldn't just shoot the tubes, which might cause a burst that'd shatter the spike, drown them all, or something even worse. "Suits!"

Rovo passed the first test. The rookie ducked aside, his hands reaching and drawing the two-piece scythe weapon he'd carried around since Wexer. The black glitch moved, its cutting lines falling along and landing, with an appropriate thunk, on the platform.

There'd been six suits on the *Nautilus*. Two had been broken apart by Gregor, but the other four, one of which Vana had worn off, likely made it here. Sai said he'd found one burned up on the island, a lucky break. Which left three.

Rovo swung the scythe at the sound, the hooked end lashing in while, with a wrist flick, the rookie sent the bar half flaring out into a nifty, if thin, shield. Aurora adjusted her aim, but the suit still had the water-bearing tubes on its other side, making a missed shot fatal. The suit's pilot blocked Rovo's swing with a long, thick knife, the same blades they'd had on the *Nautilus*.

Aurora moved left as Rovo fell into a defensive posture, blocking more than attacking. His opponent seemed to be taking a measured approach, jabbing and poking to test Rovo's reflexes, rather than pressing in a frantic attempt to even outnumbered odds.

Which meant . . .

Already turning when the second *thunk* sounded, Aurora once again sacrificed her rifle to block an enemy's attack, this one a slashing stroke cutting in towards Aurora's face. The rifle took the strike in its center, splitting the weapon's power pack and sending the ionizing gas leaking, harmless, into the air. The knife caught itself inside the rifle's guts, and Aurora wrenched the big gun, throwing both weapons to the ground where the knife, buying into the same weave as the suit it came from, filtered black to match the platform's ground.

"Really hate this tech," Aurora muttered, jumping at the space the slash had come from.

Without the bright blue tubes behind it, the suit didn't give itself away, and Aurora's leap missed. Aurora hadn't tackled, simply, nothing in so long the momentary floating sensation felt loose, strange, before ending in a hard hit-and-roll on the lift's surface. Pressing her hands on the ground to stop the slide, Aurora then threw her left arm back towards the platform's center, where she hoped the suit had moved itself.

A second knife slashed in, hitting Aurora's arm and leaving a gouge in her armor. The visor flared red with the threat, locking onto the suit and giving Aurora a target to aim for. Gregor had mentioned the assistance in his own battle on the *Nautilus,* and now Aurora saw the red high-light as her only chance to counter her invisible opponent.

Pushing back to her feet, Aurora drew her own long knife, the refined blade meant as a last resort for a Defense-Corp soldier who'd exhausted their ammo. She had pistols, but the damn tubes kept Aurora from going back to the energy weapons. Instead, she struck out right ahead, a stab that would've stuck the suit in the gut if the same knife hadn't darted back to deflect.

The move gave Aurora's left hand an opportunity to deliver a kinetic-boosted punch, one the invisible suit did its best to dodge. A normal punch, at normal human speeds, would've flown right over the ducking suit, but one thrown at a faster rate than biology alone would allow caught the suit mid-move. Aurora felt the hit shudder up her arm, heard the rolling clanks as her target bounced across the floor.

And saw that sweet second knife fly out and embed itself into the spike's wall, falling out of reach as the plat-form descended. Aurora ignored it, heading forward and scooping up the first knife from the floor, its camouflage causing Aurora to grab it by the blade. She ignored the cuts into her gloves, flipped the weapon over, and came in towards her visor-marked enemy for a the finishing touch.

"Some help here?" Rovo shouted, pulling Aurora's attention away to her right.

The rookie had lost his shield, the thing lying on the lift to the rookie's left. Rovo worked his hooked weapon back and forth, trying to keep what looked like two knives at bay. Rovo's power armor showed that strategy wasn't working too well, with deep grooves and a few sparking bits littering his chest and waist.

Holding her stolen knife up, Aurora let her visor find the other fighter. With a hard toss, Aurora launched the knife at the target, nodded as the blade embedded into the suit's back, causing the suit to stumble. Rovo delivered a hard kick, knocking the enemy to the ground.

"Thanks," Rovo said, planting a boot on the suit while Aurora grappled hers in a headlock. "Apparently I need more hand-to-hand training."

"You need a lot of things," Aurora replied, then turned her attention to the captives.

Or, she would have, except the lift hit its end, slotting into the spike's base. Waiting for them, weapons drawn, were several more agents. Among them, arms folded and glaring, stood the reason for the attack: Vana, herself.

"Every time I see you, I hope it's the last," Vana said. "And every time, it's not. Let's change that trend, shall we?"

TWENTY-TWO

Down and Up

Ten levels down, Sai left the capsule with his katana raised, ready for anything.

Except food.

The capsule had dropped him to a greenhouse, a level packed with plants pumped with so many fertilizing proteins that the things crowded into every centimeter allotted them. From the capsule platform, Sai could see the aisles, monitored by rolling bots that snipped and grabbed fruits, herbs, and vegetables. A faint mist filled the air, ensuring the plants weren't thirsty. Not a living soul in sight.

"So no ambush," Sai said, lowering his katana as he continued looking around.

No agents popped up to blast him, no danger rose to end his life.

Raising his wristlet, Sai tapped out a message to Eponi and Gregor, asking where their capsules had sent them. It seemed obvious someone with access to the capsules had muddied their transit, but the question now became why?

What did they gain by sending Sai to the fruits and veggies floor?

Sai shook his head. Not his problem to try and figure it out. He turned to his right, ready to get back on a capsule heading up, and saw the reason. The platform going up had tape all over it, signs marking the loading dock as unstable. Cracks in the glass tube behind the tape showed it wasn't a lie. Someone must've botched a loading job.

The tape answered why Sai had been sent here. A delay. More time for Vana to get to her ship and blast off world. Eponi and Gregor were probably encountering problems of their own.

He had to move.

Swiping on his wristlet, using access Raquel had given each of them, Sai flew through to the floor map for his level. The stairs, naturally, sat on the level's opposite end. Guess he'd be taking a hike, and maybe grabbing a snack while he was at it.

The march through the greenhouse wasn't exactly unpleasant. Spending so much time in space, Sai rarely saw plants in any form of natural bloom. These were lush, happy. Dynas had wildlife, true, but that planet was a swampy slog with death lingering in every step. Much easier to take in a flower or two with sturdy ground beneath his feet and harmless bots trundling on by.

Sai felt the urgency—really, he knew he had to keep moving—but Vana wouldn't be pulling tricks like this if she had much of an answer to Sever's attack. This move wouldn't delay Sai by more than a few minutes, so either Vana was desperate and pulling anything she had, or . . .

He brushed away an overreaching apple tree branch and broke into a jog. Vana had split Sever up, sure, but Eponi and Gregor would be doing just what Sai was: trying to get back to the ship. If Vana had sent each Sever to a different level, then each one might get back at a separate time. What would've been a difficult fight for Vana's agents with the trio together might be an easy one with each coming in their separate turns.

Sai again checked his wristlet as he reached the level's far side. No response.

Not good.

The stairway door didn't have a lock, though the entry did have a helpful sign suggesting the capsules instead of the many steps leading up and down. Beyond the sign lay the stairs themselves, shallow steps treaded with concrete nubs and bearing water's glistening hallmark. Drips and drops sounded throughout, and Sai felt one splat against his head as he made his way in.

Salinity, apparently, didn't care overmuch about its stairs, and the leaks that might make their way in here.

Not that it mattered. Sai had seven levels to climb before he reached his target. Scaling the first set, jumping two steps at a time as his katana swung on his back, Sai considered breaking through into the next level and grabbing a capsule. That, though, might take even more time, and who knew what the next level might be: an encounter with a surprised security guard or a bot tasked with keeping out unauthorized guests might take more time than Sai cared to lose.

Three levels later, Sai and his heart rate regretted his decision.

Two levels after that, huffing and pounding on the wet stairs, Sai nearly ran into the person waiting on the next landing.

The man had a wide grin on his face, loose clothes that suggested a lot of lost weight without a new wardrobe, and a pistol in his hand.

"You're late," the man said, raised the weapon, and fired.

Ordinarily, wet steps would be a safety hazard. Ordinarily, Sai would've considered the fools that let their pathway up become so dangerous to be, well, fools.

The fools saved Sai's damn life.

Seeing the man, with Sai's focus so utterly on moving one step to the next, startled Sai into such a jerk that his legs slipped. Sai fell back, the laser flashing overhead into the stairwell wall behind him. The life-preserving slip exacted its vengeance a half-second later as Sai hit the steps, his katana providing an awful first contact. The whack knocked Sai's breath away, though he barely had time to consider that before Sai's weight drove him back down the steps, crumpling him in a heap in the landing below the man.

Who laughed, who cackled like Sai's fall was the funniest thing he'd seen all day.

"I've never seen a dodge like that one!" the man shouted, leaning over with his hands on his knees, pistol off to the side. "Falling down the stairs? Classic. Just classic."

Sai fought against competing objectives: figuring out why he kept running into maniacs with these agents, and getting his body moving again.

"I mean," the man said, between wheezing hoots. "Vana said you were the best of the best, but here you are, like an extra in a bad movie." He shook his head, wiped away apparent tears. "Almost hate to fry you, buddy."

"Then don't," Sai said, catching enough of a breath to reply. "Who's forcing you?"

Sai's left hand, working at the pistol on his belt, came closer to the trigger.

"Forcing me?" The man looked at himself. "I'm forcing

me, man. I don't have a choice! It's like, if I don't get the next dose, it all goes to hell, you hear what I'm saying?"

The next dose?

"No, I don't hear what you're saying," Sai replied, continuing to work at the pistol. He had it free from the holster now, still keeping it buried behind his back. He needed to get his left hand oriented, ready to flip it out and fire in a single motion. "What do you mean, dose?"

The agent slipped into a subtler grin, getting ahold of himself. Aimed that pistol again, and Sai shot. The bolt streaked up the stairs, pegged the agent right in the chest. The agent looked at the burning hole, shrugged, and Sai fired again, let hand bringing his own pistol out for better aim. The agent shot back, drilling Sai right in the vest.

Enough heat spread through to let Sai know the vest had done its work, that the vest shouldn't be asked to do too much more. The agent wasn't quite so lucky: Sai's second blast struck where there wasn't any coming back, and the man hit the ground hard.

"Going to have to thank Raquel," Sai muttered as he stood, started up the steps.

Salinity supplied the vests, after they objected to sending in Sai, Eponi, and Gregor in full on power armor. City-wide panics were bad for business. They compromised with the laser-sucking fabric, which worked just fine so long as the enemies aimed at the chest and only hit a couple times. Given Sever's average, Sai would be a dead man before long.

Sai looked at the agent as he went by, trying to parse what the man had been saying. Talking about a dose, and that laughter, like someone losing their hold on themselves . . . reminded Sai of Abbad, Renard and Vana's henchman. Sai would've chalked it up to a strange coincidence, except he'd had a deep, intimate encounter with a virus not all that long ago.

Maybe Helix hadn't stopped. Maybe Kaia's blood wasn't the only genetic toy Vana played with.

Sai took the last few stairs at a run, pistol out and ready for any more surprises. None interrupted the journey to the salvage level, marked by scrawled white lettering on the heavy door. No lock on this one, nothing beyond an ordinary handle. Stepping to the side, Sai opened the way slow, keeping the door's bulk between him and what lay beyond.

The Spiral

THE CAPSULE WENT to the bottom. Gregor watched the level counter descend, the lights around the tube and the stop frequency slowing as the distance between each level grew. Somewhere along the drop, the capsule went beneath the water's surface, a sensation marked by nothing more than an indicator next to the levels: a little blue-lit water line.

After the first few seconds acclimating to the falling sensation, Gregor made the reasonable assumption that Vana and her agents had adjusted Sever's capsule inputs, sending them to different places. The question now became whether those places were chosen with a reason, or at random.

Hard to believe a random number would pick the deepest spot available.

Gregor kept a tight grip on his hammer as the capsule opened. Unlike the other platforms above, this one had only two tubes. One going up, one going down, both ending right where Gregor stood, bathed in a deep blue light, as if the designers here decided to play up the under sea vibes. Not that many would see it.

Kaiyo's spike narrowed to a surprising end. Gregor had expected a small room, maybe some consoles tracking various things Kaiyo wanted to monitor. Instead, the capsule pushed Gregor out into a mushrooming space. Not all that large, but beautiful.

Reinforced glass arced away from the capsule platform, billowing out into a circular chamber. This far down, any surface light had ceased its journey and dissipated, leaving a darkness meekly penetrated by soft white diodes lacing the glass in straight-line patterns. Sea life, perhaps drawn to the structure's heat, or light's novelty this far down, clustered around, swimming into visibility and then vanishing into the shadows.

Stunning, in a way, and Gregor decided he didn't really mind Vana's trick, if only because he'd never have seen this.

Beyond the sea view, though, the chamber adopted more functional purposes. A marked stairway offered a chance to descend further for any necessary maintenance to Kaiyo's deep anchor, running below Gillane Four's ground. A sizable console did make its presence known, squatting against a wall, with Salinity's logo glowing against a locked screen. A protein and water vending machine sat opposite, nearby a table, chairs, and what appeared to be a couch that could pull out into a bed.

Someone ran shifts down here, keeping tabs on the absolute bottom.

Gregor let his hammer slide off his hands, clank its head on the floor. Without an immediate threat, and without any other way to leave this level, Gregor went to the upward capsule call, and stood on it.

Too late. The capsule he'd been on rushed around and

up before Gregor made it, vanishing towards the surface. Who knew how long he'd have to wait for another one to make the trip this far down.

As his hammer's clang petered out, a response echoed up from the stairwell. The steady stomping of feet on steps. The intermixed sounds led Gregor to think there might be more than one person coming up, possibly several. Given the single couch down here, it figured Salinity would only have a lone worker this far down at a time.

Which meant odds weren't zero something was amiss.

Which meant Gregor ought to pick up his hammer and get to a better spot.

Leaving the capsule pad, Gregor went to the stairwell's far side, waiting where anyone climbing up the steps ought to have their back turned. As the well sank right into the floor, only a slight metal railing served to part Gregor from his approaching target, and the big man could get in a hammer blow over that rail without issue.

Yet, when the time came, when a ragged mop of patchy blond hair appeared, Gregor didn't swing. The juicy opportunity passed because Gregor saw the Defense-Corp crimson uniform, with the black bars marking an agent career. That alone wouldn't have stopped the swing, except the uniform hung on the man's shoulders in tatters, and beneath it was something that stopped Gregor cold.

You don't forget a sight like Felix.

The one-time human, on Dynas, had been an early sort-of success for the viral work going on there. Gregor never quite figured out the goal, but Felix had been sequestered deep in the planet's swamp, where the man had endured tests and been kept alive as the viral muta-tion remade his body. Felix had been able to spread the virus to guards and other people that'd made the mistake of getting close to him, and the mark of that spread came in shadowed, pulsing dark growths along the victims.

Marks that looked real similar to what he saw now.

When Gregor last saw Felix, the man had been a shell hollowed out by the infection. The virus, so Felix said, ate and ate and ate until nothing remained. That time, Gregor had swung the hammer and delivered Felix from his torment.

This time he'd ask a few questions first.

"You can stop there," Gregor said as the man neared the top step. Behind the man, a second person, this one a woman and looking even worse off, followed, slouched. "Another step and it will be your last."

"As if that's a threat," the man spoke like whistle through gravel. "You can't expect the condemned to care about an early send-off."

Then, as if he found his own words hilarious, the man let loose a dry chuckle. The woman, below, joined in, her voice as faint as a whisper.

"Because you are infected?" Gregor asked.

"It's that obvious now?" The man turned around, daring Gregor to swing, and almost fell down the stairs. With a hand, the man caught himself on the stairwell wall, throwing a look at Gregor as if to say, isn't this fun? "Only two days since they cut us off. Two days, and this is what happens."

Gregor left his hammer in his left hand, drew his pistol with his right. He didn't see a weapon on the man, and the woman, who'd dropped to her hands and knees on the steps, didn't seem capable of anything dangerous.

"Who cut you off?" Gregor asked. "And why are you here?"

The man, apparently deciding standing took all too much effort, sat back on the top step, cocked his head

Gregor's way. Beneath the man's chin, dominating his neck, sat another growth, black and wriggling. Gregor's stomach turned. He didn't fear death, but this?

"You're the one we're supposed to attack," the man said, nodding towards Gregor's hammer, "Kill you, Vana said, and we'd get our doses." Another laugh, wheezed and short. "As if we'd live that long, even if you were kind enough to die for us."

A whooshing noise drew Gregor's attention beyond the man, back towards the capsule tubes. His call had been answered, and a new capsule sat waiting. Gregor could ditch these two, head back up, where Eponi and Sai might need him. The mission called.

But, so did Felix and the man's memory. There were answers waiting here, ones Gregor might never find if he left now.

"I have seen your infection before," Gregor said, choosing to go with the blunt truth. These two were too far gone for any games. "On Dynas. That one didn't live long."

"Helix," the man answered as the woman, crawling slow, came up beside him on the steps. "A front, but a big one. Renard had so many convinced the breakthroughs were almost there. A controlled environment, free to test."

"Three years," the woman said, and Gregor had to focus to hear her voice. "Three years we were there. Watching, tracking, protecting Anaskya and her work. This is what we get?"

"Renard promised we'd never have to worry about cash again," the man said. "If Helix worked well, Defense-Corp would have an unending supply of fanatical, invincible soldiers. No planet could resist. Those of us on the front edge, who worked with him, would be rewarded."

"A false promise," the woman added.

"I don't think so," the man replied, frowning at her. "Renard believed in it. I think he would've done it, too, if she hadn't showed up."

Gregor tapped his hammer on the floor, turning both heads back his way, "You mean Vana?" They nodded, slow and together. "When did she arrive?"

The two looked at each other, then back at Gregor, "After the *Nautilus*. Renard was desperate, and Vana had the answers for all of us. She said you would be following, and that we had to prepare. We had to be stronger."

Weeks had passed between the fight on the *Nautilus* and Sever's arrival on Gillane Four. More than enough time to change strategy, for Renard and Vana to convince their agents that this was the way forward. However, Gregor needed to find a missing piece.

"Where did the virus come from? The doses?" Gregor asked. "They would not have been on the *Nautilus*."

"How do you know?" The man replied. "That ship is large. A lot of secrets on there."

"I know," Gregor said. "Deepak would not allow a contagion like yours on his ship."

The man shrugged, but the woman leaned forward, almost falling down the stairs, "Promise us and I'll tell you."

"Promise what?"

"We already took care of the poor man living down here. That was hours ago. We will need more, soon, and the only people here are ourselves," the woman said. "We made the wrong choice, and we have suffered enough. Please. Do what you came here to do."

"Nobody should have to hurt the one they love," the man said, leaning on the woman. "Not even us."

If there was sympathy to be found for the two agents, Gregor didn't go looking for it. The pair had made countless decisions leading them to this point, including years on Helix. A single day on that planet, in that cursed city, should have revealed their mistake.

But, Gregor could trade mercy for information.

"You will get what you deserve," Gregor said. "Now explain."

Working together, as it seemed both needed frequent chances to catch halting breaths, the two colored a grim story about the aftermath of the failed *Nautilus* insurrection. Several hundred agents packed into the large transport, soon joined by Vana, Renard, and their hostage. That they hadn't succeeded with the *Nautilus*, that a message had been sent out across DefenseCorp warning of similar uprisings, ruined the would-be triumph that several experimental suits, along with the knowledge of Kaia's whereabouts, had been captured.

A straightforward flight towards Gillane Four had one interruption that changed everything. An intercept with a battered ship, piloted by a hired hand and holding a dismal doctor. Gregor knew the name before they said it, Anaskya having left a large enough stain on his memory. She parlayed her knowledge, and Renard arranged for fast shipments from the remnants of Helix's work on Dynas to meet the transport in orbit over Gillane Four.

But the injections were Vana's idea. Renard shuttled Anaskya away to some other facility, along with the process for making the suits. Preparing for when the agents had captured Kaia.

"Vana, though, had been talking with your man, the hostage," the woman said, drawing into the story's end. "He kept telling her that we didn't stand a chance. That we would be overpowered. So she told us, and so we believed that Helix's great secret had been its success, and we would be the first to usher it into the galaxy."

"Look at us," the man laughed. "And damn the laughing. A side effect, apparently, of the doses that kept us alive this long. So much power, and now Vana throws us to our deaths."

"She miscalculated," Gregor said, hefting the hammer and stepping around the stairwell. He'd heard what he needed to hear, and now his part of the deal came due. "No drug can replace skill."

"Not yet," the woman said, pulling closer to the man. "But tomorrow? Maybe."

"Ready?" Gregor said, in position.

Their embrace served as the answer.

TWENTY-FOUR

Beats

THE GRINNING agent said she wanted to play a game. For Eponi, that game started and ended in fast fashion, with a sharp kick to her head and a blackout stretch concluding with Sai creeping up the boarding ramp. The disorientation mingled with the aches-and-pains menagerie coursing throughout her body, a breath-blasting collection that Eponi could only deflect by focusing on Sai.

But she'd been too late. Her warning too slow.

Now Sai had his back to Eponi while agents climbed up the ramp to do to him what they'd just done to her. She had to help the swordsman, and, to some surprise, Eponi found her hands hadn't been cuffed. She wasn't tied down to the couch at all, but lying there as if the agent, regretting the beating, had laid Eponi down to recover.

Doubtful.

The first face made their entrance waving a big metal pipe, a corroded green-black bar that must've funneled a ship's coolant in its past life. Eponi couldn't make out much else past Sai's blocking body, so she tried to sit up.

Bad idea.

Something lurched in her stomach as she made the move, more bruises revealing themselves, and Eponi's eyes popped as she tried to keep her insides down.

"Don't move," Sai said, as he holstered the pistol and shifted the katana into a ready stance. "I'll handle this."

Most days, Eponi would push back on Sai needing to do anything for her, but today? Now? She didn't mind giving Sai the go-ahead. Valor and vanity and all that could wait till her guts didn't feel like rotten fruit falling apart.

Besides, if these two actually came at Sai with scrap for weapons, he wouldn't need the help.

Sai seemed to think so too, because he straight up asked the approaching agents what they were doing.

"Strange to approach a target without firing a shot," Sai said, loud enough to carry down the ramp. "What's your play?"

"Rules are clear," replied the bar-wielding man, still closing. "We only get the doses if we don't damage the ship."

Eponi tried to parse what possible 'dose' might get someone to approach Sai and his raised katana while the bar man made his move. The agent sprang up the ramp's last meter, landing with a low swipe towards Sai's knees. The swordsman moved to block, flicking the katana down and intercepting the bar. The scrap held up better than imagined, taking the hit and snaring the katana's edge in its jagged burrs.

Whipping the bar back, the agent pulled Sai's katana from the Sever's grip, popped his face into a gloating grin, only to take Sai's freehanded punch instead. The jab stunned the agent, and Sai carried the strike into a downward hit on the bar-holding hand, knocking the weapon and Sai's sword to the ground. Before Sai could follow through, as if the battle at the ship's ramp had turned into a carnival game, a different agent replaced the faltering bar-wielder. Eponi recognized this one, the agent that'd kicked her into oblivion.

If the first agent came in heavy with the bar, this one deployed smaller scrap. Slivers, maybe a half meter long apiece, stabbed towards Sai and caught his jacket, tore the vest beneath. Sai back-stepped, feinted a reach towards the katana, still lodged in the bar, and drew the dual-wielding agent into a strong forward stab where Sai ought to have been.

The strike at nothing brought the agent up the last step into the ship, put her full body on point when Sai drew his pistol, cocked his head, and fired. Once, twice, and the agent, looking too shocked to talk, fell back and dropped off the ramp. Rather than following up, Sai went for the nearby control panel, slapping it and jerking the ramp closed.

"Nice moves," Eponi said as the ship sealed itself, with no more agents bothering to charge inside.

"Dirty fighting," Sai pulled his katana from the bar and gave the blade a once-over.

"With a crisp, clean victory," Eponi replied.

Again, she tried to swing herself off the couch. Again, the nausea, the pain almost knocked her out, but once Eponi put herself up and sitting, she found something to hold onto. A rung above a roiling acid lake, but a rung nonetheless.

"You okay?" Sai asked, watching her with worried eyes.

"Super great," Eponi replied, sending her own eyes to the ship's metal floor. Vana didn't want the craft to get dirty, but . . . "Hey, mind checking if there's, like, anything on this ship?"

"Right," Sai said, "except I don't know how long we'll

hold out. They might be able to open the ramp from out there."

"Give me your pistol." Eponi flopped out a hand. "They lower it, I'll shoot'em."

"Uh huh." Sai, though, did as Eponi suggested, and handed the weapon over. "Don't die on me."

"Oh, it won't be on you. Don't worry."

Sai forced a chuckle, slid the katana into his sheath, and went stomping off into the ship to find, hopefully, something with drugs in it that could knock Eponi back into something approaching game shape.

Drugs, doses. The agent had talked about the doses like they were cash, but better. Being willing to risk your life, a one-time deal, for a dose meant whatever Vana had cooking was big.

Hell, given the way she felt, maybe Eponi could get her hands on some. Pick her up a bit.

Especially with the ramp beeping, signaling an outside unlock. Sai's panic move had bought them a couple minutes, nothing more.

"Hey buddy," Eponi called, hating how the words burned her bruised throat. The agents had made her favorite thing—cracking wise—miserable, and that just wouldn't do. "How's that search going?"

Sai appeared as if summoned, popping back into the central chamber and sparing a frown at the ramp as it began sliding down again. His hands held a standard first aid kit, good for cuts and the occasional outer space bout of nausea.

"There's some painkillers in there," Sai said. "Not much else that might help."

"Give me," Eponi replied, and Sai complied.

Renard must've been one of those who frowned on the body-numbing pleasures of modern medicine. The kit had the least amount of good things in it that Eponi had ever seen, but she made do by slamming a few nerve-dulling pills while Sai put himself in harm's way. The effect wouldn't be instantaneous, but Eponi might be able to stand up before the agents killed them both.

"Think they'll come up single-file again?" Eponi asked.

"One can only hope."

Instead, nobody appeared. The ramp went down, touched the ground, and the control panel beeped accordingly. Exiting, entering, both were good to go and neither seemed to be happening.

Still on the couch, cradling the pistol, Eponi motioned for Sai to move aside, get his back against the ship's inner wall, clearing her firing zone. If the agents down below wanted to wait out the Sever duo, well, Sai and Eponi could sit.

Make them come to us? Sai signed, using the hand signals Sever had developed over the years.

I'm not going to them, Eponi replied, wishing the finger language had a broader vocabulary so she could put the appropriate curses where they belonged. Eponi figured her odds of standing without falling on her own face were catastrophic, so there wasn't any chance of a heroic exodus.

Sai seemed to understand and put himself into position. Outside, voices came up the ramp. Talks between several agents, rapid fire and mingling every so often with that odd laughter. Few things amplified the creepy vibes more than people plotting your demise and chuckling while doing so. Minutes went by, the conversation continued, and Eponi hit her wall.

"You all coming in, or not?" Eponi shouted through the doorway. "I'm getting bored up here!"

In response, two small dark capsules bounced up and

through the ramp. Any DefenseCorp soldier who'd spent more than a week with the company knew what those capsules meant. Eponi jammed her eyes shut, tried to bring her fingers up to her ears.

The flashbangs did their work. Tried and true tools that'd been around long before Eponi graced the galaxy with her living presence, the damn things earned their keep by flaring through her closed eyes, by popping her ears with such force that her already woozy head rang. Unable to hold any real composure with her body in panic mode, Eponi pitched forward off the couch and hit the ship's metal floor hard.

The fall saved her life.

Her ears ringing, her eyes blinded, Eponi couldn't hear, couldn't see. She could, though, feel. Tremors coursed through the floor and touched her fingers as feet pounded up the ramp. Eponi traced those shakes, pointed the pistol in their direction and hoped to hell she wasn't about to shoot Sai.

She pulled the trigger. Once, twice, three times. The pistol's flashes added to the colored pain behind her eyes, but Eponi felt the heavier thud as someone's body hit the ground. Before she pulled the trigger a fourth time, though, the pistol left her hands, skittering across the floor. A foot stamped hard on her left arm, and Eponi felt a bone break. Sharp agony, a scream, and only the adrenaline, only the painkillers she'd swallowed, kept her from sliding into total blackness.

Looking up, her eyes coming back into gray focus, Eponi saw the agent standing on her. The man had that wide grin, had his foot planted, and what looked like a dark shadow growing on his neck. The agent fiddled with a combat knife, getting it in both hands for a plunge into Eponi's back. She couldn't get her legs in position for a kick, and lying on her chest, arm trapped beneath the agent's leg, didn't give Eponi much for options.

"Don't move now," the agent said, stabbing down.

Eponi curled. Rolled onto her side, gasping at the searing pain from her broken left arm, and took the knife in the side. The plunge, a committed stab at an enemy that wasn't supposed to dodge, cut through Eponi's midsection, but didn't go deep, snaring mostly clothes on its way to the floor. Eponi kept moving, getting her right hand on the agent's left leg, using the pull as leverage to sweep the agent off his feet.

That move wouldn't have worked if the man had been on level ground, but Eponi's arm, busted though it might've been, didn't provide stability. The agent fell back, hit the floor ass first. Behind him, Eponi saw Sai, disarmed, struggling with another pair. They also seemed to be working with knives, taking care not to damage Vana's sacred ship.

Eponi saw her pistol too, lying a couple meters away on the floor. Pushing with her feet, Eponi scrambled towards it, dragging her aching arm along. The agent rose, laughing all the way, and chased her. Eponi tried to throw a kick as she crawled, but the man wasn't fooled this time. He went past her, reached down and picked up her chosen pistol. Flipped the grip, and mashed Eponi aside with it, a hit that had her vision blurring.

A hit that ran Eponi to empty. Her batteries done, her race finished. She tried to move, tried to find the effort to keep fighting as the agent raised the knife again. Her body wouldn't respond, couldn't climb that mountain over the pain, the shock, the overload. Like a kart that'd been thrown through one maneuver too many.

A heavy thud rippled through the ship, coursing through Eponi's fingers. Reinforcements, maybe. Dooming

Sai too. The agent, though, paused in his killing blow, face turning towards the ramp, grin falling into a frown. Eponi would've turned too, except her neck didn't seem to wanna work that way anymore.

"No." One word, more growled than spoken.

Eponi's hope found a flicker there. And when the hammer whistled over, smashing into the agent and bringing his ruin to the room's far corner, Eponi's hope found a flame.

She blacked out a second later, to the utterly sweet, sweet sounds of Gregor doing what he did better than anyone.

TWENTY-FIVE

The Climb

For a moment of triumph, taking down the two suits in the spike sure didn't last long. Rovo, fresh off a somewhat stable attempt at using the scythe, flipped hard from enthusiastic victory to simmering rage when Vana and her circle of friends appeared, pistols in hand, around the descended lift.

Rovo's power suit gave him a near-solid red outline over his vision, showcasing the potential threats in literally every direction except straight up. Unfortunately, the power armor wouldn't let him fly. Also unfortunately, Aurora seemed to be negotiating with Kaia's kidnapper.

"Hand over the girl and we'll let you leave," Aurora was saying, still keeping a hold, like Rovo, on her suited opponent that she'd pinned to the ground. "You already have what you need from her."

"A bold statement when we have you surrounded," Vana replied. "I propose a different exchange: you let us leave this world with the girl, and we let you keep your lives."

The offer struck Rovo as a tad strange: why wouldn't

Vana simply fry both Severs here and now, then bargain with Salinity, who'd be a more neutral entity in the whole affair? Raquel already stated her primary goal was to keep more of Gillane Four's citizens from dying in the conflict. She'd be pliable.

But maybe Vana didn't know that.

"You heard my offer," Aurora countered. "This isn't a negotiation."

Vana sighed, "Then you're willing to die for the girl?"

"I am," Rovo spoke up. "Like Aurora said, you don't need her any more. Why are you doing this?"

"An insurance policy." Vana seemed like she wanted to continue, but her wristlet buzzed. This time, the sigh went deeper than before. "But it seems like my insurance isn't quite as good as it once was. Perhaps, Aurora, I will take your deal."

Rovo blinked. He did not see that turn coming.

"Then where's the girl?" Aurora said. "Hand her over, we'll head up and clear out, and then you can leave."

"She's not here," Vana waved around at all the pistol-wielding agents. "Do you think this is any place for child? Once we did the draws, I had her moved. After we've left, I will send you the coordinates to find her."

"Like we can trust you," Rovo said.

"Like you have a choice," Vana replied, and Rovo hated how Vana always sounded so calm. As if everything seemed to be going according to her plan. "Protest, fight, do what you want, but if you want to find the girl, you will need my help."

Aurora glanced Rovo's way, and in that face Rovo saw the answer he was looking for. The rookie wanted Kaia alive, wanted her safe, but he couldn't trust Vana. Not after the traps, the double-crosses, the continued coercion. Raquel and Salinity had the planet under close observation. The agents wouldn't be able to get her out, and Salinity would track the kid down without too much trouble.

Rovo had to believe that, because the inverse, letting Vana go now . . .

"I'm placing a different bet," Rovo said.

"What?" Vana asked, and Rovo answered by whipping the stolen knife over the surrounding crowd.

The blade struck the thick tube running water through the heating coils. The glass, meant to withstand earthquakes, to handle heat, wasn't built to deal with a direct stab from an object designed to cut through armor. The knife pierced, the tube cracked, and the spray began.

"Life boats!" Vana's shout cut above the sudden panic as boiling water blew into the lift chamber.

Two doors, leading to somewhere Rovo didn't know, clogged as agents rushed to fill them. None thought about taking pot shots at Rovo and Aurora. None thought to get in their way as the two Severs took a different path.

Aurora made the faster move, jumping from her pinned soldier to grab Vana as the agent leader broke for one of the doors. As Aurora snagged Vana's arm, the water tube cracked more, glass folding in with the spray, turning it to a deluge. The structure started to rattle, alarms cried, and agents continued to flee.

"Raquel?" Rovo shouted into his wristlet, stepping off the pinned suit and letting that agent, too, run for the doors. In a suit like that, the man would never fit in a lifeboat anyway. "Get your people off this thing!"

"What's happening?" Rovo could barely hear Raquel over the noise.

"Little problem with the spike! Watch for agents leaving in lifeboats, they'll need pick-up. Or you can just shoot'em."

"Rovo!" Aurora shouted, and the rookie realized the water in the spike had reached his ankles, growing quickly. "Time to move!"

The Sever captain had Vana held tight in her left arm, with Aurora's right pulling the power armor grapple free and prepping to throw it up. Above, the long spike stretched with its blue—and now flickering red alarm—lights. They could've gone through the exits after the agents and hoped their enemies left them room on the lifeboats.

Not likely.

So that meant up. Racing the water.

For a brief moment, Rovo considered just swimming. Treading in the water as it rose. That thought died quick when his visor alerted him to the growing heat at his feet. This wasn't cold seawater, but near-boiling liquid super-heated as the spike fulfilled its purpose. Beyond that, the spike had been damaged. Circuits potentially exposed. Any moment might turn the growing pool into an electrified death trap.

Cool.

Aurora jumped, throwing the grapple as she sprang. The hook bit into the water tube farther up, catching into the glass and holding fast. With the leak down below, more water didn't spray out from the new crack.

"Nice throw," Rovo said, reaching down to snag his lost scythe shield from beneath the water and slotting it into his belt. "Let me know if you need a hand."

"Just move," Aurora called down.

Rather than use the grapple, Rovo pulled out his combat knife, put it into his left hand, while keeping his long-hooked scythe in his other. Turning on the kinetic boosters, Rovo leaped from the knee-deep pool and bit his weapons into the spike's wall. The metal, like the glass, hadn't been designed to resist sharp thrusts, and Rovo's blades bit in well.

Now the rookie had to do something he'd never done before: climb, using knives for hands.

Rovo started with the scythe, a jerking reach that moved him up a meter. The combat knife didn't give as deep a hold, and it took a couple jabs to get the weapon stable enough for Rovo to put any weight on it, but he moved. The power armor compensated for its own weight, doing what it could to add grip strength.

All the same, Rovo felt like he was lifting a truck.

Aurora, on the opposite side, took a different approach. One that seemed, frankly, smarter. Using the power armor's boot clamps, Aurora pinned her legs to the spike's side, using the suit's own stabilizers to help her sit upright, with Vana cradled into her chest, while Aurora removed and then threw the grapple further up.

Vana didn't seem to be struggling. Maybe she didn't want to get cooked in the boiling froth beneath them.

A reasonable choice.

After the third stretch'n'move with the scythe, Rovo abandoned his combat knife and adopted Aurora's flow. Rovo had pride aplenty, but he could see when he'd made the wrong choice. Reaching for his grapple, Rovo targeted the tube on his side, launching the grapple towards the glass. The hook caught, like Aurora's, and Rovo had that brief thrill that comes when you replicate a mentor's move.

With a tug on the grapple, the power armor kicked into action, winding up the grapple's metal thread and pulling Rovo higher. Beneath him, the water continued to deepen, but not so fast that Rovo felt much threat. It wouldn't be a quick climb to the top, but with the grapples, they'd make it. No problem.

Unless the spike decided to break.

The structure hadn't been handling the water influx all that well. Its alarms blared, the lights flashed, but the growing pool had the walls shuddering as Rovo and Aurora, with Vana nestled against her, climbed. Loud groans rumbled through the air, punctuated by pops as gaskets and molding split, broke, and splintered around them.

"Thinking we should hurry!" Rovo shouted across the spike. He'd been keeping pace with Aurora, having caught up to her now. It seemed bad form to ditch the captive-carrying captain. "Can you go any faster?"

"If I dropped Vana into the water," Aurora called back, launching the grapple up again.

Not the worst idea. Rovo had confidence Salinity could find the child, but if Sever had Vana already, it seemed like a decent play to keep her alive. Until, anyway, they had Kaia in their hands.

Rovo had snapped one neck on Gillane Four. He could make it two.

The thought shook the rookie as he climbed up another reach on the spike. Nothing like a little self-reflection in the midst of a crisis. And yet, Sever always seemed to be in one of those. Had the continual battering against Rovo's own will ground it down until he had nothing more than frustrated anger? Where the ends, saving Kaia, more than justified murderous means?

Any answer to that question would have to wait, because the tube Rovo had been using for his grapple peeled away from the wall. No, the wall itself was breaking apart. Water spilled out between metal panels, showering Rovo in icy liquid. The cold seawater plummeted into the hot pool below, billowing up steam that turned the view inside the spike into an impenetrable fog.

Rovo dug his scythe deep into the wall, hoping this

section wouldn't break away quite yet. Raising his wristlet to his mouth, he told the thing to contact Raquel, and the wristlet followed its orders.

"Rovo?" Raquel's voice came through, patching into the rookie's visor. "Where are you two? I have the last skiff, we're waiting—"

"Open the top hatch," Rovo said. "Please, now!"

"On it," Raquel said while Rovo felt his grapple break loose and fall away. Without being able to see, he'd have to go back to the manual climb. "How close are you?"

"Can't tell," Rovo said. "Getting closer. Hold tight and we'll get there."

"The spike's not doing so—"

Raquel's connection cut as Aurora's voice, taking squad band priority, broke through, "Rovo, go. I can't grapple with this fog. Get up top, drop your line and we'll ride it out."

A race against water now rising fast with more pouring in from all sides. Maybe not as skin-boiling hot, but even the best swimmer wouldn't be able to escape getting entombed in the collapsing spike.

The steam-fog broke when daylight shone in from above. Raquel had made her move, opened up the hatch, and Rovo kept climbing towards it, falling back on the knife and scythe combo, sticking around faltering wall panels, until he made it to the spike's top. Now he had to go horizontal, climbing along the spike's ceiling while the structure disintegrated around him.

You know, just a normal day in Sever squad.

Below, Aurora and Vana clung to the wall, the water catching up to them. The churning mess continued to billow up steam, though at least the alarms were dying now, their generators faltering as the spike continued its collapse to the ocean's floor.

Rovo tried driving the scythe into the ceiling, but the walls here were thicker, meant to support landing craft. The weapon wouldn't bite, much less hold Rovo's weight. He'd need a different tactic. Using his boot clamps, Rovo re-oriented, turned himself to face the spike's center. He dropped a meter, leveraging the scythe, to give himself a better angle.

"What're you doing, Rovo?" Aurora's voice, still taut with authority, picked up a worried edge.

"Being awesome," Rovo replied.

Punching the energy, Rovo kicked off the wall in a jump more horizontal than vertical. The leap brought the rookie over the center gap, haloed him for a hot moment in the daylight. Rovo reached up, extended with the scythe, and nearly tore his arm off when the thing caught. Dangling over the spike's shaft and a very, very deep watery grave beneath him, Rovo refused to look down.

Instead, he punched what little energy remained from the jump into the boosters in his boots. The kick, without something to push against, wasn't much, but the scythe held, and Rovo's left hand managed to get up enough to catch a grip. More hands fell around it as Raquel and a couple loyal Salinity guards rushed in, ready to tug as Rovo made a lunge with the scythe.

The weapon bit into the spike's surface, and with the power armor assisting, along with the sorta helpful human trio—the power armor had too much weight for their tugs to be anything more than minor—Rovo crawled onto the spike's surface.

And nearly rolled.

The spike listed to the side, turning the level platform into a hill. The two skiffs that remained close weren't actually docked anymore, but hovering nearby. That list, though Rovo hadn't realized it inside, made it possible for his desperate jump to succeed in the first place. Sometimes, disaster works in your favor.

"Rovo!" Aurora's voice cracked through. "Any time now!"

Turning back around, Rovo dropped his grapple down towards Aurora. Bathed in the flickering blue remnants, coupled with the daylight, his captain and her captive, with the water kissing Aurora's heels, looked fantastical. Aurora slipped the grapple onto her belt, then kicked off with her kinetic boosters, launching towards the exit.

Vana climbed first as they came close, moving up on Aurora's shoulders. Rovo reached down, grabbed Vana's hand. He'd get her up, hand her over, then reach down for Aurora. Simple enough.

The agent came up readily, hitting the spike's surface.

"Thanks for the save," Vana said. "But you really shouldn't be so nice."

Rovo, already moving to reach for Aurora, glanced Vana's way, "What?"

"You'll always get hurt in the end," Vana said, and as Raquel, her two guards, went for her, Vana punched the grapple release on Rovo's suit.

The cord sprang free, whistling over the edge. Aurora, holding onto the grapple's end, dropped with the cable, disappearing into the roiling sea.

TWENTY-SIX

For A Swim

AURORA HIT the water with a calm that came from a thousand life-threatening situations conquered. The power armor reacted similarly, pulling on its prescribed programming to slam shut every little valve and crease to keep Aurora dry and, more importantly, breathing the oxygen stored away in power armor pockets for situations just like this.

Not that DefenseCorp advised its power armor wearers to take deep dives—the suit would, eventually, ruin out of energy and the ability to keep any real air flowing through it, leaving its pilot immersed in a forever cocoon at the bottom of some ocean or another. The same principles applied to vacuum, though outer space at least gave its doomed traveler a better view before turning them to ice.

Aurora took in all those thoughts in a quick flash as the suit sank through a spike she'd already spent far too much time inside. Vana's trick lingered as Aurora took out her own grapple, found it useless in the water, and then tried to swim. Her legs and arms, boosted by the kinetic power coursing through the suit, did an admirable job kicking Aurora upwards. The water that'd been boiling, ready to cook an earlier version of the falling Sever into a steamed dinner, now only tripped the medium heat sensors in the armor, apparently cooled enough by the ocean around.

"Switch this out for a swimsuit and I might enjoy it," Aurora muttered as her kicks reached the spike's outer edge.

What had been smooth wall crumpled and bent as water pressure tugged the building apart. In a way, this made it easier for Aurora, as that wall now had handholds aplenty. Aurora found a grip and pulled, bringing herself up one burst and grab at a time. The surface sat not all that far away, sparkling in the daylight.

The contest, now, became less a battle with drowning and more about whether Aurora could make it to the surface before the spike gave way and collapsed completely. Swimming in the power armor came hard enough, doing it while dodging falling metal plates?

"Aurora, you still there?" Rovo's voice crackled through the comm, on Sever's squad band.

"No, I've vanished," Aurora snapped. "I'm climbing up."

"Make it fast. The skiffs are having a hard time keeping level with the pad now."

"Where's Vana?"

"Raquel's with her. They're going back to the Salinity base."

"You're not?" Aurora wanted to punch Rovo, but she settled for another reach and pull. Another meter or two and she'd be back in fresh air, ready to make the final ascent. "Why did you let Vana go?"

Rovo didn't reply right away. Good. At least the rookie had the sense to realize when he'd done something stupid.

"You always say the squad matters most," Rovo replied. "I didn't want to leave you."

"I'm not surrounded by enemies or bleeding out, Rovo," Aurora said. "Can you get on that skiff?"

"It's already gone."

Aurora's curse coincided with another pull, one that broke her over the turbulent surface. Roiling water slapped across her visor, confusing its sensors as they tried to find the best spectrum. Not that it mattered: she'd have to be totally blind to miss the big, sparkling hole in the spike's middle.

Less easy to see but no less critical was Rovo's arm. The rookie had it extended down in a long reach, dangling for Aurora to make a swim-kick jump. Sever's captain did as the situation demanded, pushing up as hard as she could, adding an extra kick with her suit's last bit of kinetic energy—charged while treading water. Like some metal, ugly dolphin, Aurora broke the surface and stretched.

In a movie, Aurora felt the moment would've played in slow motion.

In real time, she never had a chance.

As Aurora broke free from the roil, Salinity's spike had its last moment as a sound structure. The fibers keeping the thing standing straight bent and snapped under the water pressure, providing an excellent crack to Aurora's flashy move while signaling that same move's failure.

The top-level landing pad slanted to the side, lurching Rovo back from his perch and out of sight. Aurora heard the rookie's surprised shout carry through the band, mingling with her own yelp as the leap brought her within slapping range of the spike's top, with no grip to be had. Her right hand slipped off the metal, and Aurora fell face forward.

Water ran around according to physics laws decidedly

not in Aurora's favor. Instead of a plummet back into the deep pool, Aurora hit a rushing water wave pushing her towards the hole Aurora had been trying to reach. Only this time, instead of a helpful hand and a pull to a valiant escape, the water flushed Aurora through, out into the air far above the ocean's surface.

Aurora's head, exiting first, pulled her body into a tumble as she reached for and snagged the landing pad's lip. Kicking her boots around, Aurora activated the clamps, digging them into the flat surface. Water poured over and around her, the visor keeping it from her eyes.

"Where are you?" Rovo called, a surprise seeing as Aurora figured he'd have plummeted to a back-breaking smash to the water's surface.

"Hanging onto the spike's end." Aurora's assessment had strict accuracy for the moment, but the spike's continued fall, a slow-motion collapse as the structure snapped its top half from its base, would force an evacuation any second. "Where are you?"

"Jumped to a skiff," Rovo said. "We'll come in, grab you."

"Negative," Aurora said, feeling the spike's top continue its rotation. "Pick me up from the water after."

The water roared up its fury, then slowed to a dripping trickle as the collapse continued, splitting away the spike's top from the ocean flow below. Aurora's stomach did a flip as Sever's captain swung back-first towards the sea, now hanging upside-down thanks to her boot clamps. Snapping cables and cracking plates made a shrieking cavalcade as the spike began its straight down plummet. Aurora's visor calculated the drop around a hundred meters, and she'd hit the water followed by who knows how many broken metal kilos.

Not great.

Aurora sucked in a breath. DefenseCorp didn't have any training for this—normally, artillery or orbital bombardment collapsed any important buildings before Sever arrived. Instead, she had to draw on instinct. On momentum.

Releasing her grip on the landing pad's lip, but keeping her boots locked in, Aurora pushed herself into a swing. At the apex, as the spike fell towards the ocean, Aurora released the boots. Unlocked, with the power armor's weight pulling her along, Aurora flew—so much as someone in a bulky suit could fly—down and away from the crashing spike.

The additional speed drove Aurora into the water like a missile, and she speared her arms to slice through the waves, plunging her deep. Her aim brought her right to the spike's still-standing structure, its underwater lights giving Aurora a target even as the collapsing half entered the sea behind her. The falling metal pushed water forward in a gushing spurt, tumbling Aurora ahead until she smashed into the spike's lower half.

Her power suit groaned along with Aurora's muscles, and her eyes flashed a few cool colors as her brain took a rattle. The water's moving pressure kept Aurora planted against the spike's side for a long breath, but the reverse sucking began quick. Using those boot locks—Aurora wanted to find who'd made the things and gift them as much cash as she could spare—the Sever captain sealed herself to the outer wall, watching the water rush back around her.

The spike's top half drifted down, bubbles rising all across the massive structure like a natural funeral procession. Aurora watched it glide past her, heading further down into the ocean's depths. She'd just been inside that thing, just been trying to get to its top, and now there it went, gone forever to a darkness Aurora hoped never to penetrate.

"Captain?" Rovo's voice, scratchy getting through all that water, broke through.

Aurora didn't answer at first. She breathed. Waited. Reconciled the fact that she wasn't about to die with what'd just happened.

"Aurora?" Rovo put in some edge this time, a little panic. "Please tell me you're there."

"I'm here," Aurora said, not moving. Not daring to unlock her boots. "I'm underwater. Locked to the spike's remains."

Swimming to the surface, or climbing to it, seemed an impossible task. Her visor said she had enough air left for thirty minutes. Aurora could afford to put herself together.

"Are you hurt?"

Aurora closed her eyes, "Not hurt. Tired, but not hurt."

So often, only after the moment had passed did Aurora feel any fear, any worry over what'd happened. In those split seconds, locking the boots or making the leap for Rovo's hand, the objective held prime in Aurora's mind. The physical actions necessary to complete that objective ran roughshod over any emotions that could get in the way.

Now? Now Aurora had time to piece the whole thing back together.

"That was a good shot," Aurora said.

"What?"

"To break the spike. Did you know that would happen?"

Rovo laughed, the weary, excited sound of a victor, "I had no idea. I thought it might spray some water. Maybe trigger an alarm for us to use as a distraction. Take'em by surprise."

"Instead, you've cost Salinity a lot. Raquel won't be happy."

"But we're alive," Rovo said. "That has to count for something."

"We'll see how much," Aurora replied. Taking another big breath, she sighed. "Bring my ride down to the surface. Close to what's left. I'm going to make the climb."

"See you soon, captain."

THE SKIFF, with Rovo and Aurora crushed into the back seats, made its way back to the Salinity facility with as much speed as the pilot could coax out of it. Aurora's suit dripped a puddle onto the floor, its white-and-black paint glistening under the daylight, a pretty contrast to its pilot's frustrated face. They'd left the agents in their emergency pods, floating on the open waves. Salinity security would come for them later, charge them with who cared what, so long as the agents were kept out of commission.

"Raquel's still not answering?" Aurora asked Rovo for the fourth time in the hour since they'd flown away.

"No, but she's probably busy," Rovo replied. "Maybe."

Raquel had taken Vana, supposedly to the same facility Aurora and Rovo were heading to now. Putting the agent, a strong fighter with, clearly, nothing to lose, in a skiff without any Sever alongside her had been a dumb call. Raquel's silence could mean the woman was involved in putting Vana in a cell, but Aurora knew which way her bets would lie.

An equal concern came from the other three. Gregor, Sai, and Eponi had completed the mission, planting the EMP grenades on Renard's ship, but it hadn't exactly been a stealth success. The agents had known Sever would make some attempt on the craft, and Eponi had been soundly beaten up. Sai and Gregor had torched the agents keeping guard, and both believed nobody saw the grenades get planted, so that part of the plan might still work.

If Vana even bothered with the ship, knowing now it was compromised.

Either way, the three were on their own skiff, burning back to the Salinity facility to talk next steps. To, hopefully, find out from Vana where she'd stashed Kaia.

"Try the facility," Aurora said. "Raquel should've made it back by now, right?"

"Should have," Rovo replied, then did as Aurora asked. The call went out, came back almost immediately.

Raquel hadn't landed, and her skiff hadn't made any calls.

Aurora would've swore, but instead, she did what she had to do: she started making plans. Next time, she'd be the one on Vana.

Nobody else.

Scars Past and Future

With Gregor carrying Eponi and Sai wielding his katana as a guiding, protective beacon, the trio left Renard's ship and broke across the salvage towards the capsules. With Gregor's help inside the craft, the attacking agents had been reduced to mauled gristle and bone. While the ship had escaped serious marring, the insides would, nevertheless, need a strong cleaning to make them whole again.

Modern combat, often laser-filled, tended to take a cleaner approach. The burning bolts cauterized wounds, leaving victims wounded or dead, but without the telltale physical display. Even Sai's katana, sharp enough for clean cuts, avoided major messes. Gregor's hammer, however, harkened back to the old, brutal days: its bashing left a barbarian's tale behind, one that shadowed Sai's steps.

Sever and Sai had danced with death too many times since Dynas. The variety had Sai wincing as the trio took capsules up. The wait while Eponi loaded hers slow, while Gregor squeezed into his careful, replayed the damages suffered. Sai had found himself nearly shoved into vacuum, injected with a murderous virus, on the business ends of who knew how many pistols, rifles, and starship turrets.

At some point, you had to look around and wonder at how you still lived.

The answer, of course, moved before him, with Gregor helping Eponi climb into her seat. Only together did Sever stand a chance against the enemies that kept appearing before them. Only together could they help each other through the scrapes and stabs and scars accumulating on their bodies and souls.

Sai, facing back into the quiet salvage with his katana ready, alone on the platform, chuckled to himself. Being dramatic again. He could be prone to such things, a far off perspective that, Sai had to believe, sprang from his children and the widening of Sai's universe that came with their place in it. For a long time, he'd been able to quiet the insistent call to return to his family.

But with every shot Sai took, with every punch he threw, that call grew louder.

The cry for cash, meanwhile, fell quiet.

Sai knew he stayed now out of loyalty and love for the other four that journeyed beside him. That was, and would have to be, enough to bring him from this fight to the next.

Because there would always be a next.

SKIFFS TOOK the trio back to the Salinity facility outside Kaiyo serving as Sever's de facto base. Whereas before the Salinity officers and workers treated Sever with mixed deference and annoyance—intruders on their home turf— they now grumbled openly when Sai went past. At first, the expressions confused the three, but when Raquel's absence, her kidnapping on a botched raid led by Rovo and Aurora, became known, Sai understood.

DefenseCorp was vengeful. Wrong its outfits and, regardless of the contract, DefenseCorp would spare no resources in hunting you down and destroying you. The stance came part and parcel with protecting DefenseCorp's reputation as the galaxy's foremost destruction purveyor. Sai himself, both before and after he'd joined Sever, had played parts in missions designed simply to teach a lesson with fire and flame.

Vengeance, though, required a target. With Raquel and the other troopers in the skiff with her missing, and their presumed captor vanished, the frustration all too easily found a mark on the intruders. The strange squad that'd dropped onto Gillane Four and brought so much chaos to the lives of family men and women, to people who'd thought themselves long retired from days filled with laser fire and nights watching their backs.

Sai understood, but when he helped Eponi off the skiff and towards the facility's medical unit, a three bed place meant more for headaches than broken bones, he didn't have much sympathy left to share.

"You'll bill the time to whomever you damn well want," Sai told the on-site physician and her supporting bots as they clustered around Eponi, staring at the wounds and enduring Eponi's cocky description of how they came to be. "This isn't about cash, it's about getting a player back in a game you can't afford to lose."

"Can't afford to lose?" The physician looked as doubtful as Sai had ever seen anyone, both eyebrows raising and mouth sliding into a smirk. "That's a bold statement from a bunch of DefenseCorp terrorists."

A strong choice of words there. Sai would've picked up that insult and ran with it another day, but after this one, with his muscles screaming rest with his brain telling him that Sai needed to find Aurora and put together some strategy for what came next, the man chose not to push it.

"Just, just help her," Sai said. "I know it's not what you expected, and I know you might not like us, but she didn't do this to herself. We're trying to save a child. That's all."

If Sai had been more on his game, he'd have mentioned Kashmal, that Kaia was a daughter of a Salinity employee, but those logical arguments splintered and flew away in the mental breeze jumbling up Sai's skull.

Amazing how a man could go from slicing and dicing with precision to, a few hours later, barely holding it together.

The physician must've noticed, because that doubting stare fell away fast into a frowning reply, "I'm not sure she's the only one that needs some help. Tell me you're not going back out soon?"

"That depends on when we find the girl," Sai replied. "Because when we do, I'll be ready."

The physician looked back towards Eponi, pursed her lips, "Then I'll do what I can to make sure she is too."

"WE PLANTED THEM ALL," Sai said, back on the open overlook as evening crept in over the horizon. Aurora had the same table, and Sai joined her. No alcohol this time, no party. Grim and grittiness seemed the vibe. "Three grenades, all tied to my wristlet. Unless she gets off-world without us knowing, I'll be able to trigger them."

"At least we had one success today," Aurora said.

"I heard," Sai replied. "The rookie brought down an

entire spike? I'd call it impressive if I wasn't worried the cash was going to come out of our accounts."

"That's a fight I'm not having now," Aurora replied. Her hand, with a fork, picked at the vegetables on her plate, an orange and green medley losing steam to the chill outdoors. "When you said how scary it felt on Dynas, when you went below the waters in the swamp to get that mine?"

"Yeah. Power armor isn't much for swimming."

"Now I know." Aurora stiffened. "After all the times we've gone out, I've never been that far under the ocean. The oxygen timer really does a number on you."

"The constant ticking, telling you how long you've got till you choke out and die?"

"Makes it hard to focus," Aurora said. "Especially when you have to tell a rookie what to do."

Sai started a grin, left it half-formed until Aurora matched it. They burned a few minutes eating while the patio filled up with Salinity employees catching their own dinner. With Eponi in the med bay, Gregor catching a nap, and Rovo off dealing with his own demons, the two kept things quiet.

"Kaia wasn't there at all?" Sai asked when the sky hit the best shade of orange. "Vana played you?"

"I don't think so," Aurora replied. "She's been ahead of us this whole time. Always ready, always leaking the right information to get us where she wants us."

"Hold up," Sai said. "That's your mood getting you. We're winning this. We've taken out so many agents, Renard, and now we have her only ship sabotaged? Vana's walls are closing in, and she's going to get desperate."

That word caught Aurora's attention. She held up a finger, waving it through the air at nothing in particular. A habit Aurora had, one that Sai had picked up on after watching his captain work her way through countless missions gone awry.

"You might be right," Aurora mused. "Desperate. If we believe Vana that she managed to get Kaia's blood off-world already—"

"Likely, no matter what Raquel says. Gillane Four has air traffic everywhere, and an agent could get onto a transport."

"Then the only reason Vana's still here is that she hasn't found a way to get herself and Kaia into orbit without risking her life," Aurora stopped again, this time turning to tapping on the table to grease up her mind. "She's losing agents, she's losing hiding places. If this keeps up, there's only one end, and Vana's going to know it."

"So she'll throw everything she has into one last shot."

"It's what I'd do," Aurora said. "Hell, it's what DefenseCorp would do. They never settle into long, draining engagements. DefenseCorp always blows it out, uses every ounce of force they can muster."

"Which is what?" Sai folded his hands across each other, fingers clasped, almost as though the katana's hilt sat between them. "Vana can't fly out commercially. We didn't leave any evidence on the ship that we planted anything."

"She'll think it was an attack, one looking for her or Kaia. She'll go back to the ship and use it. She has to." Aurora sat forward, elbows on the table. "You said, also, that the agents were strange. Gregor mentioned the same thing. Now it sounds like the agents might be dying."

"We shouldn't have let Anaskya go."

"Another time." Aurora waved the regret away. "The agents aren't mindless. They'll turn on Vana if she isn't giving them a chance to survive."

"A hospital," Sai said, tracing the lines. "Vana will set them on a hospital. Say there's a cure there. The agents will move in, cause a panic. Salinity will respond, and in the chaos, Vana breaks for orbit."

Aurora didn't quite jump on Sai's suggestion. She sat back in her chair, sent a stare towards the horizon, as if the scattered clouds might provide a better thought.

"No?" Sai asked.

"I don't know," Aurora said. "That . . . seems too simple. If this disease is new, how would a random hospital hold a cure?"

Sai shrugged, "These agents didn't seem all there, Aurora. Whatever Anaskya's doing to them, they aren't the same. Vana could fool them."

Aurora still didn't seem convinced, but any further conversation came to an end when Rovo tromped in, carrying his own tray and looking harrowed.

"I've checked every band," Rovo said, sitting at their table. "Scanned all DefenseCorp frequencies with the Bug. Nothing. No word about Kaia or Raquel. Just usual noise about contracts, and how we're making a big mess."

"Can't argue that," Sai said. "Way to destroy an entire spike, Rovo. I'm proud of you."

Rovo shook his head, apparently not ready to have a laugh. Which, Sai could get that.

"I did learn something useful, though," Rovo said, perking up a bit. "Salinity's picked up a new arrival in system. Deepak's here, with the *Nautilus*."

Aurora's smiled, the first genuine one Sai had seen since getting back to the facility. Sai, too, couldn't help but match it. The cruiser's arrival marked the definitive end to Vana's chances of escape. Once the big ship closed, its fighters could put an orbital net around the world. Nothing would leave without a thorough inspection.

"That's it, then," Aurora said. "We wait and watch. Vana will have to make her move soon, or Deepak's going to trap her here. Get some rest, but keep your weapons handy. When Vana tries anything, we'll catch her."

"Along with Kaia and Raquel," Sai added, more for Rovo than anything.

The rookie looked like he needed some cheer, just like Sai needed some sleep.

TWENTY-EIGHT

A Beautiful Night

THE NAP WENT LONGER than Gregor anticipated, but he hadn't set an alarm and deserved what he wound up with: a late evening awakening, with the kitchen closed and the only food coming from some vending machines. The soft glowing things offered protein-spun products, synthetic vitamins, and every other snack designed to last until infinity and beyond. Gregor rubbed his eyes, stared at the unappealing list.

Back on the *Prisa*, the other squad members, Eponi and her medical needs excepted, were all collapsing or nearly there after the long day. Salinity's facility echoed the hour, with most personnel who were spending the night—many took skiffs back to Kaiyo at day's end—already ensconced within their quarters. The solitude made Gregor's decision all the harder.

A man of action, Gregor looked at the disappointing array and couldn't find an easy answer. He needed someone behind him, prompting Gregor into a choice. Instead, and Gregor figured this could be a fault of his nap bringing him to the in between zone of sleep and waking, he muddled through the lineup again and again, slowly clearing out rows and their branded options.

"That one," Gregor muttered, more to some invisible specter watching and waiting than to himself.

His choice, a bacon-flavored vitamin and protein medley, clunked to the slot after Gregor's wristlet beamed his cash account details to the machine's satisfaction. Taking the wrapped solution to his rumbling stomach, Gregor made his second significant choice:

He'd eat the thing on the deck, rather than returning to the *Prisa*'s cramped quarters.

If nothing else, the deck wouldn't remind him of possibilities as yet unfulfilled. Eponi hadn't had a chance, yet, to get to the *Prisa*'s cockpit. When she did, the pilot would likely notice Gregor hadn't made any use of the communications relay, and the needling would commence. Gregor could put a stop to it, could head back to the ship right now and beam off a short message to the universe.

Yet he went the other way, along low-lit hallways, passed empty control centers and conference rooms. While Gregor didn't know everything Salinity ran from here, the facility seemed to be the company's foremost base keeping Gillane Four running. The Kaiyo headquarters handled more corporate duties, while the back-end kept itself out of sight here among the waves. The office life felt like a foreign thing, a path never open to a man born on a spinning space rock and one Gregor had never felt a compulsion to explore.

Seeing the empty desks, the empty chairs, the break rooms with notices for various potlucks and corporate events, the pull again failed to capture Gregor's desire.

But Gregor could and did find solace in the quiet deck. Illuminated by soft red lighting laced around the outer edges, a concession to light pollution that gave Gregor a luminescent view of the starlit map overhead. Constellations unfamiliar and sparkling danced with one another up in the dark, another alien vista calling to Gregor with all those unknown planets and their problems.

How could you settle for just one home when so many others waited to be explored?

The thermal chairs made a sit down comfortable, gave Gregor a chance to finish the cheap food in relaxed peace. The sounds, which Gregor noticed when his own footfalls weren't added to them, didn't quite match the view. The facility felt noisier this night than most, with its nightly duties kicking up a heavy whine and thrum down below. The buzzing echoed off the waves, wrapping up and around, so that it seemed like a million insects flew about in concert. Punctuating that steady noise came periodic and random thunks, light strikes on metal. A pipe or two in need of maintenance, or a generator struggling to stay consistent.

For a company as thorough as Salinity, the discordant sounds seemed unusual. Then again, with Sever and Vana blitzing around their planet, such routines might've been pushed back. The *Nautilus* had surely bumped its schedules after the fighting through its corridors.

"Soon enough," Gregor muttered, "we'll have you back to normal."

A chill cloud puffed away with his words. Gregor's sweater and sheer body mass kept him comfortable, but Gillane Four, especially away from the cities and their warming biomes, embraced a windswept, cool climate. Even with their stay on cold Wexer, Gregor hadn't overcome the sweaty horrors on Dynas, and the man, having finished the snack, stood and went to the railing to catch a windy kiss before heading back to the *Prisa*.

Far below, starlight coated a ghostly ocean. Shallow

waves marched across its surface, their tension coming and going like forms struggling beneath a trapping net. Gregor received the icy smack he'd been looking for, inhaling the air and feeling it deliver a shocking, sweet caress to his lungs.

Few things were more refreshing.

His eyes returned to the waves, drawn by a flicker that at first seemed like nature playing a trick. A wave tilting the wrong direction, the rippling black more solid than it should have been. The line—no, the block—kept moving, drawing in closer to the facility. Gregor figured the craft would be only a few meters above the water's surface, and the telltale ripples of its passing, now that Gregor looked for them, made an appearance for moments before the next wave washed the evidence away.

A Salinity vessel, making a late night approach at surface level, without running lights?

Gregor followed the thing's path as it swept towards the stout pillars anchoring the facility to Gillane Four's crust. The craft angled to Gregor's right, and there, hidden partly by the facility's bulk, Gregor saw something that made his blood ice more than the chill wind ever could.

The lightless skiff wasn't alone.

Several more black blocks lingered around the pillar, and climbing up the metal pole were many smaller forms. Those thunks Gregor had been hearing rose as the distant bodies struck grapples into the pillar's sides, and the whining? The skiffs, hovering over the water.

No friendly visit started with a midnight, stealth entrance.

Gregor brought up his wristlet, intending to radio out to Sever and signal an alert. When the little computer came up to his lips, a body came up over the balcony's edge. With her right hand grabbing and pulling Gregor's wristlet away from his mouth, the agent kept Gregor from calling to his squad. With her left hand, stabbing a knife toward's Gregor's stomach, she tried to keep him from calling to anyone ever again.

But one surprise cost the other: Gregor stepped back from the balcony's railing, enough that the knife only nicked his skin. The step yanked the agent, still holding Gregor's wristlet, over and onto the balcony main, where Gregor grabbed the woman's knife arm. Swinging her, Gregor threw the agent into a table-'n-chairs mix, clattering the bunch into a tangled collapse.

Cursing his decision to leave the *Prisa* without a weapon, Gregor again went to his wristlet. This time, a shot came from behind. Hard and burning, the bolt crashed into Gregor's shoulder, the pain pushing him forward in a turning dive. Another laser flashed where his head had been, streaking its blue-black light over the sea.

"Stop shooting!" shout-whispered the agent Gregor had thrown, picking herself up from the pile. "Not till we get the clear!"

His right arm felt like fire as Gregor picked himself up, facing the agent that'd shot him. That man swapped his pistol for another of the combat knives, long-toothed things with edges meant to pierce body armor that'd fizzle a laser. The agent behind him would be on her feet in a second. To Gregor's left, potential salvation lay inside the facility.

Gregor feinted forward, as if he meant to rush the second agent. The man bit, falling back and putting himself into a defensive stance even as Gregor kicked off towards the balcony door. Gregor's long strides should've made it an easy getaway, but the agents were damn agents for a reason: they always had another trick to pull.

Something bit hard into Gregor's left leg, and while he

felt the grapple rip free—taking no small amount of skin with it—the sudden resistance threw Gregor off balance. He pitched forward, getting his arms up in time to keep himself from a gnarly face-plant to the textured surface. Gregor hit and rolled, facing up as the woman followed her grapple shot with a leaping stab towards Gregor's chest.

With his left hand, Gregor found a chair and brought it sweeping across, catching the agent in mid-air and mashing her to the side. She did a helluva job keeping quiet as she crumpled. Gregor sat up in time to catch a hard kick from the agent's buddy, a blow that jumbled Gregor's thoughts, sent the world spinning.

But instinct was instinct, and Gregor's had been honed to a razor's edge.

Ignoring the pain in his shoulder, the blurry starlit world, Gregor rose and threw himself at the other agent. With his right hand, Gregor gripped and forced the agent's knife away while his left delivered one jab after another to the agent's gut, chest, and anywhere else Gregor could find purchase. The hits kept coming as Gregor walked the agent back out, all the way to the edge, and with a final push, Gregor shoved the man up and over the railing.

This one didn't go so quiet. The man's panicked shout rang out as he plummeted to a hard smack in the water far below.

Wheeling around, Gregor saw three more agents had joined him on the balcony, ringing him with pistols drawn. Behind them, Gregor saw Vana's soldiers making their way through the balcony's doors, rushing inside the facility. No alarm rang, no calls to get ready. Soon, there wouldn't be anyone left to hear an alert if it came.

Gregor punched his wristlet, opened the transmission to Sever's band. If he was going to die, he'd do it saving his squad.

"Come get me!" Gregor yelled, loud enough for the mic to pick it up. "Or are you cowards too scared to die?"

The middle agent cocked his head, laughed, "We fail here, and we're dead already. Kill him and let's go."

Gregor faced the barrels with a wide grin, then broke right. He would die, but he would die fighting. As Gregor started to move, the soft red lights flared bright white. Other lights came up, bursting on as someone in the base realized things were wrong. Blaring alarms squawked, shattering the quiet. The flash, the sound threw the agent's shots by millimeters. They burned Gregor's back, slashed his hair and left a scar along his neck. Glazed his left elbow and left his sweater burning.

But they didn't kill the Sever monster, and that was a mistake.

Gregor reached the agent to his right, picking her up in a crushing hug and whirling, using the agent to catch the next few pistol shots as Gregor kept up his back-pedal, falling back into the balcony's corner. The shots stopped as the agents realized they were peppering their friend.

"Drop her!" Shouted the same one that'd spoken before.

Gregor ignored him, kept backing up until he felt the railing at his back. His right hand moved, finding what it sought along the agent's belt.

The agent repeated his order. Gregor's hostage groaned, barely alive. Barely would be enough.

"Neither of us die today," Gregor said. "If we are lucky."

Holding the agent tight, Gregor kicked them back, up and over the railing. Together, they plunged through the starlight, down towards the roiling waves.

TWENTY-NINE

Recovery Rumble

Eponi hated waking up. Sleep always felt so much better than the event ending it. Today, no, tonight wasn't an exception, a gradual de-hazing of her murky eyes into a room she didn't recognize, with dim monitors, a plugged in IV, and a mushy cot that left her back questioning, as it often did, Eponi's life choices.

Eponi pieced together the ride back to the Salinity facility, followed by anesthesia and an operation Eponi didn't remember that put her left forearm in a thick cast. The thing itched in the blue-gray light. The sensation prompted her body to finish waking up, hitting a biological floor reminding her that Eponi had been absorbing fluids for hours without having a chance to use the bathroom. A reach confirmed a catheter, confirmed her body also still had bruises all over and the aches that came with them.

To her right, Eponi saw the call button for the facility's nurse. Or nurses? Eponi couldn't recall how big the medical wing happened to be, and, frankly, she didn't care. After getting carried by Gregor, sitting in a skiff, and then getting plunked into this bed for most of the day, Eponi wanted to move. Wanted to feel, just for a moment or three, what it felt like to operate under her own power.

She removed the catheter—pull a stint or two in a DefenseCorp med bay and you figure out how to get yourself some freedom—swept her legs off to the right side, dodging the IV pole and, with a groaning rise, Eponi achieved the same thing she'd managed at one year of life: standing on her own two feet.

Dizziness punched in. The monitor to her left, a helpful screen laying out all that health data Eponi would rather not know about herself, beeped an alert. The sound died when Eponi tugged off the monitors. She waited for the nurse to come bounding in, asking Eponi what the hell she was doing. Instead, wrapping her gown around her, Eponi counted down ten seconds before she took another step, and then another, making it all the way to the room's door without any interruption.

"Slackers," Eponi muttered, pulling the IV pole along with her.

The liquid miracles, as Eponi liked to call IVs, were the one thing Eponi would keep attached as long as she could. The water, and any drugs included, tended to keep her feeling better than the alternative. Worth riding out, even if the pole made walking an awkward dance.

The doorway from the room didn't lock from the inside, so Eponi rose to tap her wristlet against the scanner, only to remember the damn computer now had a cast running over it. Useless. Back on the *Nautilus*, they'd give crew members with busted wristlets or casts like Eponi's a special card to carry for door opening, food ordering, etc. Here, though, she could only hope a finger press would work.

To leave a patient's room? It did.

Salinity's medical wing took up four rooms around a

nursing station decked out with monitoring consoles. Eponi wasn't sure what Salinity did that put its employees in enough risk to require the hospital space, but the distance from Kaiyo might mandate the equipment. Either way, the small ward glistened in soft white, darkened for nighttime. Monitor beeps and the occasional device buzzing through its processes provided standard ambience.

Eponi went towards that nurse station first, its screen armada shielding the desk and its occupant from view. Ideally, the nurse could help get Eponi's IV out and clear her for a return to the *Prisa*, or at least an update on when she might get free. Piloting a ship with a cast on wouldn't be the easiest, but lying in this room all day while Sever went out looking for a fight wouldn't play either.

Vana's agents had done this to her, and Eponi wanted some vengeance.

Those bloody thoughts flew away when Eponi saw the nurse, or what had become of her. Slumped over the desk, with a precise cut to her neck, the nurse had cared for her last patient. Eponi took in the sight for a half-second, cataloging all the potential reasons—crazed patient? Accident? —and settled for getting the hell outta the medical ward as soon as possible.

Wheeling around, Eponi caught the black-clad form rushing towards her, the man's knife the only thing catching any light. Eponi swung her IV pole, the unwieldy thing crashing into the agent and tripping up his legs. The man fell past her, a sting shooting down Eponi's arm as the tube tore free. One more ache to add to all the others.

Facing a choice, Eponi went for combat. She could've broke and ran, trying to get free from the wing and out into the broader base, but one black-clad agent meant there had to be more—after all, who would choose the medical wing as a primary target for a solo assault?—and leaving the ward unarmed and panicking to run into the agent's friends would, uh, not go well.

Eponi kicked, striking the agent once, twice as he tried to untangle himself from the pole. The blows were good ones, but the agent hadn't come on this mission protected by paper. He grunted, continued moving, and rose up, backing away as Eponi worked her feet again.

A losing strategy, that one. If Eponi let the agent get stable, he'd be free to knife her just like the nurse. If she fought him, Eponi would be going in one-handed and beat up. Also not good.

So she ran.

Back to her own room.

Three steps in, a finger press on the panel shutting the door behind her. A second slap killed the lights. Already short, Eponi crouched, took a breath, and prayed the agent took her for a Salinity worker in a panic.

She heard the IV pole move, the agent laughing softly to himself as he regained his footing. The laugh keyed Eponi back to the earlier encounters in Kaiyo. Did this agent need a dose, or had he already found one?

Did it even matter right now?

Again, Eponi eyed the cast on her left arm, covering her wristlet. Not that there were good times to break an arm, but there were definitely *better* times than this very moment.

Steps came closer, trembling the floor beneath the room's door and sending vibrations running through Eponi's feet. The agent could've been quieter: the sloppy move meant he didn't take Eponi seriously, meant Eponi had at least one drop on the man.

Dumb. Everyone should expect to find a Sever in the med ward. They were always getting hurt.

Eponi couldn't lock her room, and the agent didn't

bother to be circumspect. He slapped the panel loud enough for Eponi to hear, and the door slid away, showing the agent looking straight ahead, knife ready to put an end to the poor patient that'd gone for a walk at the wrong time.

Instead, Eponi gave the agent a kidney shot, followed by Eponi standing quick and butting her head into the agent's chin. She heard the man's teeth crunch, ignored the added instrument the head butt added to her own pain symphony, and went for the agent's knife arm. The agent's training had enough life left to attempt a half-hearted stab, one that Eponi snagged in her gown as she pulled the stabbing arm by her.

Eponi planted a foot, helped the agent's stabbing momentum carrying him on by. The trip sent the agent falling to the floor. He hit, shifting to a roll that caught on the room's doorway. Moving his hands beneath his chest to push himself up, Eponi reverted to her kicks again.

This time, she went for the skull.

This time, the agent collapsed, lights out.

"Gregor would be impressed," Eponi muttered as she stripped the agent for parts.

The hospital gown didn't provide a place for a knife, but Sai or Gregor had been nice enough to bring some clothes. Eponi, slowly, carefully, pulled the outfit on. Using the ties from the gown, Eponi rigged up a workable thigh holster for the knife, and kept the agent's pistol in her hands.

Leaving the room, Eponi's triumphant flush died an ugly death. One agent had stalked the med ward, likely to make sure no resistance could emerge from the sick and wounded. Odds seemed slim that one agent represented the entire raid, an attack planned only to off Eponi, or maybe the nurse. If Vana's agents were hitting the facility, and no alarm had triggered, then things might be . . . grim.

Eponi's first move brought her back to the nursing desk, seeking some way to trigger an alarm. The workstation tied itself to a Salinity ID, presenting Eponi with nothing more than a useless, albeit friendly-looking, lock screen. The nurse's wristlet had died with her, and no big red button offered itself as a way to save the day.

If only more organizations took to possible assault and invasion as seriously as DefenseCorp, which littered its vessels with ways to trigger a ship-wide response.

A quick sweep of the med ward confirmed to Eponi that she was the only patient still there: three empty beds and quiet rooms meant she could leave the nurse as the sole victim. Eponi paused outside her room and the agent's unconscious body, glanced back towards the nurse. She held the pistol, and in open combat, Eponi wouldn't hesitate to fire a killing bolt.

But Aurora had castigated Rovo for killing Renard, ruining a potential information source. This one might help Sever understand what happened here, and then Salinity could take out its own vengeance on the man.

Of course, all that depended on the night going Eponi's way.

She crept into the hallway, a wrap-around corridor looping the circular Salinity structure. Every so often, the hallway would open into other areas, with central spokes splitting the base into four quadrants. The docking bays sat opposite where Eponi stood now, with the cafeteria and various meeting rooms between them.

Noises greeted Eponi as she stalked from the med ward, the constant patter as boots hit metal, accented by the occasional muffled shout or the thud as another body hit the ground. The agents had come in force, then.

Left would take Eponi to the cafeteria, and a few bangs out that way seemed to indicate a fight in the offing. Even on her best days, Eponi would've been loath to dash towards an engagement without power armor, and now she only had one arm and a body that belonged in bed.

Right took her towards the facility's productivity core, where offices, conference rooms, and the labs designed to help Salinity improve its water quality did their work. If Eponi had it right, all these spaces swarmed beneath the other three quadrants and descended all the way down to the ocean floor. Not that Eponi would be getting in another capsule to confirm.

It'd be a long time before she went into one of those again.

Sneaking quick glances behind her, Eponi dashed as quick as she dared along the blue-lit corridor. To her right, walls gave way to windows and the dull furniture beyond them, waiting for morning meetings that definitely wouldn't be happening.

"Kill me then," came a hoarse voice from around the corridor ahead, covering up cowardice with momentary courage. "You're not getting past this door."

"We don't have to kill you," came the reply, sounding as slimey as anything Eponi had ever heard. "We can, though, make you wish we had."

Eponi couldn't help an eye roll at the line. She'd hoped for better from the agents, because the damn shadows were still DefenseCorp, and you didn't deserve to work for the galaxy's bouncer if you couldn't come up with a better threat.

Slowing her walk, Eponi let her eyes lead around the bend, showing two agents holding a man in what looked to be a maintenance uniform up against the wall. Behind him, a locked door looked to lead further into the facility's guts.

"Then get to it," the man replied. "Most of our people are down there, sleeping, and if you think—"

The agent pressing him to the wall pulled a knife, stuck it up to the hostage's throat.

"We don't care about your people," the agent said. "We want Sever Squad. Where are they?"

"Never heard of 'em."

Was the man covering for Sever, or had he never actually heard the name of the power armor-sporting soldiers currently squatting in his base? Eponi wasn't sure, but she did know she wasn't going to let that knife do its job.

"Hey there," Eponi said, rounding the corner. "Looking for me?"

Both agents whirled. Eponi shot the first, the one holding the knife up to the maintenance man, and dropped the agent with the aforementioned killing blast. The second hugged the wall, bringing up his own pistol as Eponi fired a second, missing effort. The agent didn't get a chance to act on the spare moment, because the maintenance man made great use of his newfound freedom to bash the agent's head from behind.

The clobber did its work, sending the agent to the ground and paving the way for another Eponi search-n-find. Two pistols, one handed to the maintenance man, the other stripped of its power pack. Two knives added to Eponi's thigh rig.

"Thanks," the maintenance man offered, already pulling up his sleeve and tapping away on his wristlet.

"Tell me you have some alarm system."

"Best we've got is a fire," the man said. "It'll get the lights on, people moving, though."

"Then do it, and follow me."

But the man didn't take after Eponi when she started along the corridor towards the bays. When she threw a frustrated, curious look back, the maintenance man had his locked door open, was about to step through.

"My friends are this way," the man said. "I'm not letting them die alone. You save yours, I'll save mine."

Brave, stupid. Eponi gave him a nod and took off as the station's lights came on, accompanied by a loud, clanging alarm. Every other time, Eponi took those sounds as obnoxious, annoying, reminders of the obvious.

This time, the noise gave her hope.

Through the Noise

Rovo's HEAD hit the low ceiling over his cot, a bunk room shared with Gregor on the *Prisa*. The noise prompting the sudden sit-up, alarms ringing throughout the ship, had Rovo rolling out and into some semblance of a combat-ready uniform. The *Prisa* wasn't a luxury cruiser, and its tight quarters offered built-in lockers for every Sever member, two stacked cots, and not much space between them. Rovo snagged a shirt, some actual pants, boots, and, resting in the locker's rear recess, a rifle.

As he pulled on the clothes, his bleary mind tried to figure which alarm sounded now. Every one had a different pitch and cadence, from a fire to an intruder to the ship's shields getting blown. The sharp, insistent pinging here fit the second definition: someone was trying to get access to the *Prisa* who didn't deserve it.

While Rovo pulled on the clothes, arms and legs going everywhere, he realized he hadn't bumped into Gregor yet. The big man should've taken all the room in the place—it's why Rovo always had to wait to come or go till Gregor had himself sorted—but nobody pushed against Rovo, nobody grumbled that the rookie moved too slow.

Gregor's cot was empty.

Either the hammer man had heard the alarm and responded without waking Rovo up, which seemed unlikely, or he'd left earlier. Either way, a question Rovo couldn't answer and couldn't waste more time considering.

Sai bumped past Rovo as the rookie left his quarters, the swordsman looking far more poised with a laser-sucking vest on, katana at the ready in one hand and a pistol in the other.

"Take the cockpit," Sai said, heading towards the curling steps leading to the *Prisa*'s middle. "Aurora's already at the ramp. I'll back her up."

"Where's Gregor?"

"He's your bunkmate, isn't he?" Sai replied without stopping.

Rovo followed orders, stumbling down the curling stairs after Sai and veering left from the *Prisa*'s center towards the cockpit. The *Prisa*'s two seat rows were empty, the pilot's chair looking lonely without Eponi sitting in it. Rovo chose the co-pilot's slot, sliding in and tapping the consoles awake while his eyes ventured out through the glass to the chaos beyond.

The trigger touching off the alarms didn't take much to spot: Aurora danced a laser-fire ballet with an agent band, all darting between the *Prisa*'s struts to find cover and deliver death. Two smoking, black-clad bodies indicated the current score went in Aurora's favor, but the agents seemed to be spreading out. If enough broke behind Aurora, she wouldn't have cover, wouldn't have a chance.

Rovo's hand went to his rifle, and for a second, he thought he'd have time to get back to the *Prisa*'s center, rush out and cancel the ambush before it started.

He didn't have to.

Sai bounded into the fight with mild fury. An entrance slowed by the man's scrapes and beatings over the last few days, but Sai still delivered shots that counted. One caught an agent looking towards Aurora, frying the man's chest and sending him to the floor. A second grazed a wall, pushing Sai's target to her strut's other side, right where Aurora's rifle made quick work.

The other agents, seeing the odds flip, broke and ran towards the small bay's only exit. Firing en route, their pistols had Aurora and Sai keeping low, with Aurora using a strut and Sai slipping behind the boarding ramp to stay alive. Rovo watched, considered whether he ought to light up the *Prisa*'s main guns.

Sure, they'd tear through the facility like it was paper, shredding the building and burning up anyone from here to the ocean . . . but he'd get the agents.

"Raquel's going to be mad enough as it is," Rovo muttered, watching the trio reach the bay door.

Three flashes solved Rovo's dilemma. The agent trio dropped, the latter two still focusing their fire back towards Aurora and Sai when pistol shots crashed from the other direction. Walking in, with more than a little shake to her step, came Eponi. She held her pistol ready for more, with an impressive knife array around one thigh. The cast on her left wrist only made the look more ridiculous, and Rovo couldn't suppress a grin.

Just like Sever to turn an ambush into an opportunity to show off.

"You going to kill those alarms, or do you want me to go deaf?" Aurora's voice came in hot over the *Prisa*'s comm.

"On it, sorry." Rovo did as ordered, tapping away the squawks on the console.

Except the noises didn't all stop. The main alarms died, but an insistent beeping continued from the speaker right near Rovo, the one meant for cockpit alerts. Swiping through the various programs on the console, Rovo found the cause: a message, coming in with high priority from Kaiyo.

Renard's old ship was lifting off, and Salinity needed to know what to do. They had fighters ready to scramble, to blow the craft apart.

"Hey," Rovo said, opening the comm band as Aurora and Sai helped get Eponi into the craft. The swordsman and Aurora looked like they were going back into the base to help fight off the agents, and Rovo couldn't let that happen. "Vana's making her break."

Salinity's employees on the base would be in trouble, but Raquel's security forces were sending reinforcements. It'd take 'em a while to get out to the facility, but choices had to be made. Aurora didn't argue with the assessment when Rovo finished laying out what he'd seen.

"Vana makes it away with Kaia, and it doesn't matter what we do here," Aurora said. "She could come back with more, in suits, and no Salinity security guard would stand a chance. Eponi, get us in the air."

"What about Gregor?" Sai asked.

"He called the first alert," Aurora replied. "Woke me up." The captain frowned, glanced at her wristlet inside the crowded cockpit. "He's either dead or hiding, but his location shows he's below us."

Eponi squeezed by Rovo, took her spot in the pilot's chair while Aurora and Sai tried to get a better bead on where Gregor had gone.

"You okay to fly?" Rovo asked.

"Just because I have a broken arm, I'm only a few hours outside of surgery, and I've just survived a thrashing," Eponi said, cocking an eyebrow, "doesn't mean I can't fly."

"Okay then."

With Eponi's request, the Salinity facility responded with its automated operation, opening the bay and letting the cool night blow in. Starlight replaced overhead lamps, masking the dead or wounded agents in a silver glow. Rovo didn't spare much time for the view, though, as the console demanded his attention.

"She's angling for orbit," Rovo said. "We don't have much time."

And yet, as Eponi brought the *Prisa* up and out, Aurora told the pilot to swing the craft down and around. They'd found Gregor's location, and the man appeared to be near the ocean. If Gregor had splashed down, they couldn't leave him swimming.

A younger Rovo might've protested. Suggested that any time not spent blitzing after Kaia and Raquel—assuming the two hostages were with Vana—was a step in the wrong direction. But every time he veered away from Aurora's squad-first principles, things seemed to go wrong.

Besides, now they had another alternative.

"Sai, what about the EMP's you planted?" Rovo asked.

"They're still in signal range," Sai replied, sitting behind Rovo as Eponi swooped the ship out and around the facility. The entire base had its bright lights on, with plenty flashing red as the alarms continued. Shapes moved within, though Rovo couldn't tell if they were agents or Salinity personnel. "If Vana was still on the ground, I'd blow 'em. But now?"

Rovo could follow that logic well enough: disable the ship in mid-flight, and Vana plus the hostages would nose-dive into the cold waters. A bad end to a bad move.

"So then what?" Rovo said. "What's even the point of planting the bombs if we can't use them?"

"Orbit," Aurora replied. "They'll kill the engines in space. Life support too, but if we're following, there'll be enough oxygen to last till we rescue them."

"So long as they don't get beyond signal range," Sai added. "Which, we might be in trouble."

"There's our guy," Eponi interrupted, pointed with her cast arm towards the windshield. She'd been flying single-handed, her right hand wrapped around the flight stick while the left used its free fingers to tap anything needed.

Rovo hadn't quite understood what it meant to join a squad like Sever back when he'd signed the employment agreement. Special missions, the brief had said. Danger-ous, but highly compensated. Professional group, advanced skills required.

Apparently advanced skills meant being able to fly with a single arm.

"Rovo, Sai," Aurora said, "Gregor's not responding. Need you two to handle pick-up."

Rovo swapped spots with the captain, following Sai towards the *Prisa*'s aft. As they went, Rovo heard Aurora's voice opening up a transmission with Salinity, telling them to scramble their fighters. To follow Vana, not to fire.

And, if they could, send a rescue shuttle too.

Whether that shuttle would be saving hostages or picking up bodies remained to be seen.

Eponi opened the *Prisa*'s boarding ramp as she swiveled the ship into position. Rovo took his first look at Gregor, hanging limp with his arms wrapped around an equally unconscious agent. They hung a few meters over the roiling waves, sea spray flying up as the *Prisa*'s jets swirled the water.

"How?" Rovo asked, as the two bodies appeared to float in the dark.

"Grapple," Sai said, heading down the ramp. "Look for the line."

Rovo saw it as he followed Sai, both taking their steps carefully. The dark line shot up to the facility's narrowing base, gouging into a side wall not all that far above. A great throw to make while falling, though that didn't explain why neither Gregor nor the agent seemed to be conscious.

Together, talking it through with Eponi the entire way, they eased the ramp's end close enough for Rovo and Sai to grab the twin danglers and pull them on and up. Setting both bodies down, Rovo ran some checks. Pulses came back positive for both, though the agent looked like she had some serious laser wounds.

Getting tossed on the *Prisa*'s hard floor seemed to shock Gregor into a slow waking, his eyes fluttering open, giving Rovo a questioning stare.

"You're home, buddy," Rovo said. "Welcome back to the party."

"What party?"

"The best kind," the rookie replied as the *Prisa* lurched up and away, speeding towards the stars. "Where we get to save some good people and bash some bad ones."

"Those are good parties," Gregor nodded, then winced. His hand went up to his head, where Rovo saw a bruise beginning to form. "I have learned, when stopping a fall with a grapple, watch out for your friend's head. The stop hit us both."

"Well, you won that fight," Rovo nodded to the agent. "She's in rough shape."

Gregor sat up, Rovo helping him along, "What about the others? The agents came in force."

"We took some out. Now we're running."

"Running? Us?"

"Vana's breaking for it, Gregor," Rovo said. "We can't let her get away."

"Then after, we go back and finish the job."

Rovo expected a grin, the cocky sort of confidence he'd come to see in Gregor, Eponi, and the others. Gregor, though, held serious. This wasn't a jest. The agents had wronged him, and the hammer man would see them held to account.

Rovo felt no pity for the poor bastards.

THIRTY-ONE

Priority Target

BY THE TIME you made it to a DefenseCorp command, you'd seen the hard decisions made a hundred times or more. The choices to abandon units, which ones to re-arm, when to retreat or advance, and who to sacrifice in the charge to victory. When Aurora put on Sever's mantel, the precedents and their moral burdens had been made well clear.

Didn't do anything to make the choices easier.

After Eponi mopped up the agents running from the *Prisa*'s bay and Vana made her break for orbit, Aurora had to decide between grabbing power armor and laying waste to the remaining agents assaulting Salinity's civilian work-force, or breaking away and chasing after Vana and her presumed two hostages.

The moment or the mission.

That Vana already had some of Kaia's blood colored the choice further. If her scientists—Anaskya, who should've been spaced after Dynas—figured out how to replicate its special properties, then it wouldn't matter whether Vana made it away with the child at all.

Aurora had planned to hunt the agent once they'd saved Kaia. With Deepak's support, Sever would've tracked Vana to the galaxy's farthest points until they'd captured or killed her and her plans. The real decision here weighed those Salinity lives against taking Vana now, before she could cause further destruction.

Put that way, Aurora didn't hesitate. Vana was the target, and on her order, Eponi gave chase.

"We've launched our two fastest fighters," Deepak said, his face blurry on Aurora's wristlet. "It looks like Salinity has some of their own going with you?"

"A lot of people want Vana dead," Aurora replied. "Can you find the transport? She had a lot of agents here. It has to be in system."

"Not for long." Deepak shook his head. "We picked it up when we arrived, and apparently the *Nautilus* scared it away."

"Did you track it?"

"It vanished behind one of this planet's moons. I have people plotting possible exit vectors."

"Good," Aurora said. "Let me know when your fighters get close enough to help."

She cut the transmission, looked through the windshield. Gillane Four's dark sky showed the first transitions to dawn, with starlight shining bright as the *Prisa* screamed towards space. Sai and Rovo had moved to the ship's twin turrets, ready in case Vana decided to put up a fight.

"Think she has them with her?" Eponi asked, keeping the *Prisa* steady with a single hand. Vana wasn't taking on any tricky maneuvers, just angling straight away from the system. Easy enough for a compromised pilot to track. "Raquel and Kaia?"

"Yes," Aurora said. "Without them, Vana has no chips to bargain with. We'd blow her up without thinking twice."

"Naturally. That rescue shuttle's coming up slow behind us, but if Sai's grenades do their work, it should be ready to dock."

"No," Aurora replied. "The shuttle's only there if something goes wrong. When Vana's safely out of the atmosphere, Sai's detonating the grenades. Then *we* dock. Take control. I'm not letting anyone else watch Vana except us."

Except herself. After Rovo's unfortunate choice, Aurora wouldn't be letting anyone else keep guard over Vana. Maybe Gregor, though he might kill the agent out of spite.

Aurora wouldn't mind that much.

Normally, hitting weightlessness and feeling her body go through the familiar lurches as its balance, direction, and general sense of reality twisted would be lost in repeated mission detail reviews, arms checks, and ribbing directed towards whichever squaddie most deserved it. Now, though, Aurora took in the shift and embraced it, using the signal to confirm Vana's craft had also passed beyond Gillane Four's immediate gravity.

In other words, disabling the damn thing now wouldn't cause a quick plunge to the ocean's depths.

Eponi had the *Prisa* closing, with Salinity's fighter quartet hanging further back with the rescue shuttle. Like the security guards on the surface, Aurora figured Salinity's pilots hadn't fought in years. Few things posed more risk than inexperienced, armed people in a fight, so Aurora had given them the reserve role and the pilots, showing more sense than bravado, accepted the assignment.

"How long till we hit attack range?" Aurora asked, watching the distant sparkle the *Prisa*'s windshield marked as Vana's ship.

"Three minutes," Eponi said. "She's starting to speed up."

"Can we match it?"

"More than. The people we took this ship from ran high risk cargo along high risk routes. You wanna buzz Vana, let her kiss our jets, we can do it."

"I'll keep that in mind. For now, get within range and stay there."

While Eponi saw to the engines, Aurora used the copilot's console to reason with the enemy. She sent out a hail, beaming a frequency and an identifier straight across the vacuum to Vana's ship. If the agent accepted, the pass-back would link the band between the two ships. Aurora would see Vana's face, Vana would see Aurora's, and together they could discuss who lived and who died.

Vana didn't keep Aurora waiting. Sever's captain didn't finish a full swallow of the Rovo-prepped coffee, quick and dirty stuff meant for a sharp jab to the psyche, before Vana's straight-laced face popped in.

The agent looked tired, older than Aurora remembered, even from the spike's fight the day before. As if what must have been a mad scramble to take the skiff, return to Kaiyo and get things ready for the departure had taken another decade or two off the agent's life. Behind Vana, the small visible cockpit ended with a closed door.

"All alone?" Aurora asked.

"People are so hard to trust these days," Vana replied. "My scanners are telling me you're getting close. Do you plan on shooting me down?"

"I'd rather take you alive," Aurora said. "That, of course, is up to you. I'll toast your ashes just fine."

"And Kaia and Raquel's? Will you be happy to send them on their final, everlasting flight?"

"Don't be poetic. The only way you live is by shutting down your engines and surrendering. You can't get away."

Vana shrugged, "And yet, I must try. To do anything else is to betray everything I've worked for."

"You mean everything Renard's worked for. You just came at the end," Aurora said, using her hands to tap out a quick go command to Sai. Time to set off those grenades and stop Vana dead. "I'd start working on your apologies, Vana. If you're lucky, Salinity will listen to them before they stick you in a cell to rot."

If Aurora admired anything about the agent—a big if—then it would be Vana's ability to stay endlessly composed. At Renard's name, at the insinuation that Vana, like a co-opting parasite, had cut in and cut off the true drive for the suits, the virus, Vana pulled up a glare like none Aurora had ever seen. The agent's lips shook back into a snarl, teeth showed, and Vana's eyes narrowed further than slits, like knives meant to slash Aurora's insides.

Before any curses, denials, or worse left Vana's lips, the image died.

"Done," Sai's voice came through the *Prisa*. "She's dead."

Aurora looked over at Eponi, "Confirmed?"

"Her velocity's not increasing, and the ship's entered a slow tumble. Think our man's still got it."

"Nice work, Sai. Get ready for a boarding party," Aurora said. "Let's bring our friends home."

Following the order, Aurora let Deepak and the Salinity force know the situation. They'd hang back, ready to assist with any clean-up. Meanwhile, everyone that had it, put on the power armor. Save Eponi, who's job kept her in the cockpit. The foursome cramped into the *Prisa*'s central chamber minutes later, with Eponi's regular updates pacing their moves.

The agent providing Gregor's grappling escape, barely alive, had been stun-cuffed to a cot.

"First up, get in position," Eponi called, voice coming through the squad band. "I'm going to hit the main hatch first, so if Vana's got something planned, you'll get all of it."

"Thank you," Gregor said.

From anyone else, Aurora would've treated the words as sarcasm. From Gregor, you never really knew.

Gregor would go to work, cracking through the hatch and breaking the vacuum seal on Vana's ship with enough force to ensure that, if Vana tried to separate her craft from the *Prisa*, the hammer-sized hole would suck the agent into the void. Following him, Sai and Aurora would help clear out any enemy force. Rovo would come last, tasked only with finding Raquel and Kaia and getting them out.

A simple operation, one that could get complicated if Vana, as Aurora suspected, decided to put a knife to the necks of her two prisoners.

In that case, Sai and Aurora would take the shots, accept the risk. The game had been going on long enough.

The trio assembled in the line leading to the *Prisa*'s airlock: its boarding ramp door just without the ramp activated. The airlock's spot on the *Prisa* necessitated a tunnel connection, deployable with a button tap or two from the console next to the door. Gregor had his hand placed, ready to launch, when the whole trio felt the *Prisa* shift in a sharp jerk away, as if the craft had been hit.

Eponi's cursing filled their squad band, and Aurora spun around and pounded back towards the *Prisa*'s center.

"Talk, Eponi," Aurora ordered, leaning on that authority to punch through Eponi's frustration.

"She's launched them both," Eponi said. "Renard packed two lifeboats on that thing, and they're both gone now. One almost hit us."

Disable the ship, sure, but lifeboats, escape pods, whatever you wanted to call them were designed to be dumped manually. If Vana wanted to flee, she could definitely shoot herself away, but you couldn't disappear in one of those things.

In short, it didn't make any sense.

"Why?" Aurora asked the squad band.

"She's hailing us on a short wave. Must be from her wristlet," Eponi said before anyone else could offer an answer. "I'll patch it through."

"Rovo," Aurora warned, "Stay quiet."

The rookie, wisely, said nothing.

"I'm glad you picked up," Vana's voice came through thin, none of the simmering anger left in her tone. "You're running out of time."

"To pick you up?"

"I'm still here. It's not me you have to worry about."

Lines connected to dots. Possibilities spun.

"Together, or separate?" Aurora asked.

"Every little girl has to grow up sometime," Vana said. "Your choice."

Aurora closed her eyes, cut the line. The moment or the mission.

"Eponi, what're the lifeboat trajectories?"

"Umm, opposite. They'll both hit the planet. Neither are jetting up, though. They'll hit hard. Too hard."

Lifeboats could be launched manually, sure, but they were still devices. Sai's grenades would do their work. Hit a thick atmosphere like Gillane Four's at speed, things would get real ugly, real fast. If Kaia and Raquel were in those things, they would be dead in minutes.

Enough minutes, maybe, for Vana to restart her ship.

"Aurora," Rovo's voice, ironclad. "You can't. We have to try to save them."

The moment, then.

Shuttle Shot

How DO you prepare for a launch through vacuum without a tether?

You check all your damn systems and make sure they're good to go. As soon as Aurora started through on the new plan, Sai had his power armor review all its seals and refresh the oxygen supply stored in pockets throughout the suit. The things weren't exactly designed for long-term outer space exposure, but they could keep a soldier alive long enough for a rescue, or to perform one.

As to just what Sai would do after he propelled himself across the void, he hadn't quite pieced it together. Getting to a lifeboat, and a likely dead one at that, wouldn't do much except add another body to the casualty list. Even so, if Sai arrived and found, say, Kaia clinging inside the lifeboat without any alternatives, he could still . . . abandon her and catch the rescue shuttle.

Sai already knew he wouldn't be able to make that choice.

Which might be why Aurora picked him in the first place.

"Almost aligned," Eponi said, voice coming in clear, focused into Sai's visor. "Get out there, killer."

"Hopefully not killing anyone this time," Sai replied.

Behind him, Gregor stepped back from the boarding ramp and sealed off the compartment. The *Prisa*'s unused cargo hatch sat before Sai, a little circle in a shiny, gray metal floor. Beyond it, the *Prisa*'s engine room hummed. Not the best design to put all that valuable equipment near the boarding ramp, the door easiest to breach in a fight.

Who was Sai to talk: DefenseCorp dumped their soldiers in drop shuttles all the time, and those things were little more than cheap metal death traps.

"Opening the hatch," Sai said, touching the tiny console mounted to the wall on his left.

The device did its job, confirming a tight seal split Sai's self from the rest of the ship. It beeped once, twice, and a third time to make sure Sai really wanted to open the cargo hatch without any cargo attached. When Sai made no effort to reverse his action, the hatch shot open and Sai saw the stars.

The stars pulled him forward.

Getting yanked by vacuum didn't feel like a human's pull. There wasn't any build-up, any sense muscles tightened. One moment, Sai stood still. The next, his body slid across the floor towards the hatch. As he went out, Sai hooked his hands on the hatch's outer edge, playing that momentum into a swing.

No gravity meant his legs splayed, relying on Sai's efforts to keep them in line as he danced with his hands on the hatch's ring. The power armor helped, the gloves and their textured grip digging into the imperfections on the hatch and letting Sai hang on. Tucking in his abs, crunching his waist, Sai brought his chest and stomach into contact with the *Prisa*'s outer hull. His knees came after, marking a soundless bump. Sai brought those knees up, still keeping a grip on the hatch.

Here came the hardest part. Do it wrong, and Sai would lose his grip and float off.

Do it right, and—

Sai refused to overthink it, rolling his ankles while releasing his hands. The power armor followed the commands Sai spoke at the same time, activated the locks on the boots as they skimmed, soles down, the *Prisa*'s hull. The sudden latching had Sai lurching back, as though a hand had caught him as he fell.

"Ready," Sai said. "You can close the hatch."

"Nice work," Aurora replied. "Eponi can hold this position for another five seconds. Get set and go."

Sai would've hit back with a cocky reply, but there wasn't time. Instead, he looked straight up and told his visor to find the target. The escape pod was too far away for a good visual, but the visor's radar pings found it easy enough. With his kinetic boost charged, the visor helped Sai lean forward, bend his knees to hit the perfect launch position.

"Here we go," Sai said, then hit the boosters and jumped free.

Sai shot off like a rocket, the frictionless launch blitzing him into a free flight. Outside of simulators, Sai hadn't ever sent himself rocketing through the stars before. No reason to, really, unless a mission had gone awry.

Or you had to save somebody.

Despite the urgency, despite the risk, once he'd launched, Sai couldn't do much except absorb the ride. Without any propulsion, he couldn't alter his trajectory. Without anything to catch or bounce off of, Sai drifted. Gillane Four's bulk glowed blue beneath him, a stunning backdrop that washed out all but the brightest stars.

Behind him, the *Prisa*'s dwindling form flickered as Eponi rerouted the ship into an all-out dive towards the other pod.

Looking straight, Sai couldn't see Vana's craft, but off to the left, a glowing pair showed evidence that Deepak's fighters streaked towards their enemy. Hopefully they'd catch the agent, blow her to dust.

"On target?" Aurora's voice pinged through Sai's visor.

"So far. Pleasant ride." Sai stopped. "Aurora, you know what to say if this doesn't work out?"

"Not having this conversation, Sai."

"But—"

"Connect with the pod. Stabilize it. The Salinity shuttle's matching your velocity," Aurora said. "Those are your orders. We'll see you on the other side."

The soft click came through: Aurora dropped the call. She'd never been one to consider unpleasant futures, particularly those involving a dead friend. Sai had that discussion time and again with the captain, trying to tell her what he wanted for his family, but she always brushed him off, always played it as an eventuality whose time hadn't yet come.

Maybe because Aurora, herself, didn't have anyone to tell. Sai didn't know if she had plans for after, what would happen to the cash in her account, to any remains that might be found.

The power armor yanked Sai back from his stargazing, drawing him to the declining oxygen meter—plenty left there—and the similarly falling distance between Sai and the target. The lifeboat hadn't lost much speed since Vana ejected the thing, but Gillane Four's gravity wouldn't be denied: the pod's orbital decay increased by the second, and the lifeboat's entry into the atmosphere would be a fiery disaster if Sai couldn't get the pod ready for the rescue shuttle.

Designed to handle pick-ups from drifting derelicts or in-atmosphere saves from isolated dangers, floating skiffs, and other relatively stable situations, rescue shuttles were the craft sent in after an engagement to snack on the bones and see what happened to survive. The Salinity shuttle, like the DefenseCorp ones, looked a lot like a cylinder covered with hatches. Each one could extend an airlock, and each fed into a central space dominated by medical equipment.

The shuttle was a big can, and had all the maneuverability to match. It couldn't form a seal with the lifeboat, couldn't catch it as the small thing fell from orbit.

Not unless Sai could manage a miracle.

He saw the lifeboat now, a smudge that'd grown to a skiff's size as Sai closed in. Mottled gray, with DefenseCorp's logo shining on the outside in a silver glitter, the lifeboat did everything Vana's—Renard's—ship didn't, showcasing itself to any potential rescuers in every method possible.

Sai flipped his band to an open broadcast and shot a call forward, "Hey there, this is your would-be friend, coming along for help. Do you read?"

Nothing came back. Not surprising. Sai's EMP grenades would've blown out the lifeboat's systems as well as the bigger ship's. He'd have to do this the quiet way.

Impact came with a catch. Technically, Sai wasn't speeding towards the lifeboat so much as his slower velocity let the lifeboat catch up to him. The difference, in meters per second, meant that Sai could still get squashed like an insect on a skiff windshield if he didn't position himself right.

Every escape pod built itself differently to match its parent ship's needs. This one looked like a wedge cut in half, with a sloping side on one end narrowing to a point. That point should've been making the entry into the atmosphere, serving to reduce drag and deflect heat away from the fatter end, where all the desperates would be hanging out. Instead, the powerless launch had the big end leading the way, where it would eventually slam into Gillane Four with all the elegance of a man landing belly-first into a pool.

Reaching to his waist, Sai pulled the grapple. Took it in his right hand. Using targeted pops from his stored oxygen packets, each one dropping his air supply by nerve-twinging segments, Sai positioned himself to get his legs out of the lifeboat's way. The big thing screamed towards him now, aiming to pass by beneath an upside-down Sai, so that Gillane Four's blue bulk loomed directly over Sai's head. The lifeboat would cut between, and Sai dropped his grapple into that space.

He had to bet the lifeboat's hull would be thick enough to take the grapple. If Sai tried to use his grips, tried to lock on with his boots, he'd only have a split second. A miss would send him bouncing into a long death into the void.

"Hope you're all having a better time than me," Sai said, beaming the message back towards the *Prisa* as he let the grapple fly.

The lifeboat went by in a flash, filling the space between Sai and the planet, the swordsman straining his neck to look. The gray metal, the shining silver logo, and a glassy sheen with what might've been a bit of skin tone. A hint of a human trapped inside. Then Gillane Four's shiny blue.

The tug hit, the grapple catching its prey and bringing Sai along for the ride. He tried to let the cable out slow, reducing the tension ever so slightly. That didn't work, the sheer speed running out the grapple's full line in a couple seconds. The grapple whipped Sai around, a force not really felt and yet absolutely sensed by the sudden increase in Gillane Four's shifting clouds below.

Sai stretched around with his right hand, reaching for and grabbing the grapple line. Pulling, Sai turned himself to face the lifeboat, riding along behind it like some space-bound huntsman with his dog. Metal bits flashed around Sai in an instant cloud, the debris kicked up by the grapple's contact. Sai watched for more, waited for the lifeboat to crumple or explode if the grapple exposed its insides to vacuum.

But, somehow, the line held, and the pod didn't crumple to crumbs.

Taking his first breath in who knew how long, Sai offered himself a slight smile and set the grapple line to reel him in. Sai caught up to the lifeboat's point in seconds, catching himself on the bulk as he slowed the grapple's draw. This close, he could see inside, could see the face staring back at him with a confused mixture of panic and hope.

Raquel. Bruised and favoring her left arm, but alive.

THIRTY-THREE

The Prize

ONE WAY TO describe a DefenseCorp career would be by cataloging the injuries suffered in and out of missions. Gregor's scars, bruises, bent bones, and a head subject to so many concussions told a story with a certain ending: the action would catch up to him, and Gregor's body would run out of room.

That day, however, did not appear to be today. Despite the knock-out blow suffered when Gregor used the agent and her grapple to save his life, despite the searing shoulder ache dulled by leftover salve Sai handed over—a lingering reminder of the swordsman's own bout with burns, Gregor had his power armor on, had his hammer leaning against the *Prisa*'s wall while he waited for Eponi's go-ahead.

After Sai's jump into darkness, the *Prisa* re-sealed itself, closing the cargo hatch and once more opening the path to the ship's engines. Gregor stood alone in the narrow hall, with Rovo back up the ship's curling stairs. Eponi and Aurora kept up running chatter, dropping info on the lifeboat's location, and whether they'd still catch Vana.

"We're closing in," Eponi said. "Gregor, ten seconds till

we try for a seal. We get one, you get that door open fast and anyone inside out. We're close enough to atmosphere that I don't wanna play dice."

A bold admission. Gregor figured Eponi would gamble anything at almost any chance. For her to emphasize the risk meant she found real danger in the rescue. Not that atmospheric skips were anything to joke about. Gillane Four had the thick air, the heavy heat layers to make a high speed entry at the wrong angle a catastrophic one, and the *Prisa*'s profile wouldn't get any favors from the escape pod's ungainly form dangling like a pointed parasite.

"I will get it done," Gregor replied.

Steadying himself with his hallway-spanning arms, hands planted flat on the walls, Gregor counted in his head till the appropriate number. Eponi gave the go on cue, and Gregor felt, heard the clicks as the *Prisa* made its rendezvous. Outside, in vacuum, an interlocking quartet found their partners on the lifeboat's doorway and made contact. Sliding together, the two ships created a seal to keep air inside.

Like Sai, Gregor swiped at the cargo hatch's console, prompting the dividing doors to slide shut on Gregor's either side. Not exactly the normal docking procedure, but Gregor wouldn't chance anything. Vana's agents could be in the lifeboat, could be planning a surprise assault. Now, all that would get them is a quick trap inside.

And when Eponi jettisoned the escape pod, she could force open the hatch and ditch the agents too.

"Opening hatch," Gregor said. "Stand by."

"You have your hammer?" Aurora asked.

"Always."

Gregor held the weapon in his right hand while his left made another swipe at the console. The *Prisa*'s hatch complied with orders, spiraling itself open beneath

Gregor's feet. A more cautious person might have waited off the hatch, stood on the narrow band the *Prisa* reserved inside the two sealing doors. Gregor preferred to drop in, to sink right through any ambush before they had a chance to prepare.

Zero gravity wouldn't give that kind of boost by itself, so after swiping, Gregor's left hand went to the hallway's ceiling and pushed. The force should've sent Gregor floating into the escape pod. Instead, Gregor went down a centimeter or two before he hit hard metal.

The lifeboat's hatch didn't open.

"It's still closed," Gregor said. "You sent the signal?"

"I don't need to," Eponi countered. "It's automatic."

When the *Prisa*'s hatch opened, the ship should've triggered the same response from the escape pod. Two possibilities, then. Either the agents inside weren't ready for an ambush and had locked the escape pod's door, or the little craft had no power to act on Eponi's request.

Both options offered the same solution.

"I'm breaking in." Gregor stepped off to his right, putting his back to the *Prisa*'s engine room. "This might make a noise."

"Be quick about it," Eponi said. "It's getting hot up here, and I'm not going to sacrifice us all for whatever's in that pod."

"You won't have to."

Gregor swung, twisting the hammer's haft as he moved to send rippling kinetic energy, just like the power armor, to the hammer's head. When the weapon struck, all that extra force overwhelmed a poor lifeboat hatch designed for accessibility, not defense. The curved, tooth-like plates making up the hatch resisted for a fractional moment before bending, breaking inward.

Straddling the hatch, Gregor looked inside the lifeboat

and waited for his visor to find any potential threats. About the size of the *Prisa*'s cockpit, the pod's interior took its light from Gillane Four's reflection, a silvery blue smattering through the small windows. Crash couches lined the lifeboat's sides, extending up almost to the pod's very end where Gregor stood. Packed in on the hull's other side from the engines would be emergency aid kits, crash flares, the sort of things one might need if they didn't, say, burn up in the atmosphere.

The visor found nothing dangerous. Gregor's eyes didn't pick out any threats the old fashioned way either. No sounds came from the dead craft.

"Looks empty," Gregor said. "A decoy?"

"Confirm it," Aurora replied.

"That means going in. We have time?"

"You have five seconds," Eponi said. "After that, we're losing Vana."

The mental count started in Gregor's head as he brought his legs together and pushed off the ceiling again. He went in, straight through the hatch and into the lifeboat. Kept up his momentum to the lifeboat's point, fully intending to bounce off the plating there and rocket back into the *Prisa* without an enemy in sight.

The visor caught the flinch, not Gregor. Splashed out a questionable silhouette in bright blue as Gregor re-oriented.

A very small silhouette.

"She's here," Gregor said, getting a better look. "Kaia."

"We're about to not be here," Eponi replied. "Get her off that pod."

Kaia hunched in the pod's corner, crouching low and looking at Gregor with worried eyes. Darkness covered her, making her almost invisible except for the damn visor and its awesome powers.

"Kaia, grab the hammer," Gregor spoke as he kicked off the lifeboat's bottom plate. "Come now, quickly!"

Gregor had no way to know if the girl would respond to a command coming from a person, all suited up in heavy armor, that'd just bashed into her cramped, doomed home. The last time he'd rescued Kaia, she'd been isolated on a rooftop, cut off from Rovo and about to get taken, or killed, by the same people that'd sent her on this one-way trip to Hell. That time, Kaia didn't get a choice.

This time, the girl made the right move.

She jumped as Gregor pushed himself up, launching towards the hatch with his feet. Kaia didn't so much catch the hammer as the big weapon caught her. Gregor let the hammer head drop as he approached the hatch, with Kaia holding on. The thinner profile let Gregor shoot through first, with the man bringing up his knees as he exited to clear some room for Kaia.

"Jump off now," Gregor told the girl as he pulled her up through the hatch, feet resting on the hammer head like some sort of princess. "Get near that door."

Again, Kaia obeyed orders without a question, yet her eyes, the rigid way she let the hammer go, showed she might not be quite as confident as she appeared. Right now, though, Gregor didn't have time to get comfortable.

"Seal the hatch and go," Gregor said, routing the words through the squad band. "Kaia's on and safe."

"Nice work," Aurora said, about the highest praise you could expect from her.

Eponi didn't speak, but acted. The cargo hatch, with legs and other limbs clear, shut beneath Gregor. A thunk followed as the lifeboat disconnected, ready to continue its disintegration journey. The *Prisa* swung again, something Gregor felt as the walls, the floor around him turned as Eponi re-settled the ship on a course back out towards Vana.

"Gregor?"

The voice came so meek, so quiet that Gregor didn't catch it at first, as the sealing doors keeping Gregor and Kaia locked near the cargo hatch retracted with a *whoosh*.

"Is that you?" Kaia asked again, repeating Gregor's name.

She stood central in the hallway, hands at her side, face screwed up with the nervous question. Someone had tied Kaia's hair together, and while the smooth athletic clothes the girl wore didn't seem an exact fit, they were clean. Not a scratch marred her face.

"You got it, kid," Gregor said.

"No," Rovo announced, rushing down the steps. "We got you, Kaia. We got you."

"Rovo!" Kaia spun at the rookie's words, sparking into that special laughter that's equal parts joy and relief.

Gregor watched the reunion for a long moment, maybe daring a grin of his own, before Aurora blew new orders in. Eponi had power pouring into the engines, and the weapons. They were going to catch Vana, and Sever had to be ready to fire.

"Get her somewhere safe," Gregor said to Rovo as he went by.

The rookie paused ruffling Kaia's hair, put a hand on Gregor's shoulder, "Thank you."

"It's not over yet." Gregor's grin widened. "But it's getting closer."

Kaia started asking what was getting closer, and Gregor took the cue to continue on up the stairs.

"Rovo's on guest duty," Aurora continued as Gregor

pounded back into the *Prisa*'s center. "You get the starboard turret. I'm on the other."

The short jog to the port turret took longer because Gregor had to ditch away his power armor. Gunnery stations on a small ship like the *Prisa* weren't designed to house a bulky frame, but they could—barely—fit Gregor in nothing more than his skinsuit, the hyper-thin clothes designed to make power armor bearable.

Settling in, Gregor gripped the turret's targeting controls with both hands. The console activated at his touch, sprang up with potential options to blow into space dust. Gregor checked the screen, expecting a big blob with Vana's name all over it.

Instead, he caught a flickering pixel burst. As though the console had a malfunction.

"My targeting is broken," Gregor said, carrying the message now through the *Prisa*'s internal comms. "There's nothing to shoot at?"

"Use visuals," Aurora replied. "Renard didn't put many weapons on his ship, but it's hard to find."

"A true agent."

"An ass. Just like Vana," Aurora said. "Eponi, are we in range? And where are Deepak's fighters?"

"Just to our left," Eponi replied. "But there are bigger problems. I think Vana has the ship running again."

"So?" Gregor said, continuing to fiddle with the console. He could, of course, use the windows to aim visually, but at the distances a space battle used, that'd be like shooting at a squirrel through a thick forest. "We can catch her?"

"It's not her I'm worried about," Eponi finished off with a curse. "She has back-up. The transport never left the system, and it's closing fast."

Gregor didn't know how a big ship like the transport could've stayed hidden, but if the craft and its big guns came too close, the *Prisa* and Deepak's fighters would be in trouble. Gregor didn't worry about himself, but his wasn't the most important life on the ship. Everyone in Sever signed their own death warrants when they enlisted. The agent, locked away in Gregor's own quarters, had made her own choices to get here.

But if the transport destroyed the *Prisa*, then Kaia would die through no fault of her own.

Gregor could not, would not let that happen.

That choice, though, wasn't his to make.

One Or All

BEFORE EVERY RACE, Eponi took her kart out for practice laps. tested the machine's systems against the world's conditions, from freezing temperatures to blowing winds to geysers spitting blue fire. She'd build out a move set, map it to where on the course Eponi could use each one, and on race day, she'd deploy the tricks to climb the positions till she hit the finish line.

Chasing down Vana in the rocketing *Prisa*, with Gillane Four's primary moon showing purple against black space, Eponi punched up the engines and the ship's weapons. Vana's craft put more into stealth than defense, and Eponi already knew Vana's location. The best, easiest move? Overpower the enemy, disabling them with laserfire or blowing them up with the same.

When the agent transport pulled around the moon, the course changed. Eponi didn't have practice laps for this situation. She'd never flown the *Prisa* into combat against a ship like the transport, large and covered with heavy guns meant for supporting a land invasion. Eponi hadn't, really, flown in space combat against large ships at all.

DefenseCorp kept that fun for its cruisers.

"*Prisa*, we're not equipped to go up against that thing," said the lead fighter forming up next to Sever's ship. The two craft, scrambled by Deepak to assist in taking out Vana's ship, were fast things, designed to harass and obliterate smaller, slower ships. "Tell me you have a better idea?"

Eponi reran the *Prisa*'s weaponry through her mind. Three main cannons, two turrets on either side and a main, fixed gun center. The ship had missile options, but the launchers had been empty when Sever stole the ship on Wexer, and nobody wanted to pay cash to reload the things. Even so, the *Prisa*'s cannons had an edge over the DefenseCorp fighters, and Eponi could muster better shielding.

"Split it," Eponi said. "You two focus on Vana's ship. We'll tease the transport and draw its fire, see if we can't pull the two apart until you deliver."

"Then it's a kill command?"

"It is," Aurora broke into the line, chiming in from her turret. "We've secured the hostages. As much as I'd like Vana alive, that doesn't seem like the game we're playing today."

"Understood. Fly safe." Deepak's man cut the comm, letting Eponi focus on the mess outside.

Gillane Four's moon provided an ominous backdrop. It blotted out the stars, but not the transport's bright running lights. The big ship stretched half a kilometer across and looked like a giant wing. With enough room to hold more than a thousand soldiers and deliver them safely to an active combat zone, the transport had armor and weapons to spare. The only chance the *Prisa* had to do damage would come from removing the transport's teeth.

Turrets, for all their utility in presenting flexible aiming options, stuck out from ships at obvious angles. The magnetic shields designed to diffuse incoming laser energy had to stretch to cover the protruding turret barrels, presenting an ever-so-slightly thinner protection than elsewhere. Eponi swiped on her console, telling the *Prisa* to ditch its tracking of Vana's ship and turn its systems to the transport.

Outside the front, a broad glass pane giving Eponi the view of her target, a blue halo formed around the transport's long shape. The halo filled in the gaps between the lights, and within, green circles formed as the *Prisa* followed Eponi's command and found those turrets. Eponi swallowed as one square after another popped up.

Sever almost never used one of these in their Defense-Corp missions, given they were often sent on covert actions behind enemy lines or on tasks so targeted as to not need a full invasion. Having the luxury of so many lasers coming down, covering you and roasting the opposition, must be nice.

"Two minutes till range," Eponi said. "I'm highlighting the turrets. I'm not confident we'll punch through that thing's armor, but we might get its attention long enough for the fighters to do their work."

"Where do you want me?" Rovo asked.

With Aurora and Gregor in the turrets and Eponi, who could still press the firing trigger with her cast-on arm, Rovo didn't have a clear place to be. Eponi hesitated, not sure she needed the rookie up in the cockpit with her.

"Stick with Kaia," Aurora ordered, "until we need you someplace else. If this doesn't go well, do what you can for her."

The *Prisa* didn't have lifeboats. There wouldn't be any last ditch diving away from here. Good on Aurora not to let the little girl ride through the fight alone.

Eponi refused to think about the possible outcomes. She'd learned that long ago. Getting too tied up in how a race might end tended to screw up the flying.

Instead, Eponi dialed down the engines, pumping the power towards the *Prisa*'s shields. Sai's grenades had knocked out Vana's ship long enough for them to close. Now the fight would be about fancy flying, about survival, and who could hit a damn thing with a hot laser.

"Pick your targets," Eponi said. "There's plenty."

"Hard to miss one this large," Gregor noted.

"Then make sure you don't," Aurora said.

On the console screen before her, Eponi caught the two DefenseCorp fighters veering away from the *Prisa*, lining up for runs on Vana's ship. Another few seconds, and the fun would start.

If Eponi had a god to pray to, she'd have done it now. Instead, she took the deepest breath her lungs could hold—easy to forget to breathe in a heavy fight—and zeroed in on that big transport. She settled the *Prisa* on a straight run, its main cannon positioned to do what it did best.

Eponi's finger, the cast itching near it, found the trigger.

The console chirped. Bright, cheery, and signaling death. Eponi pressed the trigger, figured Gregor and Aurora were doing the same in their turrets. Flashes lit the windshield from below, right, and left. Lasers went fast enough that Eponi only saw them once the superhot light beams were well away from the *Prisa*, streaking in towards their target in straight, gapped lines.

The *Prisa*, sensing a fight had started, shadowed a new display on the windshield. Keeping her eyes forward, Eponi could see the *Prisa*'s energy as an overlay above the transport and the purple moon. The steady fire—hot blue, tweaked to the highest power setting—sapped energy like DefenseCorp sapped the life from its soldiers.

After three seconds, Eponi pulled back on the flight stick. Sever had fired on the transport first, engaging with lethal intent. The surprise bought Sever those seconds, let Eponi arc the *Prisa* up while kicking its maneuvering jets to flip the ship over. In zero gravity, going upside down didn't matter much to anyone inside the ship, but it let Eponi keep the transport in clear view.

The counterattack came in clear. The big ship's guns opened up, their splashy yellow fizzing out towards the *Prisa*'s original location and tracing a line towards Eponi's ship.

"Take your shots when you get'em," Eponi said, tilting the *Prisa* into an angled approach. "Every gun you take out's worth a drink on me."

"Good incentive," Gregor replied.

"Because your life's not good enough?" Rovo said.

"Cut the chatter." Aurora, doing what commanders do.

Eponi kept the *Prisa* turning. The cargo hauler didn't have a fighter's finesse, but the cycling, coupled with Eponi cutting up, down, back and forth at random, meant the transport's turrets struggled to catch up. Their yellow bolts formed a neon trail in the dark.

"Flight, you make contact?" Eponi reversed the *Prisa*'s flip as she sent the hail towards the two fighters, pushing the flight stick forward to dive her ship across the transport's bridge. "It's getting hot out here."

"We've engaged the target," Deepak's pilot replied. "She's playing hard to get."

Pulling up, Eponi sent the *Prisa* beneath the transport, getting as close to the bigger craft as she dared. The energy silhouette showed Gregor and Aurora firing away. As of yet, the *Prisa* hadn't taken a single hit, which meant Eponi was either the greatest pilot the galaxy had ever seen, or the agents manning the transport guns were, well, not great.

"No time for games," Eponi said. "We're not going to win against this thing."

A hearty shout cut through the band, Gregor's voice declaring victory, "One for me."

Aurora offered congratulations, but Eponi had to focus on the dancing. She pulled the *Prisa* left, keeping the craft beneath the transport. Hiding underneath kept half the big ships guns out of play, and others shooting across the transport's body would have to worry about hitting their own ship. The yellow bolts came sporadic now, the gunners deciding to play things safe.

"Coming back around for another pass," Eponi said as the *Prisa* neared the end of a wing. "You want to hit any part of this thing, take your shot."

She pumped energy from the *Prisa*'s shields to its guns. The transport hadn't shown it could hit anything yet. Might as well get some damage while the getting was good.

"*Prisa*, where are you?" The fighter captain came through in a shout. "We're getting blitzed out here!"

"We're hugging the transport, what—" Eponi stopped, her eyes going wide.

Sever operated alone. Eponi flew them into dangerous territory, doing everything necessary to survive. Live long enough and Sever would make it to ground, or outrun the pursuit.

Except now, survival wasn't the goal.

Cursing, Eponi lurched the *Prisa* right, heading towards the transport's front. As she swung the *Prisa* forward, Eponi saw Gillane Four's blue, yes, but golden yellow laserfire burned across its beauty. The transport's cannons rained fire towards Vana's ship and the fighters trying to bring it down. A singular black circle stuck out, the gap where Vana flew, while around it the transport laced its death.

"Coming!" Eponi said. "Hold on!"

The fighter pilot didn't reply. He didn't have to. Caught in an attack run, the two fighters had their sights set on Vana's ship. The transport's fire hit them by surprise. Not just an isolated laser, but a multitude. Eponi saw the fighters dancing as they broke and tried to run. The transport's top guns chased the two craft towards each other, pinning them in a shrinking, deadly circle.

In seconds, they'd be dead.

Eponi slapped the console, drained all the energy from the lasers and pumped it into the *Prisa*'s shields. Gregor yelped as his turret stopped.

"Eponi," Aurora said. "What are you doing?"

"Saving the fighters," Eponi replied, swinging the *Prisa* up as it passed beneath the transport.

The fighters made for difficult, distant targets. The turrets would rely on programs, telling the agents when and where to fire. Those programs would find the big, fat *Prisa* zooming close a far easier pick.

"Vana's right there," Aurora said. "Unguarded. We can strike."

"We do that, the fighters die," Eponi replied. "And we'd be next."

Aurora stayed quiet as Eponi flipped the *Prisa* into a fast retreat. The first turrets found them now, changing away from the fleeing fighters to the *Prisa*'s juicy hull. The ship juddered as impacts found her shields, as some burning light slipped through and singed the metal.

"Get clear, guys," Eponi said as she wiggled the *Prisa* every way she could. "We'll cover you."

"Thanks *Prisa*," the fighter captain replied. "Nearly got

ourselves cooked back there. Sorry we couldn't bring down the target."

"We'll get another chance," Eponi replied. "Don't worry."

The call fizzled as another laser struck home, and Eponi winced as the console noted the *Prisa*'s communications had burned out.

"She's going to get away," Aurora said, stalking into the cockpit. She took the copilot's chair, swiping at the console as yellow lasers filled the void around them. "Vana's escaping, again."

"So are we, if you haven't noticed," Eponi replied. "For the moment, anyway."

Flying straight away from an enemy not all that interested in pursuit, though, kept the *Prisa* alive. The transport's bolts dwindled as Eponi pushed the *Prisa*'s engines, hitting and then passing attack range.

She'd forgotten how to fly with a team. She'd cost Sever the mission, but she'd kept their lives.

That would have to be enough. But, when Eponi heard Aurora punch the hull beside her, Eponi knew it wasn't.

THIRTY-FIVE

Futures

KAIA HANDLED the attack and retreat better than Rovo could've imagined. He holed up with her and the captive agent in Rovo's own cabin. While he listened to the squad chatter with the Bug in his ear, Rovo kept his attention on Kaia, even using the console on the *Prisa* to pull up any kid-friendly he could find on the ship's entertainment library—a challenge arguably harder than fighting agents in open combat.

Zero gravity kept the *Prisa*'s dips and dodges from sending the trio rolling around, and Rovo, once Kaia had herself distracted, turned to the agent. She'd suffered laser burns that needed dressing changes, and the hit with Gregor's head had a nasty bruise forming beneath the agent's close-cut hair.

More concerning than anything else, though, were the dark splotches Rovo found across the agent's arms and legs. Like spilled ink, the patches felt warm to the touch, seeming to shudder whenever Rovo pressed in with a finger. Gregor had mentioned seeing similar infections on other agents, but finding a nightmare up close . . .

Rovo wrapped up the patches. On Dynas, he'd nearly died when a far larger infection tried to eat the rookie. Gregor had come to Rovo's rescue there, but visions of the black disease spreading through his body had consumed Rovo's sleepless nights ever since.

He'd thought Sever had seen the end of that, thought Dynas and its collapse would mark the disease's annihilation.

"Hey, Rovo?" Eponi's voice, on the comm. "You can come out. We're away, and they're not following."

Behind the rookie, the movie chattered on. Kaia giggled at something. He stared at the agent.

"Rovo?" Aurora now, concerned.

"She's infected," Rovo said. "The agent. She's like Felix. Not as advanced, but . . ."

The only treatment Sever had destroyed the disease through vacuum exposure. The extreme cold seemed to kill the virus, provided the host could live through the experience. They could try to do that with the agent, could try to—

"Then she goes to a hospital," Aurora said, killing Rovo's idea before it took flight. "I know what you're thinking, but we can't risk her. She's our only link, right now, to where Vana might be going. And, more than that, given time and a subject, the doctors here might be able to find a cure."

"You saw what happened with Felix," Rovo replied. "You think it's safe to keep her in this ship?"

"She won't leave the room," Aurora said. "Get yourself and Kaia away. I'm not risking a chance to find out where Vana's going."

If Kaia hadn't been in the room, if she hadn't looked at Rovo with a question in her eyes, he might've acted differently. As it was, he took the hand off the pistol still at his belt. The girl had already seen her father shot, been a hostage to a monster that wanted her blood, and been sent off alone on a crashing path into a planet.

Kaia had seen enough.

"C'mon, kiddo," Rovo said, swiping off the console and taking Kaia's hand. "Let me show you all the cool places in the ship."

"What about her?" Kaia asked as Rovo gave her a gentle tug towards the exit.

"She needs to rest, so let's leave her alone for a while."

When Rovo opened the door, Gregor stood in the small hallway, leaning against the wall. The big hammer sat next to him. The rookie met Gregor's eyes, caught the slight nod, and understood.

The agent, virus or no, would not be leaving.

ROVO LEFT Kaia with her father as evening descended on Gillane Four. Kashmal, supported by a bot plethora, nonetheless lit up when Kaia came into the room. As someone who'd kept his daughter in a closet for years, Kashmal seemed to have changed his mind, deciding that being a father was, perhaps, an opportunity and not a penalty. Not that a moment in a hospital, even a beautiful one like the teardrop Salinity medical center they were in, defined a perfect future.

Nonetheless, Rovo had another reason to leave the room.

"Looking tired, rookie," Sai said, lounging in the hall.

The swordsman had his own medical cloak on, various monitors dangling from his skin, through a gown, trying to make sure Sai hadn't suffered any permanent damage. While the Salinity shuttle completed the rescue, Sai himself clung to life in power armor with little oxygen, less heat. The man looked gray, patchy, but none-theless alive.

"You're one to talk," Rovo replied. "They keeping you overnight?"

Sai laughed, shook his head, "A little vacuum isn't going to kill me." He tilted his head down the hall. "Go say hi."

Nods ended the conversation, letting Rovo continue to the unit's other end. There, standing at the window in her room, was another patient Rovo had to see.

"That bad, huh?" Rovo said by way of a knock, leaning against the sand-shaded door. The whole hospital had a beach feel, as if to say the patients weren't being treated but were, instead, on some delightful vacation.

"So bad," Raquel replied, glancing Rovo's way. "I should've been out hours ago, but they want to watch me. Make sure I'm not like all the agents."

"What?"

Raquel waved at a chair opposite her bed, "You in such a rush that you can't come in for a minute?"

"If we weren't so beat up, we'd be gone already," Rovo replied, taking the chair.

Strange, now, to sit without power armor, without a hand falling to a pistol, without eyes tracking every exit, every window for an agent. They'd been on Gillane Four for a few days, but after the *Nautilus*, after the shooters in the building windows, Rovo's nerves had tightened so far he wasn't sure how to unwind.

"You know where she's going?" Raquel asked, taking her own spot on the hospital bed.

"Deepak and Aurora are meeting about it," Rovo blinked, looked hard at Raquel and didn't see anything strange. "You said they're keeping you here because of the agents?"

"To make sure I'm not *like* the agents." Raquel ran her hands up and down her arms. "Salinity's been rounding them up. You'd think they'd fight back, or just disappear into some crowd, but they're . . . sick."

"I know."

"You do?" More questions littered the space between Raquel's crinkled eyes, her slight lean Rovo's way. "Tell me."

"I don't know how the disease works, just that it's bad. Keep them away from everyone else, and each other," Rovo said. "It's one of the reasons we don't want to waste time chasing Vana."

"They're dying, Rovo. They're dying and they're saying it's her fault. That *Vana* had them injected. Why would she do that if she knew it would kill them?"

"Maybe she didn't?" Rovo shook his head. "I'm not sure, but when we catch up to her, she'll tell us."

Raquel frowned, "You can't think she'll cooperate."

"Don't know that until we have her in hand," Rovo said. "And if she doesn't, we'll figure it out the hard way."

Raquel's frown filtered up into a straight line, "That's how you all seem to do everything. The hard way."

"Not by choice."

"Is that how you're going to repay my planet, and my company? The hard way?"

Rovo shrugged, "I don't know what that even means?"

Raquel looked at her wristlet, swiped at it, "So, by my calculations, you caused significant damage to two apartments. Blew up skiffs and left their remnants on public property. Gregor and Aurora decimated a building under construction, and you, personally, collapsed a climate spike. That's a lot of cash."

"Uh, bill DefenseCorp?"

"Oh, I will. But you and your squad broke laws doing

what you did, without any official permission. I could take care of that, if you promise me something."

The conversation had already wheeled so far beyond anywhere Rovo expected, so all he could do was raise his hands and ask what.

"Come back," Raquel said. "Pay your debt to this planet, and to that little girl."

"So you can order me around?"

A smile, soon matched.

"You look like a man that needs some direction."

Well, Rovo couldn't argue with that.

THIRTY-SIX

Exile

THE PARK GLITTERED in the mid-morning, its leafy trimmed trees and close-cut grass showcasing a caring corporate owner and their bots. Aurora sat on a metal bench, the textured bumps in the slats slowly warming to the temp she'd selected on her wristlet. Wind teased her hair. For once, Aurora's body felt natural, rather than strung out on chemicals keeping her awake and ready to throw one more punch.

"This is a nice planet," Deepak announced, walking Aurora's way along a path clustered with passing people.

The DefenseCorp admiral had, like Aurora, dropped the official outfit for something more relaxed. Something, given Salinity's public campaign blaming DefenseCorp for the fighting around Kaiyo, more subtle. A crisp white sweater, some pants that looked like they'd been bought a few hours before and thrown on.

Aurora had the scraps from the *Prisa*. They didn't fit all that well, but the clothes were comfy, the jacket warm. Today, that would be enough.

"It's much more pleasant when you're not fighting for your life," Aurora replied.

"I'm surprised to hear you say that." Deepak took the spot next to her, crossed his legs and looked out over the green. "Don't you live for conflict?"

Aurora thought she'd have a snappy comeback, but the question snared her the wrong way. What did she live for? Did she—

No. Not doing that. Not yet.

"Right now, Vana's the only thing that matters," Aurora said.

"But you won. Kaia's back with her father. Your squad is alive. Vana can't take that away."

Those words came too glib, too easy. Aurora had been around Deepak long enough, heard him deliver enough debriefs to know when the man wanted acceptance over introspection. Why would Deepak want Aurora focused on the win, instead of the war?

"You sent two fighters," Aurora said. "Two fighters, nothing else. Even though you had to know the transport might still be in system."

"We weren't close," Deepak answered. "Nor were we expecting Vana to run when she did. You could have warned us."

"An agent who fought her way off the *Nautilus* through ambushes and tricks, and you're saying you weren't prepared for surprises?"

"In case you've forgotten, my ship nearly tore itself apart in the fighting your squad commenced. We're distracted."

Like so many of their previous conversations, this one felt like a test. Deepak evaded. His answers came too easy. It'd been weeks since the agent uprising on the *Nautilus*. Enough time to put together a new chain of command, restore ships and their pilots to operational status. Defense-Corp wouldn't tolerate slowness, because every day spent in turmoil was a day not earning cash.

"Deepak, either you tell me the truth right now, or I'm standing up and walking away," Aurora said. "I'm not playing games. Vana's nearly killed me and my squad too many times."

Deepak settled back on the bench. This time, when he spoke, he didn't look Aurora in the eye, "The fighters were never going to attack Vana. Only look like it."

"Explain, or I'm going to kill you right here."

Raising his left palm towards Aurora, Deepak continued, "DefenseCorp's changing its mind. Vana's presenting a compelling opportunity, at least to leadership. You have to admit, Aurora, that the suits would be effective. How many missions would be easier if the enemy couldn't see your approach?"

"But the agents turned against us! Against the entire company!"

"No," Deepak said, a chiding bitterness sliding in. "Your squad deserted us. The agents on the *Nautilus* had every right, under DefenseCorp code, to kill your team. Then, you pushed my troops to fight Renard first." Deepak took a breath, flashed his eyes away. A slight head shake brought him back to Aurora. "DefenseCorp's leaders won't let the company split. Vana's giving them a way to keep it together, and grow our profits at the same time."

Aurora pressed her hands flat against her pants to keep from clenching into fists. Arguments grew and died one after another as she ran them through Deepak's look. The man had the grace to show some sorrow, and those bags beneath his eyes were dark enough now to suggest Deepak hadn't slept well for a long time.

"A week ago, well after you left, I received orders to

intercept your attempt here," Deepak continued. "Sever Squad's been marked. You're a threat to DefenseCorp's new future."

Aurora stood, "Then my squad's at risk. We have to leave now."

"Stop. The message came to me, and I haven't sent it across the ship," Deepak said. "Some might know, but not enough. The *Nautilus* is mine, and the people on it are my crew. They won't move unless I say so."

Looking down at Deepak, the admiral's continued calm only served to stir up a fire. This, this had been why Sever had cut itself from DefenseCorp after Dynas. The company would throw everything away for a sliver more power, for a bit more cash, no matter how many people it murdered in the process.

"So this is, what, your warning? You're giving us a head start?" Aurora asked. "Where could we go? And what happens when Salinity decides to charge us as vigilantes for trying to rescue Kaia? We'll be wanted everywhere in the galaxy."

"I'm sorry, Aurora. I really am. Getting you the power armor, giving you this warning, I'm already risking everything."

"Sure you are." Aurora swept a look around the park. Didn't notice anyone watching, but snipers could be anywhere, recording bots hidden in the leaves. "Thanks for nothing."

Deepak flinched. Aurora thought about going one step further, giving the admiral a slug that he surely deserved, but every second Sever stayed here, thinking they were safe, was another moment risked.

"Wait," Deepak said, standing himself as Aurora started walking away. "I'm not, I don't want to see you get hurt anymore."

Aurora curled a lip, glanced back, "That was never your choice to make."

"And yet, I tried all the same." Deepak matched her stride. "I didn't come here just to warn you."

Aurora didn't reply. She picked up her pace. The walk from the park to the docking bay wasn't a short one, and the capsule ride would be tracked, watched. She started to lift her wristlet, to blast out a message on Sever's band recalling them all to the *Prisa*.

"You said before that you think Vana and Renard were doing something worse than the suits," Deepak said. "I've heard the reports on the agents here. The sickness."

"Yeah. Vana riffed on the Dynas disease. It'll kill everyone if they don't get some dose," Aurora said. "I'm sure you'll all get it too. Keep you loyal. Turn you into monsters."

"Such a plan, if it comes out, would break DefenseCorp," Deepak said. "Suits are one thing. A murderous virus? The galaxy won't stand for it."

"Are you going anywhere with this? Because I am going somewhere, and I'm not waiting for your help anymore."

"Vana sent a message. We received it yesterday. During her escape." Deepak stopped his walk, and this time Aurora stopped with him, near the park's edge where it folded into a shop-lined avenue. "The message went to every admiral, every higher up in the company. Vana's calling them to a demonstration, to a meeting. She wants them to see their future."

"And you're going?"

Deepak nodded, "They'll all go. Every last one."

"Isn't that a risk?"

A smile on the admiral, now, a slight one, "It's more dangerous to be absent when the new order is decided." Deepak held out his wristlet, swiped it to a screen for local tap transfers. "Take a look. If you want a chance to stop her, to change all this, then it will be here."

Aurora didn't hesitate, touched her wristlet to Deepak's. The devices beeped when the transfer completed all of two seconds later.

"You could have led with this," Aurora said, her anger dissipating into curiosity. "Would've made everything else easier to take."

"Because revenge is that important to you?"

"If it's going to get the hounds off my ass, then yeah, I'd say it's pretty damn important."

"You realize every major DefenseCorp official, with their guards, is going to be there. They'll all want your heads. There's no way you'll get close."

Now it was Aurora's turn to grin, "If you believed that, you wouldn't have told me."

Deepak couldn't deny it.

SEVER PILED into the *Prisa*'s center with happy attitudes that disintegrated as Aurora laid clear the stakes. Two lives now, their DefenseCorp careers and their short-lived free-lance stint, had been taken from them. Few would hire a group blacklisted by DefenseCorp. Nobody would take on a crew also hunted by the galaxy's major water supplier.

"So you're saying our only choice is to go in, us five, against who knows how many?" Rovo said. "Vana's going to have suits, going to have DefenseCorp's biggest, baddest dudes all trying to see how much stronger they're gonna get, and we're supposed to fight that?"

"When you put it that way," Eponi dripped with sarcasm, "it sounds like a bad idea."

"Or a great one," Gregor added.

"You wouldn't offer this unless you had an idea," Sai said to Aurora. "So what is it?"

"Easy," Aurora replied. "We do what we've always done. Get in, take out Vana and anyone going along with her. Find the evidence showing what they're doing, beam it to the galaxy. We win."

"That all?" Rovo said.

"That's all," Aurora replied, ignoring the rookie's tone. "We know where they're meeting, and we have some time before all our targets can cross the galaxy to get here. Eponi's going to take us to a station I know where we can rest up, hide out, and put together a plan."

"What if I don't want to go?" Rovo said, turning all eyes the rookie's way. "What if I want out of this thing? Kaia's safe. Raquel's offering me a job here. Maybe I don't want to throw my life away."

Aurora gave Rovo a steady stare, "You want to stay, nobody's forcing you to come. Sever squad, even if it's just me, is going after Vana. I'm not going to let her future win." She didn't see any other Severs popping in with objections, so Aurora went for Rovo's heart. "Kaia's going to grow up in this galaxy, rookie. You can either make sure it's one you believe in, or one that'll tear her apart."

An hour later, when Eponi received clearance from Salinity's ground control, the *Prisa* lifted into Gillane Four's brilliant afternoon sky. The blue shifted purple, and finally black as Sever soared starward.

Vana had Sever backed against a wall.

Big mistake.

READ *on for an excerpt from FURY STORM, the thrilling conclusion to the Sever Squad series!*

An Excerpt from FURY STORM

The strip-mined system had little to recommend it. Their target, Aurum Three, came into focus on the *Prisa*'s windshield. A distant blue star shot its light past Sever Squad's ship as it flew in, catching the planet and making its yellow-brown surface clear. Darker, blurred lines moved along the land, like living smudges parading over paper.

"Massive storms," Eponi, sitting in the pilot's chair, noted. "Never fun to race in those."

"Or fight," Aurora, in the co-pilot's seat beside Eponi, replied.

Both had their brimming coffee cups, waking up to the first day in months that would really matter. Skinsuits—Eponi's a soft gold, Aurora's a blood red—snugged them, allowing quick access to power armor. Eponi's left arm no longer had its cast, the snapped bone having knit itself back into shape. The pilot's left hand drummed on Eponi's thigh, anxious.

Rusted nerves. A vacation's cost.

Not that Sever had many options. As much as Aurora may have wanted to chase the agent Vana all the way to this world, Sever left Gillane Four battered and exhausted. The fighters had hardly slept, had been strung out on adrenaline and whatever else could keep them functioning for days. Laser burns, concussions, knife cuts and worse all needed tending.

But, after more than a hundred days spent recuperating, repairing, and realigning her squad to its mission and its place in a galaxy that now saw Sever as a group to be detained or destroyed, Aurora felt they'd gone long enough.

More importantly, Aurora's maybe-more-than-friend and DefenseCorp admiral Deepak sent the message saying it was time.

Vana, the DefenseCorp agent masterminding a program designing near-invisible power armor suits coupled with genetically enhanced soldiers, had decided to stand up for her claims and bring DefenseCorp's leaders to a single spot. There, according to Deepak, Vana would convince the massive, galaxy-spanning company's leaders to go along with the plan, creating a new force that wouldn't so much handle contracts as drop an ironclad shroud over civilization.

After all, who could fight an enemy that could be anywhere?

"We could've stayed," Sai said, Sever's resident father and swordmaster. His voice came over the *Prisa*'s intercom, drifting in from the ship's right turret. "The cash was pretty good."

The station, a free-wheeling centerpoint in a large asteroid cluster, had offered Sever a standing contract to provide security. While Aurora would've been fine beating up drunk miners for steady pay on the galaxy's fringe, she'd already played that role once and watched as DefenseCorp swooped in and stole the work.

"How long you think we'd last before Vana's new toys took it from us?" Rovo, the squad's resident comms expert and a third cockpit occupant, spoke for Aurora. "We'd be bored, and then we'd be dead."

Rovo had his own motivations to hit Vana. All of Sever did. That tugging, burning feeling sat wrong inside Aurora: vengeance wasn't normally an issue, because Aurora's enemies tended to die long before they became a nagging problem. Vana, though, continued to escape, to twist the fights so they weren't clear-cut laser tags until one side lay smoking on the ground. Like blocks building up into an enraging tower, Aurora had spent the recovery time on the station assembling all the reasons why she needed to turn Vana to ash.

And now, they'd arrived.

"Tell me I'm seeing things," Eponi said, nodding towards the glass.

New imperfections crossed the planet's surface as the *Prisa* approached. What had looked like splotches, normal smears across a landscape seen from afar, resolved into sharper focus. Blurred lines became straight edges associated with man-made machines. One or two could've meant Vana's own forces, but as the *Prisa* came in closer, those dots kept appearing, and growing.

"They didn't just bring themselves," Aurora said, not wanting to believe it. "They actually brought their commands too."

"That's going to burn a lot of contracts," Rovo added, as if saying that, here, would convince all those admirals to jump back in their ships and return home.

"DefenseCorp must be losing so much cash for this," Eponi agreed. "Look at all these cruisers. I don't understand?"

Aurora simmered in the silence, putting together both

an answer and an inspiration, "They're here because they want a piece. Vana's advertising suits *and* a genetic upgrade. You can't get your soldiers a dose if they're across the galaxy. But it also means we have the audience we're looking for."

"The admirals?" Rovo asked. "Didn't we know they'd be here?"

"Not them. All the soldiers. The staffers. The pilots and the mechanics. If we can show them what Vana's planning, what this virus will actually do, DefenseCorp won't be able to hide it from this many people. Not like they did with Dynas."

That planet, with its secretive experiments, had escaped the galaxy's wider notice. Sever had been sent in on a botched rescue mission to the supposedly-empty world, only to find a festering project that turned its subjects into food for a ravenous disease. Angry, destructive food, but food nonetheless.

Only with severe cold had Sever been able to eradicate the disease before it claimed them all.

"Think you're missing a step, captain," Eponi said. "We're going to be popping up on a whole lotta sensors in a few minutes, and I can't imagine they're gonna be friendly."

"Are you saying people don't like us?" Rovo asked.

"I thought everyone loved the captain," Sai said.

Aurora grimaced. Sai's sarcasm had some truth in it. Aurora's name, Sever squad's name, would be known to plenty in that swarm up in front. As the *Prisa* popped on their scanners, all those cruisers, those frigates, those fighters would figure out who flew the ship. When they did, all the missions Sever spent crashing into the enemy's heart to save DefenseCorp assets and asses might be worth something.

Or, as the *Prisa*'s monitoring system sounded off a shrill chirp, not.

"Looks like the fun's over, kids," Eponi cracked. "We're getting hostile pings. Missile locks, radar range-finders, all the good stuff. Last chance to turn back, Aurora."

"You already know the answer."

"Diving in, guns blazing," Eponi affirmed. "That's what I love about this crew. No matter how dismal it all looks, we'll just keep shooting till the odds change."

"There's a motto in there somewhere," Sai said. "Eponi, what's our allocation?"

"You're getting just enough to play with," Eponi replied. "Engines and shields get everything else. This isn't a fight, it's a sprint."

Aurora sat back in the seat, looked out at all the ships arrayed around Vana's chosen world. Eponi angled the *Prisa* towards the loosest knot that'd still give them a straight run to the surface. The pilot had ample choices: this wasn't a cohesive DefenseCorp fleet expecting attack, but an officer stew, with every individual commander deciding where to park their vessels while they dropped to the rock.

Hmm. Aurora might be able to use that.

"Eponi, give me a broadcast channel," Aurora said.

"Feeling like a speech?"

"Something like that."

Aurora's console chirped, switching the small screen over to a broad green target list. Aurora could tap along the ship names to cut them off the transmission, but she wasn't going to play favorites.

The coffee had gone lukewarm, but the liquid salved her nervous throat. Aurora could lead a thousand troops into the enemy's teeth without flinching, but delivering a bold address to thousands, maybe millions? No thanks.

The things she did for Sever Squad.

"Hailing DefenseCorp ships," Aurora began, letting the bog standard beginning warm her way into the next piece. "This is Sever Squad and her commander, sending out a notice that we're passing through your perimeter en route to the surface." A breath. Here came the game. "Despite what your systems might be telling you, we've been granted one-time passage. Fire on us, and you fire upon yourselves."

Bold words, ridiculous words. An assertion that any competent officer would laugh away in one breath and order his soldiers to fire in the next.

Except every ship zeroing on the *Prisa* right now had its backups in charge. Leaders that didn't have all the details, that didn't have the rank or the responsibility to decide if a lone approaching ship should be a friend or a foe.

"Is it working?" Aurora asked in the silence.

"We're still target locked," Eponi replied, "but nobody's pulled the trigger yet."

"Voice like honey, I always say," Rovo added. "Everybody trusts you."

Aurora swiped away from the broadcast, looked at the scanners. The *Prisa* picked up velocity as Eponi used the hesitation, siphoning more energy away from the ship's weapons and feeding its hungry engines. The scanners displayed long orange oval frigates, red fighter dots, and fat cruiser circles. The bulk drifted towards the *Prisa*'s entry path, but they all kept their distance from each other too. No coordinated strategy.

"Look at all this," Eponi said. "The *Nautilus* always flies alone. Forgot who we work for."

"Used to work for," Aurora clarified, but she couldn't deny the sight.

Outside, running lights visible now, the hulks making

up DefenseCorp's arsenal cut into the view from every angle. Huge engines many times the *Prisa*'s size lit up in glows ranging from soft yellow to hot and feisty blue. The metal hulks went below and above, and Aurora could pick out swiveling turrets moving to track Sever's ship as it passed by.

"Friends left," said Gregor, Sever's own living hulk. Snared in the *Prisa*'s port-side turret, Gregor had been quieter since Gillane Four, choosing to use his limited words with care, as if each one risked betraying some emotion, some crack in the man's armor. "Fire?"

"Keep the fingers off the triggers," Aurora said, though she fought to hide a flinch when Gregor's friends, a fighter trio, blew by the cockpit. The wave-like craft, a thin edge frothing over with cannons, made sure the *Prisa* knew it would die in a thousand ways if anything changed. "We help nothing by engaging out here."

All those officers Aurora had heard would be checking, trying to confirm, with their commanders. Vana herself would probably catch word soon. One would come back, would order Sever destroyed.

The mystery would be when.

"Is Deepak coming?" Rovo asked.

"Why is that relevant right now?" Aurora replied.

"It's not, I guess, but we're flying here," Rovo said. "Not much I can do, so, uh, figured I'd ask a question?"

Aurora threw the rookie a raised eyebrow over her shoulder. Eponi, though, seemed zoned in on keeping the *Prisa* on its path—denoted by a translucent green arrow leading through the fleet and towards Aurum Three's surface—and neither Sai nor Gregor had another update coming through.

"I don't know," Aurora gave the only answer she had.

The conversation had been painful. The park on

Gillane Four, when Deepak said Sever would be targets forever barring a miracle. Aurora didn't mind getting shots fired her way, but beneath Deepak's warning came a second, harsher truth: the two of them had, in the short time between the *Nautilus* insurrection and the fighting on Gillane Four, rekindled lingering embers. Those sparks had been snuffed out in that park, and since then Deepak had sent along only cold advice.

"Might want to see if he's near," Rovo said. "because if this goes like we're hoping, I bet we won't have many friends in this bunch."

"He knows where we are," Aurora said.

"Good," Eponi interjected. "Those locks are starting to heat up—"

"Missiles fired!" Sai shouted. "Eponi, give me some power or we're done!"

Aurora leaned forward, swiping to the scanner as Eponi threw the ship into a corkscrew, angling towards the planet. Aurora wished she'd taken one of the turrets, wished she could do something beyond watch as death came for her ship and her crew.

But Aurora would have to wait till they landed.

Then, then she would get her fill.

Continue the adventure in FURY STORM, available now!

Acknowledgments

This novel is the product of my family and friends refusing to let a dream die. My wife Nicole, for letting me write in the early mornings and making sure I don't starve. My brothers and parents for their continual comments, support, and enthusiasm.

Evan Aaseng, for being a constant sounding board and reeling me back in whenever my ideas went too far.

And, of course, you, the reader, for giving me a reason to write.

About the Author

A.R. Knight spins stories in a frosty house in Madison, WI, primarily owned by a pair of cats. After getting sucked into the working grind in the economic crash of the 2008, he found himself spending boring meetings soaring through space and going on grand adventures.

Eventually, spending time with podcasting, screenplays, short stories and other novels, he found a story he could fall into and a cast of characters both entertaining and full of heart.

Sever Squad has more adventures to come, along with new plots, settings, and stories in the future. From there, A.R. Knight plans on jumping through to other worlds and finding new stories to tell in the limitless borders of our imagination.

Thanks, as always, for reading!

For more information:
www.adamrknight.com

To Evan